Wolf's Mate

CHANTAL FERNANDO

G

Gallery Books

New York   London   Toronto   Sydney   New Delhi

Gallery Books
An Imprint of Simon & Schuster, Inc.
1230 Avenue of the Americas
New York, NY 10020

First Gallery Books trade paperback edition August 2016

GALLERY BOOKS and colophon are registered trademarks of Simon & Schuster, Inc.

For information about special discounts for bulk purchases, please contact Simon & Schuster Special Sales at 1-866-506-1949 or business@simonandschuster.com

The Simon & Schuster Speakers Bureau can bring authors to your live event. For more information or to book an event contact the Simon & Schuster Speakers Bureau at 1-866-248-3049 or visit our website at www.simonspeakers.com.

Manufactured in the United States of America

10 9 8 7 6 5 4 3 2

Library of Congress Cataloging-in-Publication Data is available.

ISBN 978-1-5011-3957-4
ISBN 978-1-5011-3960-4 (ebook)

To Natalie Ram,

For being the very best friend a girl could ask for.

Acknowledgments

Thank you, as always, to Abby Zidle and Gallery books!

To my agent, Kimberly Brower, I'm so lucky to have you! Thank you for everything you do, as always. I know I can always count on you, and I'm so grateful.

A big thank you to all my beta readers—the women who are always there for me on a daily basis.

Arijana Karcic—thank you for all you do for me. You're seriously the best and deserve the world.

Thank you to my parents for helping out whenever I need them, I appreciate everything you do for me, and to my three sons for being patient when they know their mama has to work. I love you all so much.

FMR Book Grind, thank you for everything; I appreciate all the hard work you all do for me! Rose Tawil words can't express how much I love you!

They who dream by day are cognizant of many things which escape those who dream only by night.

—Edgar Allan Poe

ONE

Vinnie

"HELLO?" I say into my phone distractedly as I throw back another shot.

I have no idea who could be calling me, since I'm at the clubhouse and everyone is here, but I always answer my phone—it's a habit. If one of my brothers needs me, I'll be there, day or night, drunk or sober. Even if I'm drunk, and it's late at night, I'm not going to complain.

When I hear Talon's voice on the other end, however, my good mood and easy demeanor disappear. There's only one reason the president of the Wild Men MC would call me, and it's a moment I've been dreading.

"We need to talk," he says. I stand up and move away from the others so I can have this conversation alone.

I walk out front and stand by my bike, admiring her as I ask, "What do you need?"

He's calling in the marker I owe him, I know it, and I just hope he doesn't want me to do something fucked-up. Recently, there was a little trouble involving another brother's old lady,

Bailey. We had our hands full, and Talon stepped in to help by keeping the troublemaker involved, Amethyst, in his clubhouse while we did cleanup. Bailey's ex, Wade, who is her daughter Cara's biological father, tried to use them to get money from the Wind Dragons MC. Luckily Irish was there. He ended up stabbed, and Wade was killed. Just another day in the life.

Of course, nothing is free, so I gave Talon my word that I'd owe him a favor, one he could collect at a time of his choosing. My honor requires me to do whatever he needs, even though I can't stand the guy and I'd rather be doing anything else right now.

Like, fuckin' *anything*.

However, I hate owing anyone, so I'm eager to get this over and done with.

"Pack a bag," Talon says on the other end. "You'll be gone for a week." He doesn't sound smug, or even like he's enjoying calling in my debt. In fact, he sounds rather solemn. Why, I have no idea, but I guess I'm going to find out.

"Do I need to bring anything?" I ask, wondering what weapons I might need. What the fuck did he want me to do for a week? Go with him on a run, maybe?

"Nope. I'll meet you at Rift tomorrow around lunchtime and explain everything."

"Okay," I reply, curious now.

We both hang up and my mind wanders with possibilities. I'm glad he chose Rift because there's no way I'm going to his clubhouse and he's not welcome here. We may both be bikers, but we're still from two different worlds, and those worlds don't mix. When I joined the WDMC, the Wild Men MC were our enemies, and even though it's not like that anymore, they aren't exactly our allies either. We own Rift, so he's actually giving me the power.

Very interesting.

"Everything all right?" Sin, my president, asks as he walks outside and spots me staring down at the phone in my hand.

I slide it in my pocket and say, "Yeah. Talon's calling in his marker. I'll be gone for a week."

Sin stills at that bit of information, then closes the space between us. "What does he want?"

"I'll find out tomorrow—meeting him at Rift."

He puts his hand on my shoulder. "If you owe him a marker, we all do. Call me anytime—you need anything, I'm there. We're all there."

"I know," I say, nodding.

And I do—the words don't even need to be spoken out loud. I've been in this club for many years and seen lots of things along the way. I was just a prospect when Sin became president, and I earned my way to being a full-fledged member not shortly after. This club is my family, my backbone. Everything that I am. I don't intend on ever getting out, and I look forward to working my way up the ranks.

That's what the Wind Dragons are all about: a brotherhood based on loyalty and acceptance.

We aren't saints, but the intention is there. We do what we have to to protect our own.

And I wouldn't have it any other way.

"I'm going to go enjoy my last night of freedom for a week," I say, lightening the mood.

Sin cracks a smile and says, "The brunette?"

I shake my head. "The blonde."

He laughs and walks with me back inside the clubhouse, where I regain my seat and refill my glass. I call over the blonde I was eyeing and pull her onto my lap, wrapping one arm around her while the other hand nurses my drink. I see Arrow speaking to Sin before coming to sit next to me, not even glancing at the woman I'm holding, or any other available woman in the room.

"When do you leave?" he asks, looking me in the eye, tapping his hand on his knee. I fight the urge to smile. Sin sure passed that bit of info off quick.

"Tomorrow," I say as I squeeze the woman's ass. It's a nice one, round and firm.

"You want me to go with you?" he asks, glancing away. "I'm sure Talon won't give a fuck if there's an extra man there to help, and even if he did, fuck him. He wouldn't dare say shit to me."

"No," I tell him quickly. "It'll be fine. I'll call you if I need you though, brother."

The last thing Arrow needs is to get into shit with Talon, who has some weird friendship that no one really fuckin' understands with his woman, Anna. Yeah, no more drama needed in that situation.

He nods and stands.

"You going home?"

"Yeah," he replies, lifting his chin at me. "You know where to find me if you need me."

I nod, appreciating the fact that he and any of the men are just a phone call away, no matter what I need or what shit I need help getting out of. After Arrow leaves, the men start to clear out. I stand with the woman still in my arms, ignoring her girlish squeals, and carry her off to my room.

Who knows what tomorrow will bring, but I'm sure as hell gonna enjoy today.

"You're kidding me," I say slowly as I stare at Talon in distaste. "Why the fuck can't you or one of your men do this?"

Talon looks away, his white-blond hair covering his eyes as he looks down into his drink.

"No one wanted to. And instead of making one of my men do it, I thought, why the fuck not make it your problem?" The bastard actually grins. "Easy way out. And it's an easy enough task. You stay with her at the house, guard her for a week, keep her out of trouble until we put the fuckers that are after her in the ground, and then you go back home without owing me shit."

"So it could go for longer than a week?" I ask, grinding my teeth.

"If it does," he says, taking a sip of his whiskey, "I'll send one of the men to swap places with you. You owe me only a week. That's fair, yeah?"

"Who's after her?" I ask him. "And why?"

His lips press into a tight line before he replies. "She's innocent, Vinnie, but her father isn't. Some people are trying to make her pay for the shit her old man's done, but I'm not going to let that happen."

It was a vague answer, and I'd have let him get away with it if it didn't affect me and how I handle the job at hand.

"The more I know, the better I can protect her."

"Her father is an accountant," he says, not looking happy about giving up added information. "He's in prison for fraud and embezzlement. Shayla worked for him, helping him with accounts or whatever he needed, except she didn't know and still doesn't really know just what kind of dodgy shit he was up to. She's not a certified accountant, she knows only what he taught her, which is fuckin' convenient for him. That's all you need to know. Keep her safe. Easy."

"Don't you think I should know exactly who is after her?"

"It's not going to make a difference; the job remains the same," he replies, making me want to punch him in the face.

Something's not sitting right with me. "If it's such an easy task," I ask, "what the fuck is the catch? It's essentially a baby-sitting gig, easy enough. Hell, I'll crack a beer and watch some fuckin' TV for a week—sounds like a holiday."

Talon throws his head back and laughs, his drink sloshing out of the glass. "It's not a fuckin' holiday. It's a test. A test of your fuckin' patience." He studies me, searching my eyes. "My cousin is a pain in the ass, Vinnie. None of the men want to watch her because she can be . . . a little difficult to manage." He cracks his neck from side to side while I process the fact that she is his cousin. I don't know how I feel about that.

"Your cousin," I say slowly.

"Yeah," he replies, eyes narrowing. "My cousin, and I'm fuckin' trusting you with her, so don't treat her like the enemy because she's my family."

Who the fuck does he think I am? I tighten my lips, not even justifying that comment with a response.

"I love her, don't get me wrong, but I know how stubborn and hardheaded she can be."

That's it? The girl was stubborn? That still doesn't add up.

"Big-ass bikers scared of a little girl?" I joke, grinning.

Talon pulls out his phone, presses a few buttons, and slides it over to me. I glance down at it and see a picture of a stunning Asian girl with long black hair, pale skin, and brown eyes. She is a petite little thing, with perfectly shaped lips that catch my attention.

Fuck.

"This her?"

He nods and takes back his phone. "They didn't want the job because yes, she's got an attitude problem at best, but also because she's fuckin' gorgeous, and they know if they touch her in that way, or in any way, I will personally fuck them up." He pauses, studying me. "I know how loyal you are, Vinnie—to your club, to whoever you care about. And I know that you'll look after her better than any of my men could, and that's the damn truth."

Better than his men?

His words were true, of course, but I'm still surprised at hearing them leave his lips. Perhaps he needed better men in his MC.

His cousin was a beauty, sure, but I'm not a man to be swayed by a pretty face.

"Message received," I reply, standing up from my stool. "I'm viewing this as a job, Talon. I protect your bratty cousin—who, by the way, I have no idea how the fuck she's even your cousin, seeing as she doesn't look anything like you—then I get my ass home and hopefully never see you again."

"Shayla's adopted," Talon explains, also standing. "Family isn't always about blood; you already know this." I nod. If I know anything in life to be true, it's that family is about loyalty, not blood.

"I'll text you the address now; they're expecting you. It'll take you about four hours to get there, depending on the traffic."

"All right," I say, just wanting it all over with. "Don't worry about your cousin. I'll keep her safe."

I can handle one girl. I don't give a fuck how much of an attitude she has.

"I know," Talon says, finishing the rest of his drink in one gulp. "I wouldn't have asked you otherwise."

He slams down his glass and leaves without another word.

My phone beeps with a message from him, the address.

Fuck.

Well, no time like the present.

I get on my bike and ride toward my new home for the next week.

TWO

I DO a double take when I see the house. No, the *mansion*. It's fuckin' huge. Two stories, all done in white and light gray—the house is modern as fuck, with big, timber double doors and a glass balcony on the top floor. I glance at the high security fence in approval and then enter the code that lets me in. I walk up to the door and knock, then glance down at my black boots and figure I'm probably going to have to take them off. I'm just sliding my feet out of them when the door opens and a large, bulky man stands there, a satchel over his shoulder.

"Good luck," he murmurs, walking past me. I watch him exit the gate, then disappear down the street before I step inside, closing the door behind me.

Well, fuck.

The house is silent.

Not knowing what the fuck I'm meant to do, I walk through the house, checking out the layout from a security point of view, pinpointing any weaknesses. The place is OCD tidy, and fancy as shit, so much so that I don't even want to touch anything.

Straight back from the front door is a row of glass sliding doors, opening onto a wide patio with a shimmering turquoise pool in its center.

I stop in my tracks when I see her, sunning on a lounge chair. She's lying on her stomach, a book in front of her face, which is half-covered by giant sunglasses. She's in a black bikini, and although I try not to, my gaze roams over her bare back and the curve of her ass.

Fuck.

It's a nice ass.

Big and round for her tiny frame.

Knowing I don't need to be distracted by her or her ass, I walk outside, meaning strictly business.

"Shayla?" I say as I approach, not wanting to scare her.

"What?" she asks in a haughty tone, not bothering to even see who she is talking to.

"I'm Vinnie," I say, hoping that she'd already been told I'd be arriving today. Last thing I want is to have to explain shit to her. "I'll be the one guarding you for the next week."

She closes her book and lifts her head, looking up at me. "Where did Mike go?"

"He already left," I say, scanning the backyard. "Seemed pretty fuckin' happy to do so too."

"I'll bet," she murmurs, reopening her book and casting her gaze down, dismissing me.

"Which room should I use?" I ask, wanting to get settled.

"Upstairs, first room on the right."

"Anyone else here?" I ask, trying not to stare at her ass and failing.

"Another guard comes at night," she says, flicking the page.

"You're the only one here with me during the day." She pauses, then says, "Although I don't know what they expect you to do."

I glance around. I have no idea what they expect me to do either.

Leaving her to her own devices, I check the upstairs and put my shit in my room, which is about three times the size of my room at the clubhouse. I'm glad it doesn't have fancy floral shit or anything; it's pretty much all white, with a giant bed that gives me ideas I don't need to be having. I want to take a quick shower but instead I head back down, wanting to be debriefed properly about the situation, but all I know is what Talon told me.

From what I understand, Shayla is the daughter of some accountant who is Talon's biological uncle. He had clients who required him to be creative in doing their books, which landed him in prison. Apparently there are rumors he's working with the feds, so there are men after Shayla who plan to use her against her father. Not only do they want to threaten her life, they think she has the information her father needs. She's his weakness. Talon thinks it's the Mafia, since they were a huge client of his, but he isn't really sure. No one has shown their faces. I have no idea why her father turned to Talon when he'd already hired guards, but here I am. I'm here to protect her, for a week, until they move her again.

This is the third house she's been in in the last two months. Talon thinks moving is the solution to keep her from being found, and so far it's seemed to work. On top of my being here as her personal bodyguard, her father's hired men are also on call 24-7, and the house has camera surveillance. I personally think they're going about this all wrong, but what the fuck do I know?

I'm just a biker who owes another biker a motherfuckin' favor.

After a phone call with Talon, I take a shower and head back downstairs. Shayla has moved inside and is sitting on the couch, watching TV.

"What do you do for dinner?" I ask her as my stomach rumbles, making her jump in her seat.

She flicks her head around, her hair flying around her oval-shaped face. "Jesus, how do you not make any noise when you walk? You're freaking massive." She pauses, raking her gaze over me. "You're one of those douchey guys who spends all his time in the gym, aren't you?"

My lips tighten into a line. If I'm going to have to deal with this mouth for a week, I'm going to need something to keep me sane. Since women are out, and I can't drink on the job, maybe I should take up smoking for the week.

Yeah, I can almost feel the nicotine craving begin.

"What happens for dinner?" I repeat, not impressed one bit.

"Someone usually drops something off," she says, shrugging her petite shoulders. "At seven. Sometimes a chef comes in and makes whatever I feel like eating."

A chef?

I blink slowly, wondering which idiot runs this operation. "Do they screen this chef?"

"It's the same guy who comes," she says, looking at the TV and flicking through the channels. "He's been with us for years. He's fine, practically family."

I scrub my hand down my face and count to ten in my head. I have no fuckin' idea how this girl is still alive. If I'm going to be in charge of protecting her, I'm going to change things around here. "Who drops off the food? Why don't you just cook something? It's not like you have anything else to do here all day."

Her head snaps to me like that exorcist bitch. "Just because I'm a woman I'm supposed to cook? Times have changed, and I'm not going to be spending hours in the kitchen every day just because I have a set of tits. Why don't you cook?"

I look up at the ceiling, my jaw tighter than it's ever been. Wishing Talon had asked me to torture someone for him instead, I move to stand in front of her, blocking the TV from her view.

"Hey," she growls, looking up at me.

"I'm here to make sure you're not fuckin' kidnapped, raped, or tortured," I say in a tone that's way too calm. "Who drops the food off to you?"

She purses her lips but reluctantly answers. "One of my father's men. His name is Greg."

I'm not one to judge, and I generally don't give a shit about what other people do, but it's clear this chick is spoiled as hell and is used to getting anything she wants, including her way.

"I don't like the fact that there are all these fuckin' people coming in and out of the house," I say, crossing my arms over my chest. "Talon said I'm in charge, so don't bother arguing. The chef has to go, and no one else is coming inside. The night guard I will check out myself, and if I approve, he can wait outside; he has no reason to step inside the house."

Shayla surprises me by shrugging again and saying, "I don't give a crap. Do what you want."

I exhale and walk out of the room. I change the code on the fence, and I change the locks on the doors. To really protect the little spoiled princess I need to be able to control the environment, who enters and who has access. When Greg arrives with dinner, I thank him but tell him he no longer needs to bring the food—that I will sort it out. He seems a little suspicious but agrees and lets it go. I carry the plastic bag of food to the kitchen and search through it, happy when I see tonight's menu is apparently Japanese.

"Did he bring my katsu chicken sushi?" she asks as she enters the room.

I shrug and nod toward the bag. "Have a look for yourself."

She opens the bag and pulls out a box. "Sweet," she murmurs, then grabs some water from the fridge. I have no idea how she's being so casual about everything—including having me in her presence—without even batting those long-ass lashes. Maybe she doesn't realize how dangerous a situation she's in, but still, she seems completely at ease, even though she has people out to kill her. People so dangerous that she needs high security and has to remain hidden.

"You can have the rest, this is all I wanted," she says, walking out of the kitchen. I watch her leave, gritting my teeth. Something about her just sets me on edge. It takes me a few minutes to figure out exactly what it is—she reminds me a lot of my ex-girlfriend Eliza. Eliza came from money and thought she was better than everyone else. She was a spoiled, entitled bitch, but because she was my first girlfriend, my first regular pussy, I let her lead me by the balls. Yeah—Shayla might be beautiful, but she definitely isn't my type. I like women who aren't so high maintenance and used to having their way. This week is going to drag on, but at least I can keep myself busy sorting out the clusterfuck that is Shayla's security detail.

Let's just hope she doesn't drive me insane before the week is over.

THREE

Shayla

I WATCH from the corner of my eye, pretending to ignore his very existence, as he storms around the house as if he owns it. There's something different about him from the others who have been sent to protect me. I've seen him check the locks on the windows and doors more than once, and I can tell he's questioning the way things are being run around here. It seems like he's taking the job pretty seriously, even though I know for a fact that this isn't what he does for a living. From what I gathered from Talon, Vinnie is some badass biker just using his life experience to protect me. But I trust Talon, and if he says Vinnie can be trusted, then I believe him.

"Who does the cleaning?" he suddenly stops and asks me, running his hand over his shaved head, his brown eyes pinned on me. Seeing as we haven't been doing much of the whole communication thing, his question catches me off guard.

"Why?" I ask, lifting my head up to look at him. No one has ever asked me that before.

"Answer the question," he says, not looking impressed. "If

you get a cleaner or some shit to come in, I think you need to reassess your priorities, because a little mess is better than you being fuckin' dead."

My eyes widen at his outburst. I have a feeling this guy really doesn't like me, although I'm not sure why exactly.

"I do the cleaning," I tell him, looking away and painting my toenail a bright red. I don't know what his deal is. I finish painting the nail, then glance up again, wondering why he's still standing there glaring at me.

"The place is spotless," he points out, looking around.

I dip the brush into the bottle, then say, "I like things clean."

I can't sleep if the place isn't spotless. I don't know why, but I've always been very organized and tidy. On top of that, I like to keep busy, and being stuck in the house all day doesn't give me very many options. Since my father landed in prison, work is out of the question. No one wants an accountant—an uncertified one at that—whose father is in prison for fraud. Besides, I like to clean when I'm stressed out, or angry. It helps calm me.

"You clean," he says slowly, sounding surprised. "I'd have thought you'd be used to having a cleaner, or something."

"I did have a cleaner when I lived with my dad," I say, shrugging my shoulders.

I can actually feel the judgment pouring off him. He thinks I'm spoiled and is surprised by the fact that I can keep a tidy house. Like he said before, though, I haven't really got much else to do. I've been taking some college business and marketing classes online, for a degree, to keep me busy. If I'm not studying, I'm reading, cleaning, or working out. I feel like I'm in prison, just a really fancy, expensive one. I can leave the house if I take someone with me, but all my previous bodyguards have preferred that I just stay home, probably so it was easier for them to do their job. Still, what I wouldn't kill to be able to walk outside that front door freely and without being paranoid that someone is coming for me at any given moment.

I don't complain though.

This is my life right now, but it's only temporary. I just need to suck it up and know that so many other people have it worse than being trapped inside a luxurious house. Some people don't even have a house. At least that's what I tell myself.

"So you spend all day tanning by the pool, demanding food, and painting your fuckin' nails?" he asks, looking extremely put out.

"What exactly do you want me to do?" I ask, scanning his face. I don't bother to point out the fact that I've already told him that I clean the place. It's not like I'm sitting on my ass doing nothing, and besides, what else am I supposed to do? "You haven't even been here for a full day and you're judging me? I've been living like this for weeks now. Do you think I enjoy being locked up?"

"I'm just wondering why everyone is fighting so hard to protect someone who seems to be nothing but spoiled and shallow," he says easily, like each word isn't cutting me.

"You're a dick," I tell him, shaking my head in disbelief. "And your job is to protect me, not try to make me a better person. We have a week in this house together, so why don't you just keep your hastily drawn conclusions to yourself, all right?"

Maybe I was spoiled—my father always gave me everything I wanted.

But I wasn't shallow.

And I think it says more about him than me that he decided

what I was before trying to get to know me, even a little bit. But oh well, he wasn't the first person to think so, and he wouldn't be the last.

He ignores my rant and sits down on the couch opposite me. To make matters worse, I find myself physically attracted to him—not that I'd ever admit it out loud. He did have that whole bad-boy thing going for him, a good build, and a handsome face. Although not classically gorgeous, he still has something about him that makes me want to take a second or third look.

"I need to run to the store to get a few things, and you need to come with me."

I perk up at the thought of leaving the house. I haven't been outside since the day I walked into this house. "Okay."

"Do you know the area?" he asks, stretching his neck from side to side and not looking at me.

"No," I say, leaning back on the couch. "What do you need to buy? I can do a Google search and see what there is around here."

I'd do anything for a little tiny taste of freedom, even ignore his previous rude-ass comments.

"I saw a grocery store as I was riding in, so that's fine," he says, glancing at his watch. "I want to go to a sporting goods store where I can get some weights or something, or I'm going to go batshit crazy here." He pauses. "And maybe some swimming trunks."

Not remembering the last time I went shopping in person, I feel a bubble of excitement surrounding me. "Okay, sounds good. I can buy some new stuff too. When do you want to go? Tomorrow morning?"

He nods once. "Yeah, all right. We'll have to take the vehicle they left here—can't take my bike."

"That's no problem," I say, unable to stop the smile spreading on my lips.

"Should've known shopping would be your weakness," he grumbles, stealing the remote and changing the channel.

I don't let his comment get to me. Let him think what he wants—I don't care.

I *am* happy to be able to go shopping.

If I could take a walk in a park, or go to the library, even better—but I'm not going to push it.

"You got me there," I say, rolling my eyes. Sure, I had designer bags and clothes, but that was because my father bought them for me as gifts. I've never bought something so expensive for myself, and I don't feel comfortable spending anyone else's money. It sucks as it is that I can't work, that I need to stay hidden. My father got into some serious shit, and now I'm the one sacrificing for it.

"Must be nice to have everything handed to you on a silver platter," he says, glancing down at his phone.

I grit my teeth and try to stop myself from replying, but the words just leave my mouth. "You must be a pretty hypocritical biker to judge my life when you live yours in a certain way." I pause. "Crime, women, drugs, and who knows what else, but sure, let's concentrate on the fact that I grew up with money. Apparently that's the only thing you can use against me."

Vinnie raises a brow at me, looking extremely unimpressed. "You learn all that about bikers by watching Talon? I sure as fuck don't do drugs."

I notice he doesn't address the other issues I mentioned, so the women and the illegal stuff must be true.

I know that Talon and the Wild Men aren't innocent at all, because Talon is always tangled up in something or the other.

"Really? Must suck to be stereotyped like that, then," I sneer, flashing him a fake smile.

The bastard suddenly looks amused, his lips twitching and his brown eyes filling with mirth. "You're rich, spoiled, and you have a mouth on you. I was told about all this before I even stepped into this door, so don't act like it's completely wrong. It's not just me coming to this conclusion. It's basically fact."

"Well, if everyone thinks it, it must be true," I say in a sarcastic tone. "Everyone being Talon, since he's the only person we both know."

Talon always tells me I'm a brat, but in a fond way. I'm his baby cousin, of course I'm a pain in his ass, it's part of the job description.

Vinnie shrugs and infuriatingly says, "I'm a good judge of character."

The only thing he's good at is being an ass.

"So I'm assuming you don't come from money, then?" I ask, not rudely, but all of this has to be coming from somewhere. "What do your parents do?"

"I don't have any parents," he says in a flat tone, looking back down at his phone.

"Everyone has parents."

I mean everyone came from somewhere. I was adopted as a baby, and I don't know anything about my birth parents, except their names. Maybe one day I'll travel back to Vietnam to find answers, but for now, my parents are the ones who loved and wanted me, not the ones who birthed me.

"Not me," he says, sounding like he'd rather be talking about anything else right now. "I grew up in foster care."

He still had biological parents, just like I did back in Vietnam, but I don't point that out.

"My dad and mom adopted me from an orphanage in Vietnam," I tell him, wanting him to know he's not alone, my biological parents didn't want me either.

"Yeah, well, no one adopted me," he says, standing up. "I'm going to go outside and check the perimeter. I need to have a chat with the night guard too."

He leaves, and I'm left feeling . . . something.

He didn't get adopted.

What would my life have been like if I hadn't been? Maybe that's why I don't complain about the predicament I'm in right now.

Because my life could have been a hell of a lot worse.

FOUR

H E comes back two hours later and ignores me, so I do the same, pretending we never shared something so personal with each other. I'm reading a romance novel when he sits down opposite me again and says, "It's late."

I raise my gaze to him. "And?"

"And aren't you tired?"

"Aren't you?" I fire back, wondering what he is getting at here.

"If we're going shopping early, you better get your ass up. How long does it take you to get ready? An hour? Two?"

He's really laying this bullshit on thick.

"You're ridiculous, you know that?" I say, narrowing my eyes on him. "I'll be up and ready before you are, don't you worry about that."

"I really fuckin' doubt that," he scoffs, putting his bare feet up on the red couch. "Be ready to leave after breakfast, say, ten?"

I roll my eyes. I wake up at six every morning to do yoga, so being ready by that time isn't a big deal for me.

"I'm sure I can manage that," I say, glancing back down at my book. When Vinnie makes a sound of amusement, I lift my head again and send a threatening look in his direction. "What now?"

"Nothing," he murmurs, still grinning.

I look into his brown eyes, lighter than my dark ones, and demand, "Tell me."

He scrubs a hand down the stubble on his cheek, then points to my book. "I know the author, is all. It still amazes me how popular her books are." He pauses. "And that she writes them."

I take a deep breath and try to curb down my inner fangirl. "Are you trying to tell me that you personally know Zada Ryan? No bullshit?"

I want a signed book.

No, I *need* a signed book.

No. I need all her books signed for my signed bookshelf.

With a personalized message.

"No bullshit," he replies, searching my eyes and frowning. "What's wrong with you? Your eyes are all wide and crazy, and you're squeezing the shit out of the book in your hand."

I drop the book on my lap, trying to act cool. "I'm fine," I say, tucking my hair back behind my ear. "So, just how are you friends with Zada?"

This is huge.

"On a first-name basis are you?" Vinnie asks, smirking. He taps his fingers on the arm of the couch, and I stare at the tattoos covering his knuckles as I answer.

"I love her books," I admit, shrugging. "Aren't I allowed to be curious?"

He leans forward, resting his elbows on his thighs. "Tell you what, you behave yourself for the next week, listen to everything I say, and stay out of trouble, I'll introduce you to her."

My eyes flare. "Behave myself? I'm twenty-four, not a damn child."

Could he possibly look down on me any more? I've never met a man so infuriating in my life. It makes me want to act the way he's accusing me of just to give him a hard time.

He shrugs his broad shoulders flippantly. "You know what I mean. Don't be a brat. Make my time here a little more pleasant."

How have I not been pleasant so far?

Gritting my teeth, I stand up and leave the room without a word. Yeah, he is good-looking, with those brown bedroom eyes framed in thick lashes, his sensual lips—even if they've mainly been pursed in a tight line in my presence—and the delicious body I know is hidden underneath that black T-shirt, but he is a dick.

He wanted me to *behave*?

How old is he? A couple of years older, at the most, and he's acting like I'm a kid and he's in charge. I walk upstairs to my bedroom and lie back on my bed, the white sheets soft against my skin. As I stare at the ceiling, I think over everything he's said to me today.

He thinks I'm a brat?

A plan forms in my head.

I'll show him just how bratty I can be.

I think it's time to teach Vinnie a lesson.

The next morning, after yoga, I take a shower, washing my long dark hair, then toweling it dry. By the time I'm dressed in my jeans and a white top, and my hair and makeup are sorted, it's only 8:00 a.m., so I clean my room to pass the time. When it's spotless I grab my Chanel bag and head downstairs. I come to a standstill when I look outside and see Vinnie doing push-ups outside by the pool. It's like a view from a movie. Gorgeous pool, beautiful sunny day, and a man too sexy to be real. Where did this guy come from? I need to go there.

His body is even better than I'd imagined.

His back is perfectly muscled and covered in tattoos, a sheen of sweat glazing his skin. I press myself against the sliding door for a closer look. Who knew a man doing push-ups could be so sexy? I watch as his arms flex with each movement, mesmerized. I continue to hover by the door, just staring at him like a creep.

Why are the good-looking men always egotistical jerks?

When he quickly stands and looks up, straight into my eyes, I mutter a curse under my breath. I'm standing, body pressed against the door, perving on him, and he caught me. Just great. Trying to cover up, I open the door and call out, "I'm ready when you are," then walk away to the kitchen, mentally cursing myself. A few seconds later I hear the sliding door close before he joins me. He doesn't comment on the fact that I'm up early and ready before him. Instead, all he says is, "Enjoy the view?"

I open the fridge and look inside, avoiding having to look at him for as long as I can. "What view?"

Oh, I knew what view, but I had to try to save face. The last thing he needs to know is that I find him attractive. No, he doesn't need to know that at all, especially because it doesn't matter, since nothing is going to come from it. Except maybe his ego inflating even further.

I close the fridge and make myself look at him.

My gaze instantly drops.

Oh, shit.

His abs. They are perfect. No—they are everything. Not too ripped, but deliciously defined. Abs you'd see on the cover of a magazine.

I didn't get a good look at those before, but now I do. I let my gaze linger for only a second before I look into his eyes. "Can we leave earlier? I'm ready and eager to get out of the house."

I change the subject and hope that he doesn't call me out on it.

He smirks knowingly but replies only with a "Sure, let me grab a quick shower and we'll go."

Yet he doesn't make a move to leave.

"What?" I ask when he continues to stare at me—that smug, amused expression on his face making me want to punch him.

"Nothing," he says, shrugging his broad shoulders. "Just didn't think I'd be your type."

So much for his leaving it alone.

"That's because you're not my type," I say, crossing my arms over my chest and narrowing my eyes at him. I can't believe the things that come out of this man's mouth. If he were a gentleman, he wouldn't have mentioned anything at all. So what if I checked him out a little? I don't know any women who wouldn't, although I'll never admit to that out loud.

"Your wide eyes and shallow breathing say otherwise," he says, grinning, his brown eyes alight with humor.

"I think you must have a really big imagination," I say, tilting my head to the side and studying him. "You one of those men who needs attention from women to feel validated?"

His lip twitches a few times, like he wants to smile but is trying to fight it.

"You can smile, you know," I advise him. "It won't make you any less badass. Maybe more likable though." I take a step toward him, enjoying it when his gaze drops to my mouth. "Pretty sure you said you were going to jump in the shower so we can leave. I've been ready and waiting for a while now. Maybe you're the high-maintenance one out of the two of us?"

I flash him a smug look and then walk out of the kitchen, brushing past him on the way, my shoulder touching his lower arm. Feeling happy I got to have the last word, my foot is on the first step when I hear him mutter, "I can see why no one else wanted this job," which hits me like a shot to the chest. I pause for a second but then continue making my way to my room, pretending like his words don't mean anything to me. And I mean, why should they, right?

FIVE

Vinnie

"I CAN see why no one else wanted this job," I growl, closing my eyes and rubbing my forehead. She's beautiful. Even more so up close. I can almost ignore the mouth on her because of how fuckin' pretty the lips those words come out of are. I make sure to take a quick shower, throw on a pair of jeans and a black T-shirt, then head downstairs. She's sitting on the couch, typing on her phone, bag by her side, obviously eager to go. How long has it been since she was allowed to leave the house?

"Where are the keys?" I ask her, wishing I could take my bike instead. I'm assuming she's going to want to buy a fuckload of things, so we're definitely going to need to take her four-wheel drive. Or whoever the fuck it belongs to.

She points to the coffee table in front of her, where two keys sit, hanging off a key chain of the Eiffel Tower. I grab the keys and say, "Let's go."

She quickly shoves her phone in her bag and stands up, sliding it over her shoulder. She follows me outside and gets into the passenger seat as soon as I unlock the doors. I drive up to the gate, then put the car in park while I hop out to enter the gate code. As it opens, I get back into the car and drive through, then hop back out to close it. Glancing around my surroundings, I look for anything or anyone suspicious before I drive down the road.

"Do you want me to give you directions?" she asks, looking down at her phone.

I shake my head. "I had a look last night, it's only a few minutes' drive away. I know where to go."

She nods and looks out her window, then puts the window down and smiles as the wind hits her face.

"When's the last time you left the house?" I ask her, staring straight ahead.

"Other than to move to a different location?" she asks. "Ummm. About a month."

Fuck.

No wonder she wanted to get out so badly.

"None of the guards, or whoever, could take you somewhere just to give you a change of scene?" I ask, feeling angry on her behalf. My fingers tighten on the steering wheel. What kind of life did she have? Sitting inside a house and doing nothing?

"They prefer to have me in a controlled environment in case anything happens," she says, not sounding angry over the fact.

"Then they're obviously not very good at their job," I say through clenched teeth. "Or they're just fuckin' lazy. Yeah, it's an added risk, but if you take the proper precautions, I don't see why you can't go out now and again. If you don't, you're gonna go fuckin' crazy."

She shrugs her dainty shoulders. "I never really asked them to take me out, or badgered them about it." She sighs dreamily, the sound making my dick harden. "Really happy to be getting away right now though."

She never asked them or hassled them about it? No diva demands? Who is this girl? I'm starting to think I was wrong about her, at least about certain things. She was still rich and spoiled, but maybe she isn't so bad as a person.

Maybe.

I should probably be asking myself why was I so angry. Over someone I didn't know, and wasn't even sure I liked. I'd thought she was like Eliza, but after just a few conversations with her, I think I might be wrong. I'm not usually one to judge others, in fact, I'm usually the one to be judged, but something about Shayla has me all fuckin' twisted.

"Well, while I'm here we can go and do whatever you like," I tell her, the words flowing out of my mouth before my brain can catch up. "I'd prefer to stay away from large crowds though."

"Really?" she asks, and I can hear the hope in her voice.

"Really," I say as I park the car in front of the sports store. "Stay by my side; don't wander off anywhere, all right?"

She nods eagerly and opens her car door. I do the same, quickly walking around to her side. We enter the store in silence, and she follows me around as I grab some weights, a boxing bag, and some gloves.

"Do you want anything?" I ask her, scanning the store.

"No, thanks," she declines politely. She'll probably ask me to take her to some fuckin' expensive designer store next, one I've never even fuckin' heard of. I pay for my goods, my brows raising when she takes the bag and gloves in her hands to carry them to the car. She must notice my expression because she says, "Contrary to popular belief, I'm not a spoiled brat."

She storms off to the car, giant boxing bag in her hand, almost the size of her, making me feel a little bit like the asshole. I grab the two weights and follow behind her, opening the trunk, freeing my hands, then helping her.

"Thanks," I murmur, slamming the trunk closed. "Where to next?"

She looks down at her hands and winces, her cute little nose scrunching up. "Kind of a weird request, actually."

I stare at her expectantly. What is it? Prada? I rack my brain for another designer name but come up empty. I only know Prada because Faye, Sin's wife, once bought herself a bag and we didn't hear the end of it for a whole week.

"What?" I ask when she still doesn't say anything.

"Can we go to a pet store?" she asks, glancing up at me. Fuck, she's pretty. I've seen a lot of beautiful women over the years, but there's something about Shayla. Something that makes me want to protect her. Something that I'm sure as hell going to ignore.

"A pet store?" I ask, furrowing. "I don't think now is the best time for you to be a pet owner." I pause. "Unless you're getting an already trained German shepherd or rottweiler."

She purses her lips. "You asked, and that's where I want to go. Will you take me or not?"

"All right," I say, nodding slowly. "Pet store it is."

She never does what I expect.

I don't like it.

"Oh my god, how cute is she?" she beams, pressing the puppy's nose against her own. I watch in fascination as she puts the black puppy down and picks up a tan mastiff-looking pup.

"Aren't you adorable? Yes you are," she coos, a peaceful expression on her face.

Of all the places she could have chosen, she wanted to come to a pet store.

To hug puppies.

Not sure what to do with this information, I just watch her in her element, hugging each and every puppy, rubbing their bellies and baby talking to them. For a split second I wonder if it's possible for her to take one home, or maybe even ten, because it obviously makes her happy as fuck. It looks like this right here is her happy place.

I glance down at my watch and realize we've already been here an hour. The pet shop owner keeps giving Shayla dirty looks, probably because she knows she's here just to get her puppy fix. Every time she looks like she's about to say something though, I send my own look in her direction, which shuts her up.

"Vinnie, how cute is this little guy?" she asks, lifting up a giant puppy in her hand.

"Do you want to get one?" I ask, once again without thinking.

Fuck.

What was wrong with me?

"No," she says, smiling and shaking her head. "I'd love a puppy, but I wouldn't buy one from a pet store. I'd rather get one from a registered breeder."

I open my mouth, then close it, having no idea what she was raving on about. Why did she want to come here then?

"I just wanted to see some puppies," she says, shrugging with a small smile on her delicious lips. "Do you want to get something to eat now?"

"Sounds good," I tell her, rubbing my stomach. "I could seriously go for a burrito."

"Burritos it is," she says, easily agreeing when once again I expect her to argue. This is her chance to go and eat in a fancy restaurant or something, after being cooped up for so long, eating nothing but takeout.

"You sure? We can go eat somewhere else if you like," I say as we get back into the car, glancing over in her direction. "I can grab a burrito on the way home."

"A burrito actually sounds good," she says, kicking her bare feet up on the dashboard. "Chicken, white rice, and chipotle sauce."

I grin at that. "Fuck yeah. Looks like we finally agree on something."

SIX

Shayla

"I CAN order things online," I explain to him. "It's not my name or credit card, so it can't be traced to me. So that's why I don't really need to do any shopping." I walk by some green grapes and pick up a bag, putting them in the cart. "Grocery shopping, however . . . I'm in heaven right now."

Vinnie shakes his head in amusement and grabs some salad. "Are we going healthy then?"

I grin as I put some potatoes in the cart. "Half healthy, half junk food?"

He throws his head back and laughs. "My kind of girl."

We both look into each other's eyes after he says that, a weird tension building between the two of us. It's me who clears my throat and changes the subject. "I think the two burritos you had covers the junk food for the day."

He shakes his head, disagreeing. "There's corn and shit in there. That makes it healthy. What are we going to do for dinner?"

"You cooking?" I ask, raising an eyebrow.

"I was hoping you would," he says, flashing his straight white teeth at me.

"Since you took me out today, I'm sure I can make an exception. What would you—"

"Lasagna with breaded chicken," he says quickly, before I can even finish the sentence.

"Isn't that a little weird?" I say, brow furrowing. "Did you make that up, pairing those two together, or is it an actual thing?"

"You asked and that's what I'd like." He pauses. "Please."

"Okay," I say, dragging the word out. "Sounds easy enough. I've never made breaded chicken before, but I'll just google a recipe." I pull out my phone and check the ingredients. "Simple."

"Fuckin' awesome," he mutters under his breath, making me smile.

"What about dessert?"

"I'll let you choose that," he says, grabbing some steaks and putting them in the cart. "Anything chocolate works for me."

"How about Oreo and Nutella cheesecake?" I ask him, knowing the recipe by heart.

He stops in his tracks. "You can make that, no shit?"

"No shit."

He smiles and I return it.

"You're not so bad, Shayla," he says, turning his face away from me, but I see the corner of his lips kick up.

"Right back at you, Vinnie," I say, watching him as he bends over to pick up something. My gaze zones in on his tight ass. "Right back at you."

He stands and turns around, once again catching me ogling

him. This time though, he just smiles cheekily and sends a wink in my direction. Red-cheeked, I look at the bakery section, pretending a loaf of bread just became the most interesting thing in the world.

I hear his deep chuckle from behind me, and it makes my lips twitch. It's not my fault the man is good-looking, and he isn't even really my type—I generally go for professional men. I do love me a man in a suit, but something about his rugged looks and bad-boy charm has me curious. Yes, he can be an asshole, as I found out yesterday, but today he's being nice, playful even. I can see that he's on alert, checking our surroundings and noticing every detail, but he still manages to be relaxed. Today has almost been like two friends hanging out instead of a bodyguard and his client running errands. How things can change in just a few hours. We pay for the groceries and load them in the back of the car. On the way back to the house, Vinnie's phone rings and he puts it on speaker.

"Vinnie?" a woman says into the phone.

"Yeah, Faye. How's everything? You're on speaker, by the way."

"Am I? Oooh. Hello, whoever it is in the car with you," Faye says, making Vinnie flash me an amused glance. "I'm just calling to see how you are."

"I'm fine, Faye," he says gently, making me think he cares about this woman. "How's the princess? And the tummy?"

"Both good," Faye says, and even I can hear the smile in her voice. "It's Lana's birthday today, so remember to call her."

"I will," Vinnie says. "What are you guys doing for it?"

"Party at the clubhouse," Faye says, giggling. "Anna was supposed to make her a cake, right? We were going to make her a cake in the shape of a penis, but then Anna calls me this morning and was like, 'I can't make the penis cake; it's too hard!' "

Faye starts laughing, and I bite my lip to stop myself from laughing with her. "She didn't even realize what she said! I laughed for like five minutes before she got it. Good times."

I hear a woman yell in the background, "You try making a penis cake! It *is* hard!"

"You called me just to tell me that story, didn't you?" Vinnie asks, smirking. "What cake is Lana getting, then?"

"Red velvet with cream cheese icing."

"That we bought from the store!" I hear the other woman yell.

Vinnie laughs, then says, "Tell Anna I said hey, and I'll call Lana tonight to wish her happy birthday. You all stay out of trouble, you hear me?"

"Okay," Faye says into the line. "We miss you, Vinnie!"

Vinnie looks a little uncomfortable, but says, "I miss you all too."

Faye cuts the line, and Vinnie and I are left in silence.

"They sound fun," I say, hoping he'll offer me some information. I know nothing about the man next to me except that he's a biker, he knows my cousin, and that he's both sexy and infuriating. I'd definitely like to know more, starting with who those women are, the ones he seems to be so close to.

"They are" is all he says though, leading me to wonder if one of the women belongs to him. I ignore the feeling of disappointment that hits me, knowing it has no reason to be there. Yesterday I wanted to strangle him, and today, what? I'm upset he might be taken? There's definitely something wrong with me.

What did it matter if he has a girlfriend? By the end of the week he'll be gone and I'll never see him again anyway. On to the next bodyguard, until I'm probably hunted down by my father's enemies.

Yeah, I know just how serious the situation I'm in is. I can pretend otherwise all I want, but the truth is, eventually they're either going to catch me or I'm going to have to leave the country with a whole new identity. I spoke to Talon about the latter, and although he doesn't want me to leave, he says it's an option he's considering. I know Talon is working on something because he told me he just needs a little time. I really don't want to leave, so I'm hoping we figure something else out. I have some ideas, but I think for now I'll keep them to myself.

"Any last stops?" he asks, pulling me from my thoughts.

"Nope," I say, popping the *p*. I look out of the window. "I'm good."

"All right. See, we survived our first outing without any of those bastards finding us," he jokes, turning up the music a little louder. "We've got this."

"Don't even joke," I say, rolling my eyes. "Besides, we haven't made it home yet, and you might have just jinxed us."

"I don't believe in any of that shit," he replies, silencing his phone as it rings again. "You make your own luck."

"You don't believe in fate?"

He shakes his head.

"What do you believe in, then?" I ask, turning to study his profile.

"I believe in loyalty, my family, and working my ass off to make sure things go my way" is his reply. I contemplate his words. That was all he believed in? Why did that make me feel a little . . . sad? He was a grown-ass man, and like he'd said, his parents didn't want him, so maybe that's why he doesn't believe in fate. When he says his family, he has to be talking about his MC. For a moment, I feel a tiny bit jealous that he has that. My father is in prison, my mom died a few years back, and any friends I have are fading away as time goes on without my contacting them, so really, I'm alone.

And he isn't.

So while I was the one who got adopted as a child, he's the one who has a family now. Funny how that works out, isn't it? We can relate to each other, but at the same time we can't. Growing up in a world like this is hard enough; I can't imagine having to do it without parents, or someone to look after you. The foster system is a joke, everyone knows that, and God only knows what he went through.

"Loyalty is everything," I agree, thrumming my fingers on my thigh. "I do believe in fate and destiny and all that crap too though."

He chuckles as he pulls onto our street. "All that crap, huh? Sounds real important to you. But yes, you seem like one of those happy-go-lucky, always-look-on-the-bright-side type of people."

I don't think that that's a bad thing. There's nothing wrong with being hopeful, seeing the positive in situations and the good in people.

"You know what I mean," I say, rolling my eyes. "I'm a closet romantic. I think that everything that's meant to be will be, when the time is right."

"Jesus," he grumbles, stopping the car at the front of the gate. "Is this the shit that Zada Ryan writes? No wonder none of the men will read it except Tracker."

I jump on that. "Who's Tracker?"

"Stay here," he commands, leaving the car to put the gate code in. When he comes back I ask, "Is Zada Ryan one of your biker chicks? That's how you know her, isn't it? That's so fucking cool!"

He glances at me and frowns. "You have crazy eyes again."

Great, that's twice he's seen my fangirl face.

"You're not going to answer me, are you?" I gather.

"Nope," he says, sounding cheerful. "I told you, after this I'll organize a day where you can meet her yourself. Your own private signing."

"If I'm good," I mutter, remembering his past words.

"You planning on being bad?" he asks, parking the car.

"I was," I admit. "I was going to be a little bitch and make your life hell for judging me when you didn't even know me."

Vinnie snaps his head to me, eyes wide. His shoulders start shaking as he begins to laugh. "Are you serious?" He hits the steering wheel, laughing harder. "You were going to make my life hell?"

"Yes," I say, eyes narrowing at his amusement. He clearly doesn't appreciate how uncomfortable I could have made his situation. "I was."

"Oh, fuck," he groans, shoulders shaking some more. "Shay, you're fuckin' hilarious."

Shay.

No one I know calls me Shay, but I find myself liking it. And even though I wasn't trying to be hilarious—I was just being honest—I also like when he laughs.

"Come on, let's get inside. You can tell me more about this nefarious plan of yours."

SEVEN

"SO you were just going to be a bitch? That's not much of a plan," Vinnie says, eyes dancing with amusement. He grabs the fruit and vegetables and packs them away in the fridge.

"I was going to behave the way you expected me to," I say, opening the pantry and putting away the items in my hands. I leave out everything I need to make dinner. "You were making me out to be this spoiled little diva, so I was going to lay it on thick and make your life miserable while you're here."

"So what happened?" he asks, leaning back against the counter and watching me. "You changed your mind? You were still a bit of a bitch yesterday, you know."

"You took me out for the first time in a month, and you took me to the pet store," I say, my eyes gentle on him. "And you sat there for over an hour without complaining while I hugged puppies. Not many men would do that. So I forgave you for being a judgmental asshole because there is obviously more to you than meets the eye."

He was patient and he was kind. Yes, I saw the way he was

looking at the woman who worked there, just daring her to come up to us and kick us out. He had my back, giving me something when he didn't even understand why it meant so much to me. I like puppies; they make me happy. I've always wanted a dog, but my mom was allergic, or so she said. I personally think she just wasn't an animal person, but either way, I never got the puppy I asked for, even though I begged every birthday and Christmas. There's nothing puppies can't cure. If you've had a stressful day, cuddle a puppy.

Vinnie surprises me by throwing his head back and laughing. "Fuck, Shay. You can't just go around calling bikers names and shit. Not all of them might be as nice as me."

"Well, lucky for me I got stuck with you," I say, opening a chocolate bar and taking a bite. "Do you want some?"

He eyes the chocolate and nods, opening his mouth. I lift my arm up high just to reach his mouth with my hand, placing the treat at his lips. He leans forward and take a big chunk out of it.

"That wasn't a bite," I protest. "That was half!"

"Look at the size of me compared to you. Since I'm almost double you, it's only fair that I get more. Do the math, Shay."

I quickly shove the rest of the chocolate in my mouth before he makes a play for that too.

"Sexy," he comments, smirking as I struggle to chew with my mouth so full.

I simply shrug and throw away the wrapper, then say, "I'm going to start cooking. Are we doing anything tomorrow?"

"What do you want to do?" he asks, crossing his arms over his broad chest, his back still against the counter.

"Do you think we could go for a run? Along the beach or

something?" I ask, thinking how amazing that would be. "Maybe get some ice cream afterward?"

He studies me, considering. I flash him a hopeful smile and point to the ingredients for the lasagna and chicken I was about to make him, just to remind him how nice I am.

"All right." He gives in, looking amused at my tactics, his lips twitching upward a few times. "Not like we have anything else to do." He pauses. "Besides keep you alive. Are you sure these guys are still looking for you? Either they're shit at tracking people, or they don't care anymore."

"I don't know," I admit. "My father hasn't contacted me about anything in weeks. Talon might know what's going on. He's usually the one who makes sure I'm safe, and sometimes he goes and visits my father in prison."

"I'll give him a call," Vinnie says, not sounding too happy at the notion.

"You don't like Talon?" I ask, wondering what his deal with my cousin is.

"It's complicated" is all he says, quickly changing the subject. "How long until the food is ready?"

"You realize it's not even dinner time yet, right?" I point out. "It's only like three o'clock."

He points to the meat on the table. "Yet you're laying the ingredients out and making me excited. I'm fine with an early dinner. Just make enough for seconds when we get hungry again later on."

"Demanding much?"

"Hey, I took you to see puppies, remember?" He grins cheekily, making my expression soften. "I'm going to do a perimeter check."

"All right," I say, puffing out a sigh. He playfully tugs on my hair as he passes me and I watch him exit the kitchen. Just yesterday I made a big deal about my being in the kitchen cooking just because I was a woman, and here I am, the very next day, cooking him a meal. I grumble to myself as I start to prepare everything, then decide to play some music while I cook. I put on my favorite playlist, then get to work on the lasagna.

Vinnie better love it.

"Do you dance like that in public?" Vinnie asks, making me almost drop the pan in my hands. I turn around and look at him, confused by the odd expression on his face. I'd just finished the meal and was doing the dishes, and I'm sure his timing wasn't coincidental.

"What?"

He gestures to my body. "I've been standing here for a few minutes watching you dance. Is this how you dance when you're in public?"

"Yeaaah," I reply, dragging the word out. "What's wrong with how I dance?"

"Nothing," he says, picking up on my tone. "It's just pretty . . ."

"Pretty what?" I ask, narrowing my eyes. He's about to insult me, I know it. What the hell was wrong with my dancing? I thought I was a pretty good dancer, as a matter of fact. I danced growing up and all through high school, and I had good rhythm. In fact, people often commented how great I was at dancing when I used to go clubbing.

"Your moves are even sexier than the women I've seen at

Toxic," he says, shrugging his shoulders and clearing this throat. "They're fuckin' sexy moves. If you were mine there's no way in hell I'd want you to dance like that in public, because every man would be staring."

I wipe my wet hands on the tea towel and close the space between us. "Did you just say that I dance like a stripper?"

He puts his hands up. "Not exactly—"

"Oh, that's right," I say, tapping my finger on my cheek. "Sluttier than a stripper."

I try to keep my face straight so he thinks I'm serious, even though I'm just playing around with him. I know I'm a decent dancer, but I also know that I do like to dance sensually.

"That's not what I said," he growls, lowering his hands. "They're just sexy moves. All that winding and grinding and shit—you know what I mean."

"Clearly I don't," I say in a dry tone, hiding my amusement. "I just spent more than an hour cooking for you, and you walk in and tell me I dance like a stripper and shouldn't dance in public. Am I missing anything?"

"You're overreacting," he says, crossing his arms over his chest.

"No," I say, grabbing the plate with his crumbed chicken. "*This* would be overreacting." I open the trash can and pretend that I'm about to dump the food when Vinnie grabs the plate from me and holds it aloft.

"I can't believe you almost did that!" he says, sounding both surprised and upset. "What the fuck, Shay?"

I start laughing at his expression. "As if I'd throw away food."

"What?" he asks, checking over the food, not even paying any attention to my words.

I roll my eyes. "The food is all there, Vinnie, now take back the stripper comments."

"Sorry" by Justin Bieber starts to play. An apt sound track for the moment.

"All right," he groans, putting the plate back down on the table and pulling me against his body for a hug. Bad idea. The feeling of being pressed up against him isn't going to help with my attraction to him. "I'm sorry, Shay. I'm so fuckin' sorry that you dance like a stripper, and that you have terrible taste in music."

As his words hit me, I struggle to move away, but he keeps me pinned with his giant arms wrapped around me. "You jerk!"

"I'm not done," he growls again, lifting me in the air and throwing me over his shoulder, my arms dangling. He walks with me outside, and the second he heads in the direction of the pool, I start to squirm harder.

"Don't you dare throw me in there, you asshole!" I squeal, legs waving in the air.

"What a great idea," he says, standing on the edge of the pool. In one swift movement, he tosses me in, the cold water surrounding me in an instant. I push off the bottom and swim to the surface, where Vinnie is laughing like a fucking hyena. Pushing my wet hair out of my face, I send him the dirtiest look I can muster.

"I'm never cooking for you again. Ever," I grit out, swimming to the edge and jumping out. I look down to discover that my white top is now completely see-through, my nipples pebbled and very visible. I glance at Vinnie to see that, yes, that's exactly where his gaze is. Covering my breasts with my hands, I look at his face and wait for him to notice me staring at him. It takes a while, and I realize it's because my skirt is also pasted against my body, showing off every curve and crevice that I own.

"Can you stop looking?" I growl at him. "And get me a towel?"

"Nope," he says with a wide smile on his face, lying back on the hammock and putting his hands behind his head. "I think it's my turn to enjoy the view."

He actually wasn't going to get me a towel! I can't believe this guy. I don't think I've met anyone more infuriating in my life. Deciding to drag him down with me, I run with my hands still covering my breasts and jump on him, getting water all over him. I wrap my arms around his torso and bury my face in his chest.

"I don't know how this is meant to be punishment," he says, his tone having gone husky. I still my movements, just lying there on him, suddenly aware of the position I just put us in. Slowly, I lift my head and look into his brown eyes.

"You're wet now," I blurt out, staring at his lips. He has nice lips. Full, and firm. Sensually shaped. I wonder if he is a good kisser. Who am I kidding, of course he'd be.

"I'll bet you're wet too," he murmurs, licking his lips.

Shit.

I was wet—all over.

Outside and inside.

How can such sleazy words excite me?

"Shut up" is all I manage to respond.

He brings his lips closer to mine, and I know this is a terrible idea. The worst. But I still don't pull away. As a matter of fact, it's me who closes the last bit of space between us; it's me who initiates the kiss. The second my lips touch his though, it's like a switch flicks, and he takes over, cupping my face with his hand and deepening the kiss. He slants his head to the side, makes a growling noise in his throat that turns me on even more, then swipes his tongue against mine. I grip his T-shirt with my hands, pulling him closer to me. I can feel his hard cock pressed alongside my thigh, straining against his jeans. It makes me realize what we're doing, so I break the kiss. Both of us are left panting. It really was the worst idea, so why did I want to kiss him again? Why did I want him to strip off my clothes, then his? We watch each other in silence, the air tense and thick between us.

"I should go get changed," I blurt out, not knowing what to say, wanting to leave and stay at the same time.

His throat muscles work as he swallows. "Yeah, all right. Fuck, Shay."

That pretty much summed it up.

I slide off him and head inside without turning back around. But I have to admit, it wasn't easy to do.

EIGHT

Vinnie

STAND in the shower, letting the warm water drip down my body. I stroke my cock with my hand, up and down, thinking of Shay, imagining that she let me fuck her on that hammock, outside in broad daylight. Fuck. Her body, her taste. The look in her eye. I don't remember ever being that fuckin' hard in my life. She's so tiny and petite yet has curves in all the right places; a round, bubble butt, and tits just the perfect handful. I imagine I'm deep inside her, fucking her raw, until I come in my hand, spurting all over the tiled wall.

"Fuck," I grit out between clenched teeth, closing my eyes and letting the pleasure take over me. After I finish, I still don't feel satisfied. I don't think anything will sate me besides getting inside her. What a fuckin' mess. Talon is going to be pissed if I fuck her, although I'm sure I can make it so he never finds out. If he asks though, I wouldn't lie about it. I hate liars.

I finish up in the shower, then throw on some gray track pants and a white T-shirt. Feeling starved, I can't wait to eat—I only hope that shit isn't awkward between us. I still have another five nights to get through, not including tonight. I walk downstairs to find her in the living room, freshly showered herself, on her phone, the TV on in the background.

"Should we eat?" I ask, not wanting to be rude.

She turns to me, surprised, quickly putting away her phone. Her cheeks turn pink but her expression neutral. "You go ahead. I'm not hungry now; I'll eat a little later."

I nod and head straight for the kitchen, grabbing a plate and piling lasagna and chicken onto it. I grab a knife and fork, then return to the living room, sitting in the single chair. I cut a piece of the chicken and almost groan at the taste. "This is fuckin' amazing," I tell her, tasting the lasagna next. It was just as good, maybe even better. Even the salad was delicious.

I look up at her and say, "I'm really fuckin' sorry I threw you into the pool, Shay."

That brings a wicked smile to her face, laughter escaping her lips. "Enjoy the food, Vinnie, because it's the one and only meal you'll ever get from me."

"Oh, come on, now," I cajole. "If a certain someone wants to go to the beach and shit tomorrow, I think a hot meal at the end of the day would persuade me."

"Are you blackmailing me? After you already told me that you'll take me tomorrow?" she asks, looking half outraged, half impressed.

"You don't need to use such ugly words," I say, chewing thoughtfully. "But yes, that's exactly what I'm doing."

"Fine." She gives in but doesn't look happy about it. "But I want to go somewhere every day while you're here. Who knows if the next guard will take me anywhere."

I don't like the fact that a few days from now, another man will be here protecting her. Probably doing a shit job of it too, making her miserable and stuck inside. If I offer to stay longer though, Talon will know something is up. I'd also have to run it by Sin, which would prompt questions. Staying longer isn't a good idea anyway, considering the fact that we already kissed after only two days. I can just imagine what will happen the longer we stay around each other. An image of her, naked, my head between her legs, flashes through my mind.

"Vinnie?" she interrupts, stealing my attention from my thoughts.

"Yeah?"

"You stopped eating and were just staring straight ahead. It was weird," she says, wrinkling her nose.

"Just lost in thought," I say, continuing to eat. "Yes, we can go wherever you want to go, as long as it's not too crowded."

"Deal," she says, eyes on the TV screen once more. Apparently we're pretending the kiss never happened, and that's more than fine with me. I finish everything on my plate and then rinse my dish in the sink before putting it in the dishwasher. Grabbing a spoon and the tub of ice cream we bought today, I sit back down in my chair.

"You could just serve it into a bowl," she grumbles, staring at the tub of cookies and cream.

"You got another flavor, so I just assumed this one was all for me," I say, shrugging and scooping a spoonful.

"I got two so we could have a little variety. Do you want to eat the same ice cream every night? That reminds me, I have to make the cheesecake."

I swallow before I reply. "Shay, if you want some, then have it. We've already had our mouths on each other, so I don't think it fuckin' matters if we eat out of the same tub at this point."

So much for pretending the kiss never happened, I think, cringing to myself.

"Seriously?" she mumbles, sighing. "I think sharing a kiss is a little different."

"Pretty sure it's exactly the same," I fire back. "We share saliva either way, end of story."

She throws her hands in the air all dramatically. "You're impossible, you know that?"

"Are you grumpy because you're sexually frustrated?" I ask, sucking on the spoon. "Because I can take care of that for you if you want. I'm really good with my mouth."

She looks at me like she wants to kill me. "I think I'll survive, thank you."

"Offer stands," I say, giving the spoon one long lick. "You've been kept prisoner for a while, I'm sure it's been some time since you got any dick."

I thought my crude words would put her off, but her expression doesn't even change, once again surprising me.

"Unless I fuck all my bodyguards," she fires back, smirking.

My hands clench at the thought, but I don't believe it for one second. "You're not the type."

"Making assumptions again?" she asks, a haughty look on her face. She raises her eyebrow in a way that makes me want to strangle her and kiss her at the same time.

"I'm sure if you were fucking your bodyguards, they'd stick around longer," I say, smirking. "Poor Mike couldn't get out of here fast enough."

She might think her scowl is ferocious, but it's actually just cute. "You're such an asshole, do you know that?"

"I get no complaints from the women I'm around," I reply, closing the lid on the ice cream and setting the tub on the table. "I happen to think I'm an okay guy. Not the best, but sure as hell not the worst."

"Is one of those women yours?" she asks, tilting her head to the side.

"Wouldn't have let you kiss me if that were the case," I say, leaning back in the chair and studying her. "You didn't know if I was taken and you still kissed me. Not such a good girl after all, huh, Shay?"

Her eye twitches a little. "I didn't kiss you. You kissed me. And if you have a woman it's your responsibility to be faithful to her, not mine."

I chuckle and enjoy watching her as she squirms in her seat. We both know she made the final move for the kiss, even though I was the one to close the space between us. "If you say so. We were both there; we both know what happened."

A muscle ticks in her jaw as she grinds her teeth. "It doesn't matter who kissed who because it won't be happening again. A minor lapse in judgment, that's all it was. Like you said, I haven't even kissed a guy in a long time. I don't know what your excuse is, but that's mine and I'm sticking to it."

She returns her attention to the TV screen, dismissing me. I pick up the tub, open it again, and take another huge spoonful out, pretending like my cock isn't throbbing. But it is, even though I'd just made myself come not even an hour ago. Is it going to be like this for the rest of the week?

Because if so, I'm not sure I'm going to survive it.

NINE

Shayla

I REST my palms on my knees, catching my breath. It's been so long since I've been able to jog along the beach. It's a beautiful sunny day today, and I'm glad I wore my swimsuit underneath my workout clothes.

"Finished already?" Vinnie asks from beside me, not even breaking a sweat. "Let's do at least another fifteen minutes, then we can go for a swim."

I was pretty tired, but for some reason I didn't want him to see me as weak or as a quitter, so I nod and force myself to continue. By the time we're done I'm pretty much dying, gasping for air and already feeling the burn in my calves. Vinnie hands me some water, which I gulp down.

"You did well," he says, looking impressed. "I thought you'd come to a standstill whenever you'd had enough but you pushed through."

"Is everything a test with you?" I ask, wiping my mouth with the back of my hand. I felt like it was. He was always expecting me to react a certain way and wanting to see if he was right.

Last night after dinner we both went to bed in our separate rooms, but I'm not going to lie, it was hard knowing he was so close, and probably naked in bed the whole night. It was a long night of tossing and turning and playing out various scenarios in my mind. Part of me was hoping he'd come into my room and ravish me, but the realistic part of me was glad he stayed away. Why was everything with this man so confusing?

He studies me for a few seconds before replying with a yes.

I throw him the bottle of water back, and lift my T-shirt off, revealing my black bikini top. "Can we go in the water, please? The sun is scorching, and I just want to relax in the waves."

His eyes linger on my breasts, and then on my stomach. I let him have his fill and then slide my shorts down, revealing the bottom. I'm not going to lie, I enjoy the feeling of his eyes on me, as he continues to take in every part of me. I put my clothes in a pile on the sand and take a step toward the ocean. "Are you coming or not?"

He takes his T-shirt off, and I turn toward the water, not wanting to miss the show, but not wanting to stand there staring at him like an idiot yet again. Instead, I walk into the water, letting the waves brush past my knees. The cool water is so inviting, I decide to dive in without waiting for Vinnie. Refreshing coldness surrounds me as I swim under a wave, then push up for air. I look back to the sand but don't see him standing there. I scream as hands grab me from behind, momentarily startling me.

I hear an amused chuckle, and turn so I'm face-to-face with him. "Don't think the bad guys are out waiting for you in the water, Shay."

"Wasn't worried about them," I say, holding on to his shoulders. "More like a shark or something."

His hands wander to my waist, dangerous territory if you ask me. I run my fingers over his head. I don't know why he shaves it, but it suits him. I touch the short hairs there, liking how they prickle my fingers. My face is so close to his, so close I can see flecks of green in his brown eyes.

"Heard you tossing and turning last night," he murmurs, squeezing my waist. "Why was that exactly?"

My gaze narrows. "There's no way you could have heard anything. My room isn't that close to yours."

His lips twitch upward, and I have no idea what is so amusing until he admits, "I might have come to your door once during the night. Or twice."

I absorb that information. "Why?"

"You know why," he replies, letting go of me and swimming backward. "I wanted you, and I was tempted, but I managed to control myself." He scoffs. "Trust me, it wasn't fuckin' easy either. So next time you want to give me a little show in your bikini, you should probably keep that in mind."

"I wear my bikini every time I go swimming. If you can't control yourself or your dick, that's hardly my problem."

He makes a sound, a mix between a growl and a groan. "Coming from someone who wouldn't even watch me undress. Too tempting for you, was it?"

"This conversation is pointless," I call out as I swim a little farther out, and it was. Yes, we're clearly attracted to each other, but he's trying to ignore it and so am I. Even though I hadn't had sex in just over a year now. Hell, I can barely remember what sex is like at this point. Maybe that's why I was so tempted. Although none of the other guards had tempted me, and a few of them were okay-looking. I duck underneath the water, resurface, and then make my way back to shore. Vinnie follows. I realize we're going to have to walk back all the way to the car, and sigh heavily. Yeah, I'm going to be feeling all this exercise tomorrow. I pick up my clothes and glance over at him.

I don't know what expression he sees on my face but he grins and says, "Do you want me to carry you?"

I decline, tempting as the offer sounds. We walk back to the car in silence, and I allow myself to enjoy being in the sun, on the beach—the sand beneath my toes and the wind in my hair.

Who knows when I'll be back here.

He takes me to get ice cream without my having to ask. I have to admit, it's a very sweet move on his behalf.

"Anywhere else you want to go?" he asks, scanning the area as we sit on the grass.

"Nope. How about you? Do you want to go anywhere?" I ask, even though I was fucking tired and just wanted a shower and a nap.

"I'm good," he says, licking the soft-serve vanilla cone. "Can't remember the last time I had ice cream like this." He pauses, then adds, "I think it was when I was a prospect and Faye was pregnant. She'd make me bring her ice cream, or take her out to get it all the time."

"Faye?"

"My president's old lady," he explains, making my eyes widen in realization.

"Oh," I say, my tongue chasing some of the ice cream as it drips down the cone. "I forgot how good it was, just to get some fresh air and enjoy the simple things in life, you know?"

He nods, watching me for a moment before returning to his frozen treat. "You know you can't live like this forever, right? Something needs to be done about the whole situation. I don't get how your father and Talon can allow this to continue, with you having to hide because of whatever shit he got himself into."

"I know, but I don't really have a choice. I considered leaving the country, but I'd have to take a new identity and leave behind Talon and my father, who are the only family I'm close to. I've been hiding for a few months now, hopefully it won't be too much longer."

"I don't get it. Why doesn't Talon just hide you in his MC?" he says, sounding angry. "Or I don't know, come up with some-thing other than your being stuck with strangers and being sent here there and everywhere. It's fucked."

Talon wanted to hide me in the Wild Men MC clubhouse. In fact, that was the first thing he said to me. However, something changed, and he had to come up with a new plan. He didn't explain to me why, but I have the feeling something's going on with his MC and he didn't feel I'd be safe there for some reason. It doesn't really make sense, because those men are family to Talon, so I didn't really understand the situation either.

"He wanted to," I say, wanting to stand up for my cousin. "But something happened. I don't know what. I do know that he has a reason for not taking me there though."

"Something else to discuss with him," he says, jaw tight and clenched. "I'd feel like shit just leaving you, you know? Going back to my life and handing you over to some other dick, not knowing what the hell is going to happen to you."

"That's sweet of you, Vinnie," I say, laying my hand on his

forearm. "But I'm not your problem. You don't need to worry about me."

I don't know what is going to happen, and I'm trying to just take things day by day. It is unfair that people want to use me as leverage against my father, but there isn't anything I could do about it besides try to survive. He is right though, something has to give.

"It's not as simple as that," he says, taking a crunchy bite out of his cone. "I don't know; I need to think about it, but things aren't going to be the same when I leave as they were before I got here."

He says it like a promise, like a threat.

And when he says it—for some reason I believe him.

TEN

Vinnie

"WANT me to drive down, brother?" is how Arrow answers the phone, making me smile.

"No, but as usual I appreciate the offer," I say into the phone, looking down the driveway. "I do need a favor though. Talon's not answering his fuckin' phone and I have a few questions for him."

More like an interrogation. I don't care how much he tells me this isn't my business, he made it my business when he dragged me into it.

"I'll try to get in contact with him for you," he rasps, not sounding too happy about it, but he wouldn't complain. That's just Arrow through and through. "Everything okay over there?"

I didn't really know what the fuck to say. Everything was okay, but it wasn't. I know that Arrow will just tell me that this isn't my problem to deal with, that Shay isn't anything to me, that when I get back I need to forget all this shit.

But I couldn't.

"Everything's all right," I say, shuffling my feet. "Talon's protection operation is just fuckin' bullshit, Arrow. Having one or two people protect a woman by locking her up and moving her all the time isn't really the best plan I've ever heard."

"I hear you. You've got only a few days left though, so just look after her until it's no longer your problem. Your marker will be paid, and you won't owe that bastard shit anymore."

Just like I thought he'd say.

"Yeah," I sigh. "Thanks, brother."

"Anytime. You need me, I'm there."

"I know," I say, nodding even though he can't see me. "And right back at you."

"Anna wants to tell you something."

I can hear the sound of him kissing her before handing her the phone.

"Hey, Vinnie, how's everything?"

"Everything is fine. How're things at home?" I ask her. I actually miss the women and their crazy antics, even though my hands are full over here dealing with Shay. I think the women would like her a lot, but I don't even want to consider why that makes me happy.

"Things are great. We miss you! Guess what happened the other night?" She snickers, then starts laughing before even telling me the story. I have a feeling this story is going to be like the penis cake incident. I listen as she rambles on about their night at Rift and how a woman was hitting on Lana but she had no clue, missing every hint, until the girl asked her to go home with her.

"And now you're being the great friend you are and telling everyone?"

"Hell yeah I am," she replies, laughing. "It's revenge for the pizza story she told everyone last time."

"Well it's not anyone who would follow a random Italian

backpacker back to her car and eat pizza out of her trunk when
you didn't know how long it had been sitting there." I pause.
"Or who the girl even was."

"Ah, come on, live a little, Vinnie," she says. "She was Italian.
She knew great pizza. So is Talon's cousin hot? Are there any
added benefits to the job, if you know what I mean?"

I pause, not wanting to tell her the truth, because then everyone would be on my case and assume I was being swayed by a
pretty face.

"You're quiet, so I'm assuming she's not very attractive and
you don't want to be mean, or she's a total fucking babe and you
don't want us to give you shit over it when you get home."

"Anna," I warn, giving it away.

"Oh my god, she's a hottie," she whispers. "And you're stuck
in a house with her with nothing else to do. Have you slept with
her yet?"

"Anna, not a word," I growl, now pacing up and down. "And
no, I haven't. And I won't be. So you can relax. And I didn't tell
everyone your pizza story, so you can keep this to yourself."

"Of course," she says, sobering. "But that excludes Arrow.
You know that, right? It's old-lady law."

I scrub my hand down my face in frustration. "There's nothing to tell, Anna."

"Talon—"

"Has made it clear I'm not to touch her in that way."

She's quiet for a few moments. "Do you like her?"

"Anna, I barely know her." Which is the truth, but the answer to her question would be yes. She's beautiful and has a fire
in her that I love to play with. "I gotta go, all right? Talk soon.
Take care of Arrow for me."

"Always," she replies.

We both hang up. I rub the back of my neck, knowing I have only one option to save Shay, but it's the one I'm most reluctant to take.

She's already getting under my skin—I can feel it.

When I hear her scream, I race inside and up the stairs, my heart pounding. How did someone get in without making any noise? I made sure everything was locked and bolted—the only way someone could have made it in would be to smash the thick glass. I hear the sheer terror in her voice and know I'm going to kill whoever I find in that room with her. I slam her door back against the wall. Scanning the empty room, I hear a banging coming from the bathroom. I'm there in a second, freezing in shock when I see the scene before me.

There's no one in the room except Shay.

A very naked Shay.

Every inch of her flawless skin all on display.

My gaze lowers. Fuck. She's shaved bare, and is beautiful everywhere.

My mouth waters.

"What the fuck, Vinnie? Don't just stand there perving on me— Kill it!" she yells. It's only then I notice she's standing on the bathroom counter, pointing at a giant spider in the corner of the room.

"Seriously?" I rumble, my shock turning into a mixture of anger and lust. "You screamed like someone is murdering you over that little thing?"

"You consider a spider the size of your hand a little thing?

Can you please kill it, Vinnie?" she asks, covering her breasts with her hands. A little late, since I've already seen everything, but it brings me back to reality. I grab a towel off the rack and hand it to her, then scoop the spider up in my hand, making her whimper.

"I said kill it, not pat it like a puppy!"

"I'm not fuckin' killing it," I growl, even though if it were a human hurting her, I would have put him in the ground. An innocent spider though, I'm just going to release it outside. I leave her room and do just that, freeing it out the back, then return upstairs. This time, being the gentleman that I am, I knock on her door first. She opens it, the towel firmly wrapped around her delectable body.

"I thought someone broke in and was fuckin' hurting you," I growl, letting my expression tell her just how unhappy I am.

She surprises me by not arguing or giving me attitude—but apologizing. "I'm sorry. I didn't mean to make you think something was wrong. But it ran on my foot! On my foot, Vinnie! And I freaked out." She shivers like she's remembering it happening. "I hate spiders. And cockroaches. And moths."

"Moths?" I ask, my eyebrows rising. "The fuck?"

"They're filthy," she says, shuddering. "They attack you in the night like ninjas and jump on your face and shit. And they're all powdery, how disgusting is that?"

Ninja moths?

I look at her, sigh while shaking my head, and then head to my room.

Looks like I'll be protecting her from bugs *and* the Mafia.

Lucky for her she's cute.

ELEVEN

Shayla

I FINISH up with dinner, then put on the TV. Vinnie is outside punching his boxing bag and has been doing so for the last hour. He always likes to keep active; he hardly ever just relaxes and does nothing. I guess that explains his fit body though. By the time he comes in, I've already started eating without him.

"You should have told me dinner was ready," he says, scowling at my half-finished bowl of spaghetti.

"I didn't want to disturb you," I say, licking sauce from my lips. "I put yours in the microwave and the garlic bread is in the oven."

"I'll take a quick shower first," he says, still eyeing my food. "It smells good."

"Tastes good too."

A growl of impatience and then he's gone, leaving me to eat and watch TV in peace. He's back twenty minutes later, with his own bowl, much larger than mine. He sits right next to me, our thighs touching. "What are we watching? Where's the remote?"

"Why? You aren't changing it," I say, slipping the remote into the side of the couch. "You can watch after this is over."

"I don't want to watch men running around in kilts," he grumbles, shoveling a mouthful of spaghetti. I grin to myself and keep watching. There is no way I'm going to change the channel just because of his aversion to kilts, especially when they are one of the many reasons I love this show.

"It's actually the best show," I say, putting my bowl down on the coffee table. "Do you want to play some board games with me later tonight?"

"Not really."

"Why?"

"Because I don't want to?"

"Why?"

"Because I said so."

"Mature," I grumble. "Not like you have anything better to do."

"Maybe I'll watch some decent TV."

I tighten my lips.

"Why are you so grumpy? Sexually frustrated?" I mock.

"Nope," he replies, his tone staying the same. "Just made myself come in the shower, actually."

That takes me back a little, but I recover quickly. "Not as good as the real thing."

"Nope," he repeats, looking straight head. "But comes with less complications." He puts his now-empty bowl down on the table next to mine.

The man has an answer for every damn thing. "That's true. I was doing the same thing before that spider interrupted me."

That gets his attention. "You were touching yourself when the spider ran over your foot?"

I nod, satisfaction filling me as his eyes widen.

"So you didn't get to come?"

I shake my head. "The spider was kind of a mood killer."

"No spiders around here now," he comments, raking his gaze over me. "And I'm here to assist."

"I don't know why you bother," I say, studying him. "You're trying not to fuck me as much as I'm trying not to fuck you. You think your sexual innuendos and blunt words will work as a barrier against me, pushing me back, but it won't. Why the need to try and put distance between us, Vinnie? Worried you'll give in to temptation?"

"Aren't you?" he asks, licking his lips. "Don't you wonder how good I can make you feel? How loud I can make you scream? How many times I can make you come with just my mouth?"

I had wondered all those things, as a matter of fact—that and more, but hearing the words on his lips has my teeth sinking into my bottom lip. We're both playing with fire right now, pushing each other, and no matter how much I try to deny it, I know it's only a matter of time before one of us breaks.

"Have you thought about what I taste like? Whether I'm loud or quiet?" I reply, avoiding answering his question.

"Shay—"

"I'm loud," I tell him, being bold. "And my nipples are really fucking sensitive. If you play with them, I'll get wet just from that."

He freezes and sucks in a sharp breath. I look down and notice that I can see his cock stretching the material of his gray track pants. The rigid outline available for me to see, I groan as I see the size and width of him.

"Like what you see?" he asks in a deep, low voice.

I started this, but now I don't know what to do. One move, one word could end with both of us naked, him inside me. We can't take it back. No one has to know though, it's not like I'm going to tell anyone.

"Of course I do," I admit, inhaling deeply. "Fuck, Vinnie. What are we doing here? I don't want us to have any regrets."

"I know," he says, running his hand over his bald head. "Fuck!" He stands, and all I can do is stare at his cock. Seriously, I hope he doesn't wear those track pants out of the house. It's like women's yoga pants, there isn't much left to the imagination.

"I'm trying to be good here, Shay, but fuck, with you staring at my dick like that, what the fuck do you expect from me? All I want to do right now is throw you over my shoulder, carry you upstairs, and toss you on the bed. Then I want to eat you out until you come all over my face, then I want to slide inside you and fuck you until you scream my name."

The air thickens as we stare at each other. My body feels needy, flushed. My nipples harden, and I can feel that my panties are damp.

And he hasn't even touched me.

He moves to walk past me but then stops. Gripping my chin with his thumb and index finger, he leans down and plants a quick kiss on my lips before storming outside. That's it? I touch my lips with my fingers, feeling annoyed even though I know he's being the responsible one here. Did I need to be responsible though? Talon never said anything to me about staying away from Vinnie, although I guess it didn't need to be said. It's not like I make it a habit of wanting to sleep with the men sent to protect me. Usually I'm more worried about staying alive and out of the enemies' hands, but Vinnie has changed everything. I relax more about all else, because for some reason I trust that he'll handle it. Just like I'm sure he'll know how to handle me. Without overthinking it, I stand, my feet taking me outside where Vinnie stands by the pool.

"Not a good idea, Shay," he growls, turning his head to the side.

What does he think I'm going to do exactly?

I stand behind him and rest my hands on his back. Suddenly, the need for revenge outweighs my lust. With all the strength I can muster, I push him into the pool. As soon as I see the splash, I don't stick around to find out what happens. I run inside, upstairs and into my room where I lock the door and fall onto my bed, giggling.

That's one way to take care of his erection.

I'm still laughing when he bangs on my door, rendering me silent. I hide under the sheets, as if that can save me, like a little girl hiding from monsters under her bed.

"Shay, open the fuckin' door," he snarls, banging again.

I pull down the sheet, revealing just my eyes. "No!" I call out to him. "I'm going to sleep. We can discuss this in the morning."

My eyes flare as I hear him mutter some creative curse words. His footsteps disappear, and I relax into the mattress, staring at the ceiling. It's only a matter of time before the two of us end up in bed together, and every time I think about it, it sounds less like a bad idea and more like a foregone conclusion. I'll never see him again, and the attraction was there, so why not? Who knows when I'll have the chance to be with a man next, and never will I find another guy like Vinnie. Who knows how long I'll even be alive? With that very sobering thought, I decide to forget all the details, to stop overthinking everything, and to just let myself enjoy life a little.

Tomorrow, Vinnie is mine.

After he forgives me for the pool incident.

TWELVE

Vinnie

I SPEND more time coming up with my revenge plan than I'd like to admit. I grin into my coffee and she comes down the stairs, her steps light and unsure. She approaches the kitchen cautiously, then stands patiently as she waits for me to look at her. When I don't, she clears her throat and says, "Good morning."

I ignore her, the first part of my plan, and move to the living area, sitting down casually and putting on the TV. She follows me, sitting down and watching me.

"To be fair, you did it to me first," she says, sighing heavily. "Does this silent treatment mean we aren't going anywhere today?"

She stands and says, "I'm going to make some breakfast, would you like something?"

Silence.

As she disappears into the kitchen, I sit back and wait. One, two, three, four . . .

Her scream echoes throughout the house and makes me smile widely. Yes, the fake spider that took me half an hour to make was well worth it. She runs into the living room and jumps on my lap. When she sees me smiling, she scowls and stops her wailing, her chest panting up and down. She slaps at my shoulder. "You're such an asshole!"

I wrap my arms around her and pull her against my chest. "You deserved it."

She smells so fuckin' good, like strawberries and icing sugar. Her hair is still a little damp from the shower, and her skin is so soft and smooth. I bury my face in her neck. "You're a little shit you know, pushing me into the pool. No one else would get away with something like that."

"I don't think I got away with it," she murmurs, touching my cheek. "My heart is still racing. You successfully scared the shit out of me."

"Good," I whisper gruffly, pulling back and looking her in the eye. "What are we doing today?"

"You're letting it go, just like that?" she asks, suspicion written all over her face. "Or do you have more spiders planted around the house?"

"I'm letting it go," I say, tilting my head to the side. "At least I think I am."

She rolls her eyes and says, "What do you want to do today? Your choice."

What I really want to do is spend the day inside her and spank her ass for the stunt she pulled, so really we should get out of this house before I do just that.

Last night Talon finally called me back, and I chewed him out for how he expects Shay to live. He said right now there's no other option since shit's going down with his club, and she won't be any safer there. I told him to get control of his MC, something he didn't appreciate, but what the fuck? Shay should have the Wild Men at her back, not be hidden away because they can't protect what's theirs. You'd think having a cousin who is an MC president would have some perks, but apparently not with the Wild Men.

"Maybe we could go out for lunch, then go for a swim or something?" I suggest. "I'm guessing you didn't start breakfast."

"You'd be guessing right," she grumbles, laying her head on my chest. "You're so comfortable."

She places both her hands on my chest and slides them over my pecs, then down my abs.

"You know I'm sure we could find something fun and . . . energetic to do indoors," she says, biting her lower lip and staring up at me with her bedroom eyes. I don't know what's changed from last night to now, but something has.

I lean forward and press my lips against hers, then say, "Shay, I told Talon I wouldn't touch you. Are you going to make me a liar?"

She shuffles on my lap, letting me know she can feel my hardness. "He doesn't have to know. Do you think I talk to my cousin about my sex life?" She pauses. "Even when I had one, I didn't."

"If he straight out asks me, I'm not going to lie," I warn her. I don't know what Talon will do to her that could be worse than what she's going through now. I'm not scared of Talon, but I don't like to go against my word.

"Then don't," she whispers, glancing down at my lips. "I don't want to be selfish, but I want you. I'll worry about whatever comes later another day. This is me letting you know."

She moves to slide off me but I grip her hips to keep her in her place.

"Vinnie—" She opens her mouth to speak so I take the opportunity to kiss her. And I mean *really* kiss her. Moving my hands to cup her face, I kiss her deeply, savoring her taste, loving the way she feels pressed up against me. Her soft lips. Fuck.

She pushes her body into mine, rubbing herself against my throbbing cock. The world closes in on us as I finally get a proper taste of what I want, a forbidden taste, which makes it all that sexier. I pull back, but just so I can kiss down her neck, sucking gently, my tongue swiping across her skin. The breathy noises she starts to make drive me crazy, and I end up lifting her off me and laying her back on the couch, following her down with my mouth on hers once more.

Wanting to feel her skin, I start to lift off her dress, sliding it up her thigh, then up her stomach. She sits up and lifts her arms so I can take it off entirely, leaving her in a white lace bra and matching panties. Lana's line about women being the ones who decide to have sex if they're wearing sexy matching lingerie runs through my head, making me smile as my lips descend onto hers again.

Shay is something else—the way she goes after what she wants in her own way has me feeling all kinds of crazy. I kiss down her neck, her collarbone, until I reach the top of her breasts. I kiss there, then pull down the cups of her bra, squeezing her breasts in my hands, the perfect handfuls. I lick her right nipple, biting down on it gently before sucking it into my mouth. She places her hand on the back of my neck, the other resting on my head.

"Holy shit, Vinnie," she gasps as I move my head to her other breast. While my tongue tortures her I run my hand down her stomach and slide it into her panties, sinking a single finger inside her.

She's dripping.

"Fuck, Shay," I groan, starting to play with her clit. "You're so wet and ready for me."

I sit back and lift my T-shirt off, throwing it on the floor somewhere, then stand to remove my pants. I admire Shay for a second, lying there in her bra and panties, watching me with lust in her eyes, before I kneel back on the couch and slide her panties down. I stare at her smooth skin, and my mouth starts to water just looking at her. She opens the front clasp of her bra and slides the straps down. She's fuckin' beautiful, every inch of her.

I undo the button on my jeans, then slide them down, my boxers following suit. I see her taking me in from head to toe, and I stay still and let her do so. I can't wait until she explores my body with her hands and her mouth, after I explore hers. When she's finished her perusal she flashes me the cutest fuckin' smile and spreads her legs for me.

I'm in heaven.

THIRTEEN

Shayla

LOVE the look in his eyes as he watches me. He likes what he sees. He grabs my breasts again and nips at them. They aren't big, but he stares at them like they're the most perfect set he's ever laid eyes on.

At my age, I've come to completely accept myself and my body, letting go of any hang-ups I had. The key isn't trying to be perfect, it is accepting yourself as you are and to know that to the right person, you will always be enough. I also think men don't notice the small things we do, the imperfections we focus on.

I lose coherent thought as he starts to kiss down my stomach, then down my inner thigh. Holy shit. His brown eyes glance up at me as his tongue licks me, sliding through me before landing on my clit and flicking.

"Vinnie," I moan, lifting my hips as he grabs them and uses them to help him bring his mouth even closer. He pulls away, making me moan again, this time in protest. He stands up and lifts me over his shoulder in one swift move, slapping my ass as he carries me up the stairs and into his room. He puts me down on my feet, then lays back on the bed and demands, "Sit on my face."

Without hesitation, I climb up his body and do just that, lowering my pussy on his face and grabbing onto the headboard for support as he starts to eat me again. I moan loudly when he puts direct pressure on my clit with his tongue, and grind myself down on him shamelessly. The orgasm hits me out of nowhere and blinds me with its intensity.

"Oh my god," I yell, closing my eyes and just *feeling*, my thighs trembling and my world spinning. He continues to torture me, even after the waves cease, so I lift my leg off him, panting, and look down at him. He wipes his mouth with the back of his hand and grins wolfishly, making me shake my head and smile back at him.

Talented bastard.

"Your turn," I announce, moving down the bed. I take his cock in my hand and lick the head. There's no way I'll be able to fit all of him in my mouth, not even close, but I'll do my best. I want to give him the best head he's ever had. He threads his fingers through my hair, gently holding my head, not pushing me down like some guys do. I lick him from base to tip, then suck him deep into my mouth. He makes a sound, almost like a growl, that makes me take even more of him into my mouth. Fuck, that sound. So sexy. He makes it again, and I moan around his cock.

"Fuck," he grits out, gently pushing me off his cock. "I need to be inside you. Now."

He grabs me and pushes me back on the bed, bracing himself on top of me. He slides his finger inside me and finds me wet.

He positions himself and is about to slide inside me when we hear banging.

"Are you serious right now?"

I could cry. What was the noise? Is someone trying to get in?

"Motherfucker," Vinnie snarls, jumping off the bed and grabbing a pair of pants out of his bag. He throws me a T-shirt. "Put that on and lock the door behind me."

"Do you think they've found me?" I ask, sliding the huge black T-shirt over my small frame. "What do we do, Vinnie?"

"You stay here, and let me handle it," he says, putting a shirt on and stepping toward the bed. He opens a drawer and pulls out two guns. "Do you know how to use one?"

"No."

He hands it to me and gives me a quick demonstration. "You should be able to manage. I'll show you how to use it properly later."

He takes the safety off his own gun and walks toward the door. "Lock it, Shay."

I follow him to the door, locking it as soon as he disappears. I look at the gun in my hand and cringe. Could I shoot it? If I had to, yes, I think I could. What if they hurt Vinnie? Or killed him. What would I do? What if he needed me? If he is out-numbered . . . But he told me to stay here. I'd probably just be a liability. I pace up and down the room with the gun held awk-wardly in my hands, contemplating what to do. I strain to hear something from downstairs, but it's silent. I unlock the door without making a noise, open it, and stick my head out.

When I hear a man's deep chuckle, I think I should go down. I mean, what could be funny about this situation? Unless Vin-nie is dead and someone is laughing over his body. It isn't Vinnie's laugh—that I'd recognize. I hear murmured words and decide to just head downstairs to see what is going on. If Vinnie is dead, they'd find me anyway. Hiding upstairs in a locked room wasn't going to save me; they could open the door with one kick.

"Pretty sure I told you to stay in the room," Vinnie says quietly, his eyes pinning me the second my toe touches the bottom step.

"Oh, so you're not dead," I point out, holding the gun awkwardly by my side. I look at the man standing next to Vinnie. In his leather cut covered in patches, his large, muscled build and his mean, yet somehow handsome-looking bearded face, the man isn't someone I'd want to mess with. It is his shrewd brown eyes that have me wanting to hide behind Vinnie though.

"Don't sound so happy about it," Vinnie grumbles, nodding his head toward the man standing next to him. "Shay, this is my brother Arrow. Arrow, this is Shay."

Arrow studies me, his gaze perusing me from head to toe but not in a sleazy way, more in a way that is strictly business. He runs his hand through his beard as he says, "She doesn't look like Talon."

"And thank fuck for that," Vinnie murmurs, eyes zoning in on my bare legs and feet. "Go get dressed, Shay. It was only this knucklehead trying to get my attention. And put that gun away before you kill one of us."

Arrow crosses his arms over his chest and leans back against the wall. "And now I understand why you were too busy to answer your phone when I called you from the gate."

I cringe and look down at my hands. Yeah, so we weren't

being the most responsible of adults, but all I could think of right now was the fact that Vinnie was about to slide inside me when this behemoth of a man decided to interrupt. Just what exactly is he doing here anyway? Did everyone have the address to this supposedly secret location? Jesus.

"How did you get through the gate?" I ask, scowling. Did Vinnie tell him the passcode?

"I disabled the code and set a new one," he says, shrugging casually. "I'm pretty good with that shit."

"Where the fuck did you learn how to do that?" Vinnie asks, looking impressed.

"Faye wanted Tracker to teach her, so I sat in on that class," he replies.

I look to Vinnie, who sighs and scrubs a hand down his face. I stare at the long fingers that were inside of me not so long ago. How things can change in a few minutes.

"That doesn't sound like grade A security," I grumble, pursing my lips. "How did you even know where we were?"

"Talon gave me the address to your little love nest," Arrow tells Vinnie, apparently ignoring me. He slaps Vinnie on the back and shakes his head. "Maybe you should go home. Let me watch her for the next few days."

Wait, what?

Leave me with this scary man?

Panic fills me at the thought of Vinnie leaving. I was counting on spending the rest of the week with him, and I don't want him to leave.

My gaze immediately darts to Vinnie, who is already watching me. "Clothes, Shay. Now."

I know the two of them just want to talk about me, but still, I do as I'm told, heading back upstairs and into my bedroom to get dressed. I leave the gun on the bedside table, making a mental note to learn how to use it properly.

I need it to survive.

FOURTEEN

Vinnie

I WATCH her disappear up the stairs before I walk into the living room, Arrow close behind me. When he sees our clothes scattered everywhere, including Shay's bra and panties, he sits down and sighs heavily.

"What the actual fuck are you doing here, Vinnie?" he asks, tapping his hand on his knee. "Talon is going to be pissed, and you're getting yourself in a whole lot of shit, all for a piece of ass? It's just a few more days, brother. Plenty of pussy for you back at the clubhouse waiting for your return."

The thing was, it wasn't like that with Shay. I wanted her, not just any woman, but fuck if I was going to explain that to Arrow. I can't really explain why she's so different for me. She's just everything I could want in a woman. I like everything that I know about her. I find her little quirks amusing and find myself wanting to be around her as much as possible.

"What are you doing here? Is everything okay?" I ask, dropping into the chair and shoving our clothes into a pile with my foot. "Not that I'm not grateful. What the fuck did you do with the bodies?"

Everything Arrow just told Shay was utter bullshit.

Talon told him our location had been leaked and men were on the way, so Arrow rode up to warn us and to offer some help. He caught two of them waiting for us outside the gate. He took care of them both.

"They're kind of sitting in your backyard, hidden behind the shed. We gotta take care of it. Besides that, everything is fine. I spoke to Talon," he says, leaning back in the chair. "And I came to check on you, and apparently save you from doing something stupid like fucking a girl who is related to the Wild Men president and has the fuckin' Mafia at her doorstep.

"Although I will say, the men I just killed aren't fuckin' Mafia," he continues, tilting his head to the side and studying me. "They're members of the Kings MC. I knew they looked familiar, and then I checked their tattoos. They're Kings, Vinnie. I don't know what the fuck you think you've gotten yourself into here, but I have a feeling it's something else."

"Kings?" I ask, eyebrows lifting. "Those motherfuckers!"

An MC war is brewing—I know it, everyone knows it. And it's only time until we take the Kings of Hell down.

"I have it under control." I straight-out lie. I have no idea what I'm going to do with Shay, or just how involved I'm going to get. I have a feeling though, when push comes to shove, I'm going to get real fuckin' involved. If Arrow hadn't caught those guys, would they have jumped us when Shay and I were headed out on one of our adventures? My focus has been off this whole time, distracted by Shay, when I should've been on my game more than ever, because it's her life at stake.

"Hmmm," Arrow rumbles, not looking convinced. "Pack your shit. Time to move the fuck on out because it's only time until more come running." He then mutters something about hating all this hiding and running shit. He wasn't the only one. In fact, I'm pretty sure I could protect Shay all on my own, without instruction from Talon, who, in my opinion, had a lot going on right now and wasn't making Shay a priority.

A week, my ass. There's no way I can walk away after a week, leaving that shit on my conscience if anything happens to her. What kind of man would I be if I did that? It's in my power to help her, and I can't turn my back on her now. I don't know what there is between us, or what there could be, but I do know that she's under my skin, and that I don't want any harm to come to her. She's definitely caused my protective instincts to flare up, and I can't explain it, but I just need her to be safe. The world wouldn't be the same without Shay. At least my world.

"I need to call Sin," I announce, standing up and looking around for my phone.

"What are you going to do?" Arrow asks, forehead furrowing in concern. "This isn't your problem to deal with, Vinnie. The marker you owe finishes soon, and you get to walk away and let Talon handle his shit. Wipe it out of your mind, because this isn't your responsibility."

"I can't," I say for the first time out loud. I look down at Arrow. "I can't just forget it. I'm in it now. You just killed two men—how are we all not in this now?"

"You can't forget it, because you fuckin' like her," he surmises, scowling. "Fuck, Vinnie. You never do things the easy way, do you?"

"I've never really had that luxury," I say, bitterness lacing my tone. I've never had an easy life. Foster kid, moving from house to house. I never had a home until the men gave me one with the Wind Dragons. Something that not many people know is that the old WDMC president, Jim, was actually my uncle. He didn't know about me until I was eighteen and came to find me the second he did. I became a prospect for the club the very next day and haven't looked back since. The WDMC gave me the family I always wanted.

"I'm gonna have to either go off the grid with her, or follow Talon's lead until this shit is over."

And I really, really didn't want to do the latter.

"It won't be over until she gives them whatever it is they want, or they're all dead," Arrow says, standing and putting his hand on my shoulder. "You gonna claim her?"

If I claimed her, she'd have the club's protection. But how much shit would it drag them into? If I could solve this on my own, I'd happily take that route. Claiming her was my last resort. Who the fuck claims someone after just a couple of days? Apparently me, that's who.

Fuck.

Shay walks into the room in tight jeans and a red top. "Finished talking about me yet or do I have to go back upstairs?"

I exhale and say the words that are going to change everything for everyone. "Pack your shit, we gotta move."

But we aren't going to wherever Talon wanted us to. No.

We are going home.

After we do something with those bodies.

*   *   *

While Shay packs, I take the bodies to a vacant lot off the property and bury them in a ditch. Arrow's right: they are Kings. There's something odd going on here and it's pissing me the fuck off that no one is telling me shit.

A quick shower and we start loading everything into the car. I'm surprised when Shay comes out with only one suitcase and one huge handbag. I'd have thought she'd carry around a lot more shit with her, not because of my assuming that she was high maintenance, I learned my lesson with that. But because it surprises me that this is all the stuff she's had with her over the last few months.

"Here," I say, taking the bags off her and lifting them into the back.

"Thanks," she replies, offering me a small smile before getting into the passenger seat. Arrow gets on his bike, waiting for us. I open the passenger door and study her.

"We have a problem," I say, leaning on top of the car. "I'm going to trust that you can handle this."

"What is it?" she asks, looking concerned.

I hand her the keys. "I need to ride my bike. You'll be in the car alone, but I'll be riding right beside you, and so will Arrow."

"Okay," she says, not fazed. "How far is the drive?"

"Four hours."

She puffs out a breath but nods. "Okay. I trust you. Let's do it."

"Good girl," I say, leaning down and pressing a quick kiss to her mouth. "We'll talk more when we get there."

"Okay," she replies, sliding out of the seat. "Vinnie?"

"Yeah?"

"You're going to stay with me, right? I mean, until your time is up." Her eyes scan mine, as if searching for the truth. Did she really think I'd leave her? How could I?

"Yes," I reply, pushing her hair back behind her ear. "I will."

She nods and walks around to the driver's seat. I wait until she's settled before I straddle my bike, happy as fuck to be back on her. Arrow leads, then Shay, me right behind her. She didn't ask where we were going, so I didn't have to lie about the answer, but I have no idea how she's going to react to being taken back to the clubhouse. I never know with her.

We don't know each other at all, yet we're connected in a way I don't understand, a way I've never experienced before. The truth is, I don't know why I want to be around her, I just know that I do, and that is enough for me.

Fifteen minutes into the drive, I realize that she's a really shitty driver. I'm pretty sure everyone on the road does, with the way she speeds up and then slows down, and the way she stomps on the brakes. I decide to move back a little, just so I don't end up crashing into her if she decides to stop suddenly. I enjoy the ride but also keep a close eye on Shay and the cars around us. It feels good to have Arrow here too, another set of eyes, and a trusted brother at our backs. We work well as a team, as we've been doing it for so long, the same with all the brothers.

We're a deadly unit.

In my head, I run through the different scenarios that could take place at the clubhouse, and how I'd handle each one. I don't want Shayla to feel unwelcome, but I imagine everyone is going to be surprised that I'm bringing the woman who was meant to be a job back home to where my family is.

I'm surprised too.

FIFTEEN

Shayla

I PARK the car next to Arrow's bike and look around. Motorcycles parked next to one another, a big building that looks suspiciously like a biker compound. What are we doing here? Maybe Vinnie wants to get something, or see his friends before we leave again. I look to the left and see Vinnie park his bike on the other side of me. I open my car door, wondering if I am even meant to get out, and stand beside the car. Vinnie removes his helmet and gets off his sexy-looking bike, then pulls me into his chest.

"What are we doing here?" I ask him, glancing up. "Should I stay in the car?"

"No," he says slowly, a strange look passing on his handsome face. "You're coming in."

"Okay," I say, looking toward the entrance. "I kind of do need to pee."

Vinnie grins as he takes my hand and leads me into his territory. He takes me through the compound while I quickly check out the place. We stop at what I assume is his bedroom, which he opens with a key. "Bathroom is through there," he says, nodding toward the door. "You must be hungry too. I'll see what we have in the kitchen, or I'll get a prospect to pick something up for you."

"Whatever is fine," I say, walking into the bathroom. I take a peek at him before I close the door, seeing him opening his drawers, doing something. I really don't want him to hear me pee, so I close the door and run the tap water while I handle my business. I wash my hands when I'm done, checking out my reflection in the mirror. I look tired. I'm going to sleep like a baby tonight, that's for sure. When I return to Vinnie's bedroom, he's sitting on the massive bed, typing something on his phone. He glances up at me and grins. "At least here we can fuck without being interrupted by people trying to kill you, or Arrow checking up on me." He pauses. "Probably have all the old ladies in our faces though. It's most likely Faye and Anna who will be the biggest pains in the ass."

"Old ladies?" I know a few things about the lifestyle, because of Talon, but I don't know everything. *Old ladies* is a term I've heard before, and Vinnie has referred to Faye as the president's old lady before too. How many are there? While Talon hardly brings me around his members, and I have no idea how Talon and Vinnie even know each other, I'm picking up on things quickly.

He nods, smiling. "They'll be wanting to meet you, trust me."

"Why?"

"Because they're nosy, for one," he says, but I know from the tone of his voice he doesn't really mind.

Speaking of fucking . . . "Do you realize we were about to have sex without a condom? You didn't even ask me if I was on the pill, and no offense, but I have no idea where you've been."

He lies back on the bed and taps the spot next to him. "First of all, I'm not that fuckin' selfish to put you in any danger like that. I never usually fuck without a condom. And yeah—I kinda just assumed you were on the pill. I wasn't thinking about it too much, to be honest, all I was thinking about was getting inside you."

"You always use a condom?" I ask, eyebrow raised and tone full of disbelief.

"Where's the faith, Shay?" he asks, putting his hand on my lower back as I sit down. "Yes, I always use protection."

But he wasn't going to with me, which makes me a little suspicious of his words. "But with me . . ."

"You're different," he says, standing up and offering me his hand. "I don't think you're gonna try to get pregnant to trap me, are you?"

My eyes widen. "Women do that?"

"Exactly," he says with a chuckle. "So are you on the pill or not?"

"I am," I tell him, letting him pull me off the bed.

We stand facing each other, his thumb running across my knuckles. "If anything, it would be me trapping you. You're the rich one."

He turns to leave and I slap his ass. "Very funny."

He's laughing at his own joke as we leave his room and walk into a kitchen. There are two men in there, one with blond hair tied back in a man bun, the other also blond, but with shorter hair and green eyes. Both are extremely good-looking. The Wild Men have a few hotties, like Ranger, but these two take the cake. They aren't as sexy as Vinnie though. Then again, no one probably is.

"Vinnie," Man Bun says, putting down the drink in his hand and giving Vinnie a hug.

"Hey, Tracker," he says, smiling widely. "Miss me?"

The other man stands and greets him too.

"Rake," Vinnie says, taking my hand and pulling me forward. "This is Shay. Shay, Tracker and Rake."

"Hello," I say, smiling at each one in turn while they take me in.

"Hello, cutie," Tracker says, looking between Vinnie and me. "And what have you gone and done, Vinnie?"

"I thought you were in some remote place doing something for Talon," Rake says, looking amused, his eyes wide and his lips kicking up at the corners. "Where did you find her?"

I roll my eyes as they talk about me like I'm not standing right here. Arrogant bikers.

"I think she's what he was doing for Talon," Tracker says, peering down at me. "She's a little thing, isn't she?"

"*She* is standing right here," I say, crossing my arms.

"She doesn't look like Talon," Rake comments, then mutters, "Thank fuck."

I look up at Vinnie, giving him my best *Are you serious?* look. He rests his big hands on my shoulders, bringing me to stand in front of him.

"Shay's safest here," he says, kissing the top of my head. "I want her here, if Sin says it's all right."

I spin around to look at him. "What? You want me to stay here? What did Talon say?"

"Fuck Talon," Vinnie and Rake say at the same time. Okkkaaayyy, a lot of unresolved anger here.

He changed the plan? What am I supposed to do here? What

happens when I'm found here? The MC would have to fight to protect me. Vinnie is essentially giving me his family's protection, if Sin, who I guess is their president, will allow it. This is huge, and I don't really know how to react. I am grateful, and I realize Vinnie is going out on a limb for me with this, but this could really backfire if someone ends up hurt.

"We can sit with her, if you want to talk with Sin," Tracker offers, pulling out the chair of the dining table. "Have a seat, Shay."

Vinnie scans my face, and I silently let him know it's fine. Waiting here while he asks for protection on my behalf is the least I can do. I sit down in the chair quietly.

"Your food will be here soon, Shay," he says as he leaves the kitchen. He must have organized it when I was in the bathroom.

"What food?" Rake asks, sitting down next to me. "I want food."

"No idea," I reply, clasping my hands in front of me. "I guess it's going to be a surprise for both of us."

He pulls his phone out and starts pressing numbers. "He probably called one of the prospects. Isn't Ronan with them?"

"Yep," Tracker replies, then sits down on the other side of me and pushes his chair a little too close for my liking. "What are your intentions with my brother?"

Rake makes a grunt of amusement, while I tighten my lips. "Can you even have intentions with someone you've known only a few days?"

"He's saving your ass right now, isn't he?" Tracker says, not in a mean way, but matter-of-factly.

"I didn't ask him to," I say quietly, not wanting them to think this was my idea. "A lot has happened in such a short period of time. I don't even know how to process everything to be honest. I guess all I can say is that my intentions are pure."

Both of their phones go off at the same time. "That was quick," Rake murmurs.

"Decision time," Tracker says, standing up. "Do you want to wait in Vinnie's room, Shay? I don't think this will take too long."

"Okay," I say, standing and walking out of the kitchen. They stop at Vinnie's room and wait to leave until I'm inside. Tracker gives me a comforting touch on my shoulder, which I actually appreciate. I lie down on Vinnie's bed, just waiting.

I only hope he comes back with good news, or we might have to leave here straightaway. I don't know if my staying or going is better for Vinnie, but I have a feeling it is probably the latter.

I close my eyes and pray that, for once, things turn out well for the both of us, especially for him.

SIXTEEN

Vinnie

"OKAY," Sin starts, glancing around the table at the men. "As we all know, Vinnie owes Talon a marker, and he left to pay it. As he's just told me, he's brought the marker back with him to the clubhouse."

She is more than a marker, and I think that is the real issue here.

All eyes are suddenly on me, and I return each of them.

"Vinnie," he says, waiting for me to speak.

"They think her father gave her information that she can use to implicate them in various illegal activities. They either want her to get that information or they want her to blackmail her father to give it to them. She hasn't done anything wrong, and says she doesn't have anything. Talon's protection plan for her is fucked, and her location keeps getting leaked. I can't just leave her, knowing I could help her better than he is. The problem is I don't know exactly *who* is after her. We thought it was the Mafia, but now we think the Kings are involved as well."

"I told him it wasn't his problem," Arrow rumbles, studying me.

"I want her to stay here with me," I declare to the table.

"She yours?" Sin asks, his words short but heavy. This is the question that the brothers will want to know the answer to more than anything.

"Yeah," I say, swallowing hard. "She's mine."

"Is Talon going to be an issue?" Rake asks me, a muscle working in his jaw. "He always seems to be a fuckin' issue."

"I don't know," I reply honestly. "And I don't really give a fuck what he has to say, to be honest."

Mumbles of agreement.

I lean back in my seat and study the men. "I don't know how to fix this for her, but I'm going to try. If shit goes down though, it will be me handling it. If I have to kill someone to protect her, I will, but the blood will be on my hands, not yours. I don't want this touching the club if possible." I pause. "Although it probably will."

Who am I kidding? It definitely will.

"I think we should wait until they know we're protecting her before we set up a meet to find out exactly what these fucks want," Arrow says, running his hand down his beard. "The last thing they'll want is a war with us. Whether it's the Kings or whoever else. The two men I killed were Kings, so I know those bastards are involved."

I love how he says it like it's already a sure thing, when they haven't even voted yet.

"I'll destroy any of these fuckers who step into my path. None of them are innocent," I say, my hands clenching into fists at the thought of them with their corrupt hands on Shay.

"Anyone else ever hear Vinnie be so cold?" Tracker asks the room, as always lightening the tense mood.

I didn't think I was being cold, I was being realistic. And any of the men in this room would do the same to protect their women, or each other's women. I've seen it time and time again.

Shay just came into my life. I don't know where it will lead, if anywhere, but I know that my gut is telling me to protect her, that she's mine.

And I always go with my gut instinct.

She's worth taking a chance on.

I don't give a fuck how whipped that makes me sound, and I know that most of the men at this table right now, powerful men you don't want to fuck with, know exactly how I'm feeling. When you find something good, you fight to keep it. Even if it means fighting dirty. You look after it. You cherish it. And you don't let anyone fuck with it. Could Shay do better than me? Probably. Will she get the chance to find out? Fuck no. She became mine the second I decided to bring her into my clubhouse.

"All right, men. Yes or no to keeping Vinnie's woman under our roof, protecting her like she's our own?"

I glance at each man as they vote.

When it's Sin's turn, he says, "I just want to say that I'm voting yes because at one time or another, Vinnie, you've always been there to look after the women. You've saved Faye's ass more times than I can count, and now I'll be here to save Shay's."

"Thank you," I tell him.

The voting continues.

And it's unanimous.

Shay is staying.

"We good?" Sin asks the table.

Everyone nods.

"Shay is staying here, and under our protection. Vinnie, let us know what you need us to do."

I leave the room feeling like a weight has been lifted.

Shay is fast asleep in my bed, snuggled under the covers, when I return to my room. I decide to join her, undressing and sliding under the sheets, spooning her from behind. I release a deep breath, thinking about how nice it is to be able to relax, to hold her like this and know that for now, we're safe. I close my eyes and soon fall asleep with her scent in my nose.

"This is the cutest shit I've ever seen," I hear Faye's voice whisper. "Seriously, Anna, how adorable are they?"

"Are you just going to stand here and watch them sleep? That's pretty creepy," Anna whispers, making me open my eyes and glare at the two of them. "And I think Vinnie's naked. I don't want to see his bits."

"His bits? You're best friends with a romance author and that's what you come up with?" Faye snickers.

"It's Vinnie," Anna says matter-of-factly, "to me, he doesn't have a cock, or a dick. He has bits."

Faye starts laughing so hard Shay stirs, and the last thing she needs is to wake up with these two in her face.

"Can the both of you please get the fuck out?" I ask quietly, but loud enough so the two of them can hear.

Instead of listening, they both come closer, lean down, and kiss me on my cheek.

"Welcome home," Faye says, while Anna just smiles down at me.

You can't even be angry at the two of them.

"Good to be back."

"There's food for both of you in the kitchen," Anna says, then grabs Faye's arm and pulls her to the door.

"Food?" Shay says, lifting her head, her hair all messy and cute.

Faye and Anna stop.

"They were just about to leave," I tell Shay, burrowing back under the sheets. I then lift my head, realizing I was being rude. "Shay, this is Faye and Anna."

"Nice to meet you both," Shay says, sitting up and smiling at the women.

"You too," Faye says, beckoning. "Come and eat with us. There's pizza in the kitchen, along with garlic bread and a whole lot of desserts. Oh, and there's some katsu chicken sushi too."

"A woman after my own heart," Anna comments, opening the door. "I'll be in the kitchen."

Shay turns her head and looks at me. "You got me all that food?"

"I didn't know what you felt like," I say, nuzzling her thigh. "Plus nothing will go to waste here."

Especially with Rake in the house.

"Are you going to come and eat?" she asks, lifting the sheets and getting out of bed, trying to tame her hair with her fingers.

"I'm not hungry, but I'll come with you," I say, not wanting her to be overwhelmed by everyone.

"Jesus, Vinnie, she's fine," Faye says, rolling her eyes. "I'll even sit next to her and hold her hand. You rest, I'll make sure she's fed and well taken care of."

"I'll be fine," Shay agrees, walking toward Faye, who loops her arm through Shay's. The thing about Faye is, she doesn't try to be intimidating. She doesn't do the whole hard, cold, mean, president's old-lady thing I've seen with some other clubs. She doesn't have to—her reputation speaks for herself. All she does is be herself, someone who is funny and kind, but everyone knows that if you fuck with her or anyone she loves, you won't even see her coming, she'll just destroy you. Her baby bump isn't very visible, especially with the loose dress she's wearing. I don't think anyone would guess that she's pregnant with baby number two. This woman is the closest thing I have to a sister, and there really isn't anything I wouldn't do for her.

"You sure?" I ask, not knowing if I should stay with Shay until she gets used to everyone, or to let her find her own place here in the club, without my hovering over her.

Faye shoots me a look that clearly says she thinks I'm being ridiculous.

I smirk and snuggle back in bed as the two of them leave my room.

SEVENTEEN

Shayla

"**H**E called her a what?" I ask Bailey, who was introduced to me as Rake's old lady.

"A mad bitch," she says, eyes alight with humor.

I take a bite of the slice of pizza in my hand. "So she was going down on him and he called her a mad bitch?"

How much has changed in the dating world since I've been out of it? Apparently a lot.

"She must have mad skills," Faye says from the other side of me, "for such an awesome compliment in the bedroom."

We all laugh. I can't believe how open the women are with one another, and no one makes any judgment. If anything, they laugh about it with the person, not at the person. I've never had friends like this in my life. I went to an all-girls private school, and most of the girls were bitchy, catty, and competitive. I wonder if they know how much their acceptance is worth, because some people look for it their whole lives and never get it.

"Any other fun Tia stories?" Faye asks her, closing the pizza box. "Tell me before Lana comes, unless you want it to end up in a book."

Bailey was telling me all about her best friend, Tia, and how funny she is.

"I have more than enough stories, but none of them are recent. She's been good as of late. She's actually seeing someone, I think, but she won't tell me anything."

"AKA boring," Faye snickers, then turns to me.

Before she can speak, however, I have a question of my own. "Wait just a second. Vinnie said he knew Zada Ryan, and you just said her stories could end up in one of Lana's books. Which means . . ."

"Fan, are you?" Faye asks, looking at me and laughing. "I'll take your expression as a yes, then. Yes, Lana is Zada Ryan."

"Oh my god!" I whisper, wide-eyed. "Her books are awesome."

I need to not fangirl right now, because that is going to be awkward if I make a total fool out of myself in front of everyone.

"Wait until you meet her," Faye says, smiling fondly. "She's sweet and quiet. Very unassuming."

Anna walks back into the kitchen and sits down next to Faye. "Should we tell everyone to come over to welcome Shay? It's like half the women are missing."

Rake walks into the kitchen and grabs a chair, turning it the other way and straddling it. "Irish said Tina will be here soon. Jess will probably come after work. Who else are we missing?"

We're still missing Zada Ryan, I think to myself.

Faye looks at her watch and stands. "I have to go and get Clover. Are we just going to hang here all night? I might do a store run and get enough stuff for dinner. What do we feel like? How about a barbecue?"

"Yes," Rake immediately agrees. "I like this plan. Do you want help? Bails, do you want to come with?"

"No, I'll stay here and keep Shayla company," Bailey replies, winking at me.

"Yeah, sounds good," Faye says, looking at Bailey. "Don't let anyone scare Shay off, will you?" She pauses. "And maybe protect Lana from her."

"Very funny," I say, grinning. "I might have a few questions, but that's all. Such as where she got her inspiration for Colt."

Tracker walks into the kitchen and Faye points at him. "Right here, Shay. Right here."

"Right here what?" he asks, taking Faye's place.

"She's asking about Lana's inspiration for Colt Smith."

Tracker snaps his head to me and flashes me a slow-spreading smile. He kind of reminds me of the guy from *Tangled* with his smolder right now. He even flexes his biceps. "In the flesh."

I roll my eyes and say, "That's not something Colt would say."

Faye laughs and pulls Rake's arm. "You tell him, Shay. Colt's ego isn't as big as Tracker's."

"Colt is the improved Tracker," Anna adds, touching his man bun. "Although you do have some great hair."

"Traitor," Tracker mumbles, grabbing some pizza and taking a huge bite. "So, Shay, why don't you tell us all something about you? Favorite sexual position?"

Bailey almost chokes on her pizza.

Anna slaps his shoulder. "You can't just ask people that,

Tracker! Not everyone lives with Lana and discusses shit like this in casual conversation. Don't listen to him. Yesterday she started asking me about how many times Arrow usually makes me come in one night, while we were at the grocery store. An old man pretended to look at grapes for five minutes just to listen."

Tracker smiles, eyes gentling. "She's something, isn't she?"

No wonder Lana writes amazing, sexy love stories. She has a man like Tracker, who obviously loves her and is proud of her.

"She is," Anna agrees, then laughs. "Speak of the devil. . . ."

A pretty, dark-haired girl with glasses walks in, dressed in jeans and a plain black T-shirt. "Sorry I'm late. What's the big drama that's happening? I'm supposed to be finishing this book but I didn't want to miss out."

I raise my hand and say, "I guess I'm the big drama."

I can't take my eyes off her. This woman's mind is so creative, so twisted, I'd love nothing more than to get inside it. How does she come up with all the plotlines? She's crazy talented and I really want to hug her right now, but I don't want to freak her out.

"Hello," Lana says to me, smiling.

To me!

Zada Ryan said hello to me.

"H-hi," I say, waving ungracefully. I'm not usually this awkward, but how does one act around someone she feels like she knows through her books, but doesn't actually know at all? I know her mind, her thoughts, because she's shared them with me.

"This is Shay," Tracker says, watching me with amusement playing all over his face. "Vinnie's woman."

"Vinnie has a woman?" she asks, eyes going wide. "I'm so glad I came! Someone needs to tell me everything, pronto."

She puts her bag down on the table and looks at me. "How did you meet Vinnie?"

"She's the marker," Tracker says, pulling Lana onto his lap. "Vinnie went to pay back Talon's marker and he comes back with Talon's cousin. And Talon doesn't know yet."

"Holy shit," Lana murmurs, looking at Anna. "Who's going to talk to Talon? And what is he going to do? Does he know she and Vinnie have anything to do with each other? Didn't Vinnie just get there the other day?" She looks back at me. "So many questions."

And all I wanted to do was pick her brain about the ending in Colt's book.

Anna lifts her hands up in surrender. "Vinnie said he's going to handle it, and he should. I don't know the answers to most of those questions, but it seems that Shay is safer here, and for some reason she couldn't stay at the Wild Men MC." She looks at me and squints. "Is that right so far?"

I nod.

"And now Faye's gone to get groceries with Rake, because this whole drama has now turned into a reason to have a barbecue," Bailey adds, smirking. "I fucking love this place."

Vinnie walks into the crowded kitchen, searching the room until his gaze lands on me. He's changed into a pair of track pants and a white T-shirt, his hair damp from a shower. "Have you decided that you'd rather take your chances with the bad guys yet?"

"Who are the bad guys?" Lana asks, stepping to Vinnie and giving him a quick hug. "Did you hear? We're having a 'Vinnie brought home his marker' barbecue."

Vinnie sighs and mutters, "Jesus. Whose idea was that?"

Everyone in the room says, "Faye's," at the same time.

"Should've known."

Vinnie reaches his hand out to me, so I stand up and go to him. "Come with me. Sin wants to meet you."

We walk through the spacious clubhouse, passing what looks like a game room until we come to the back door. "You okay?" he asks, studying me.

"I'm fine. Everyone has been really nice," I say, then lower my voice. "I kept my cool around Zada fucking Ryan, okay? I think I deserve an award right now."

Vinnie stops, throws his head back, and laughs. "Fuck, I forgot about that. So you hid the crazy eyes?"

"I think so," I say, shrugging and cringing a little. "I don't really know when I'm doing them."

Vinnie laughs again and leads me outside, where a good-looking dark-haired man is watering the lawn. With no shirt on.

"That's him?" I ask, jaw dropping. "I was expecting an old man with a smoker's voice, a beer belly, and a beard."

"Sounds like Jim, the old president," Vinnie says, chuckling, then calls out Sin's name.

He turns to us, sees me, and narrows his blue eyes. "So this is who all the fuss is about, hey?"

Vinnie's hand tightens around mine, but he says nothing. Neither do I.

"Let me talk with her for a minute," Sin says to Vinnie—a demand, not a request.

Vinnie opens his mouth, seeming like he is going to argue, so this time it's me who squeezes his hand, silently telling him not to, that it's fine.

"All right," he says, letting go of my hand and returning inside. Sin turns off the hose, then gestures for me to take a seat at the outdoor setting.

He sits opposite me. "There are holes in this story. Your father is in prison for fraud and embezzlement, is that correct?"

I wince but nod. "Yeah, apparently he cooked the books for his clients. I really don't know the specifics, since he kept me away from that part of his business."

"And now that he's away in prison, where no one can touch him, you're the one everyone wants. I want to know why."

His crystal-blue eyes bore into me, making me squirm on my seat. "I don't know the exact details," I start, licking my lips, not knowing how much to tell him. "What I do know is that my father has hidden accounts and there's a ledger with lists. Names. Dates. Things that could incriminate people and get them killed. And everyone thinks I have this information."

"Do you?"

"I do have access to some of his accounts, but not all. So some of the money, yes," I admit. "As for the rest of it, no. I don't have anything."

"So you're saying your hands are clean?"

I nod my head.

"Because if Vinnie's getting his even dirtier for you, you better be telling the truth," he says, the threat clear and simple.

"I am. I wouldn't do anything to get anyone hurt," I state, being completely honest.

I want to add that I care about him, that I don't want him or anyone else to get hurt because of me, but I decide to stay silent. Sin can judge me all he wants, but I think he'll trust only my actions, not my words. Words don't mean anything at the end of the day.

"Okay," he says slowly, sitting back in his chair.

Vinnie opens the door and sticks his head out, waiting for Sin to say something.

"It's okay," he tells him, standing. "We're done here."

Sin says something to Vinnie that I can't hear, then heads inside.

"Everything okay?" he asks, his brow furrowing.

I stand up and wrap my arm around his waist. "Everything is fine."

So much has happened.

And we haven't even had sex yet.

EIGHTEEN

Vinnie

"UNCLE Vinnie!" Clover yells as she sees me walk into the kitchen.

"Princess." I grin, lifting her into my arms as she runs to me. "Ugh! Someone's getting heavy."

Clover grins and flexes her biceps. Or at least where her biceps were meant to be. "I know. Daddy says soon I can get my own motorcycle."

I look to Faye, who smiles but shakes her head as if to say, *That is never fuckin' happening.*

"I think you have to ask your mom about that," I say, lowering my voice to a whisper. "Don't tell your father, but she's the boss."

"I already know that," she whispers back conspiratorially. "Daddy gives Mama whatever she wants."

She pulls back and grins at me, and I do the same.

"Where have you been, Uncle Vinnie?" she asks me, pouting. "Mama told me in the car that you have a new girlfriend."

"Mama's been gossiping with you, has she?"

"It's not gossip when it's a fact," Clover says, making me unable to keep a straight face.

"You told her I have a woman?"

I look over Clover's head at Faye, who just shrugs and says, "Well, you do."

I kiss Clover's cheek and put her back down. "Shay is outside talking with Bailey and Tina. Do you want to go and meet her?"

"Okay," she replies, bouncing on her feet and looking to Faye. "I'm going outside to find Uncle Vinnie's girlfriend and say hi. I've never met one of Vinnie's girlfriends before. I was starting to think that maybe he wants to be alone forever, but that's okay too, isn't it, Mama? My friend told me that sometimes people live alone and just get lots of pets. I was going to get you a goldfish for Christmas, Uncle Vinnie. I wanted to get you a cat, but I don't think you'd like a cat. A goldfish is perfect though, because even I could feed it for you. Then every year I could just keep getting you more and more. I think we should name the first one Nemo. What do you think?"

When I stay silent and just look at the little girl with a larger-than-life personality, she keeps talking, just like her mother, never knowing when to be quiet. "No? Maybe a puppy then, but I'll have to keep saving my allowance because I don't think I can afford one right now."

I look at Faye, who can't control her laughter now. "You can definitely tell whose child she is."

Faye manages to get herself under control, then says, "Why don't you go and see Shay, honey?"

"Okay," Clover replies. She runs out of the kitchen, forgetting to even take me with her.

"She's getting so big," I muse, watching the door she just disappeared through.

"I know." Faye sighs, rubbing her stomach. "How are you doing, Vinnie? This whole thing is a lot to take on, don't you think?"

I nod, but say, "My gut is telling me it's the right thing to do."

"It's always something, isn't it?" she says. She places a hand on my shoulder and, with the other, snatches an apple from a basket on the counter. "But we always survive. I like her, Vinnie. I think she's perfect for you."

"You like everyone," I mutter, then add, "Except Allie."

She winces and takes a bite out of the red apple. "Do you have to bring that up?"

Allie used to live here in the clubhouse and date Tracker. Faye didn't get along with her—hell, neither did many of the women. When I first came here, I kind of had a crush on her though, and only Faye knows that. Allie died, which makes Faye uncomfortable now—she doesn't like to speak ill of the dead.

"It's one of the only things that makes you feel awkward," I say, crossing my arms over my chest. "Otherwise you have an answer for everything."

She chews and swallows, narrowing her eyes on me. "Guess what weapon I'm learning how to use right now?"

"What?" I ask, feeling amused. Faye moves from weapon to weapon faster than anyone I know. She may joke a lot, and be caring and sweet, but she isn't a woman to fuck with. She has a core of steel that nothing can penetrate. She's the perfect woman to be Sin's old lady.

"Nunchakus," she says, grinning widely.

I bark out a laugh and ask her, "Are you gonna beat someone up with nunchakus like a fuckin' ninja?"

I wouldn't put it past her, to be honest.

"Like a Ninja Turtle, at least," she replies, shrugging. "I like to keep my options open. I feel all badass when I'm waving those things around. So cool."

I shake my head at her, smile, and kiss her on the forehead. "Don't change, Faye."

"Never," she replies, her voice gentling.

We both look each other in the eye, sharing a moment.

"I can see the headline now," she says, breaking the silence. "Lawyer beats up Mafia assholes with nunchakus."

I throw my head back and laugh.

She'd do it in fuckin' stilettos too.

Clover runs back in, a cheeky grin on her little face. She puts her hand out and says, "Are you coming, Uncle Vinnie?"

I take her small hand in mine and let her lead me outside. Shay is sitting with Bailey, Tina, Lana, and Anna, and I can hear her laugh over all of theirs. She's freshly showered and wearing jeans with a tight white top.

"Shay," I say, getting her attention. I go and stand by her seat. "This is Princess. Princess, this is Shay."

She looks up at me and says, "My name is Clover, Uncle Vinnie."

Shay smiles warmly. "Hello, Clover. Nice to meet you."

"She'll always be the princess to us," I say, grinning when Clover jumps on Shay's lap. I sit down, listening to the conversation and inserting my input when needed, but really my attention is on Shay. What is it about her? She starts to laugh again, and it makes my dick harden. I love seeing everyone, and I love that they're welcoming Shay like this, but really I just want to take her into my room, lay her down, and fuck her until she screams. I want to taste her. Devour her. Since we haven't even started up the grill, I don't think that's going to be happening for at least the next few hours. Maybe I could sneak her away after we've done our time being social.

"What are you thinking about, Vinnie?" Lana asks, pushing her glasses up on her nose. "You look like you're planning something evil."

"That's exactly what I'm doing," I tell her, grabbing a chip from the center of the table when I see Arrow heading toward the barbecue. I follow him and offer my assistance, which he declines. He takes his own cool time cleaning it, then firing it up. I shift on my feet, my gaze going back to Shay. The top she's wearing makes her tits look good. I really want those in my mouth and hands right now.

"A little impatient today, huh?" Arrow asks, smirking at me knowingly. I drag my gaze away from her and onto Arrow, which instantly kills any sexual thoughts.

"Just a little. It's like everyone is going in fuckin' slow motion," I grumble, running my hand over my head.

"Go disappear for a bit," he says, eyes dancing with amusement. "Food won't be ready for another hour, my guess."

That sounding like a perfect idea, I tap Arrow on the back, and then head for Shay, one thing on my mind. I offer her my hand, and she gives me a look of confusion but takes it, letting me pull her out of her chair and lead her inside.

"Where are we going?" she asks, her steps quick as I practically drag her to my bedroom. I lock the door behind her and pull off my T-shirt. I must have a predatory look in my eye, because she takes a step back, biting her lower lip, her eyes roaming down my chest. She likes my body, I know it, and I'm not ashamed to use it to get what I want.

"We can't just—"

"We can," I cut her off, crooking my finger. "Come here."

She steps toward me, resting her hands on my bare chest.

"I want you, now."

"I want you too." She breathes, pressing her lips to my skin. That is all the permission I need.

I grip her face in my hands and kiss her deeply, lifting up her face. I show her how much I want her with my mouth, the kiss hungry and almost desperate. I walk her backward with our lips still pressed together, until we reach the bed. Then I start to lift off her top, pulling back from her only to get it over her head. Her bra goes next, and I lay her back on the bed, kissing her as my hands cup her breasts, flicking my thumbs over her nipples.

She arches her back a little, and I reach down to undo the button of her jeans, then lower the zipper. She slides them off herself, making me grin when she struggles to get them over her knees. I get off the bed and pull them down, throwing them on the floor, then removing the bright red panties she is wearing. I admire her for a second, her hair spread all over the bed, her dark eyes pinned on me. Bedroom eyes she has, devil eyes. Eyes that I want to look into as she sucks my dick, on her knees, while I hold her hair away from her face.

But now, it's me who gets on my knees, spreading her thighs and bringing her pussy to the end of the bed, spread before me like a feast. I look up at her as my mouth descends, her eyes still on me, her perfect lips open slightly. I lick her once, twice, before sucking on her clit, just the way I know she likes it. I ease up a little, not wanting her to come straightaway, no, I want her to enjoy this.

Just like I'm going to.

NINETEEN

Shayla

*H*E'S *going to kill me*, I think to myself.

After making me come with his mouth, not once but twice, he lays back on the bed. I help him remove all his clothes—his hard, thick cock beckoning me. I straddle his body, taking his cock in my hand and placing it at my entrance, before sliding down slowly, letting myself get used to the size of him. He feels so good, I never want this to end.

His dark, heavy-lidded eyes stay on mine, instead of looking down to where we're now connected, making the experience more personal. When he's all in, I place my hands on his chest, lean forward, and kiss him at the same time I start to ride him. He makes that growling sound I love so much, and grabs my hips, wanting me to go faster. I ride him faster, harder, while he sucks and plays with my nipples, turning me on even more, making me feel wild with need. He rolls me over onto my back, still inside me, thrusting into me in a perfect rhythm that has me clawing at his back and moaning into his mouth.

"Vinnie," I whisper when I can feel myself on the verge of

coming again. I don't think I've ever come this much at one time before. He kisses my jawline, then nibbles on my earlobe, "Come for me again, Shay. I want to feel it around my cock."

He reaches between us and plays with my clit, which of course makes me do just as he wants, coming with him inside me.

"Oh my god," I chant as the orgasm carries on, my thighs trembling and my eyes slamming closed as the pleasure almost becomes too much. I practically sag back into the bed when it's over, now knowing why they call it the little death. Vinnie curses under his breath, his rhythm changing. "Going to come," he grits out. "Fuck, Shay." He finishes inside me, then kisses my lips before pulling out and lying next to me. Straightaway he spreads his arm out, silently inviting me to come closer. I lay my head on his shoulder and wrap my arm around him.

There's only one word running through my head right now.

Wow.

Just, wow.

Not that I've been with too many men, but I've been with a few, and nothing I've experienced before compares to this. It's like he knew what I needed before I did, like he actually paid attention to the telltale signals a woman's body gives. I'm actually kind of speechless, but I think the huge smile on my satisfied face speaks for itself.

He sighs, interrupting my moment of awe, and says, "So that's why my gut instinct was telling me to protect you."

I laugh and slap his chest. "That's the worst pillow talk I've ever heard in my life."

But I'll accept it, because it's the best thing I have going for me right now.

There's a bang on the door. "Vinnie! Be social, you asshole!" Faye yells. I hear Sin's voice, telling her not to be a cock block.

"They have all night," she says, snickering. "We should eat all the food. They can live on sex."

I start giggling at that, shoving my face in his pillow.

Vinnie gets my attention by slapping my ass. "Amused, are we?"

"I can't go out there now," I groan, covering my face with my hands. "They're all going to give us shit."

"Better get used to it." He smirks, then adds, "If any of the girls give you shit, don't worry, we have ammunition against all of them."

"You do; I don't," I say, yawning.

"Tired?"

"A little," I admit, burrowing into him once again. "Not tired enough to not want to do that again later tonight though."

His chest shakes as he laughs. "Oh, we'll be doing that again."

"Tonight."

"Tonight," he agrees, then rolls me onto my back and stretches my hands above my head, pinning them into the mattress with his weight. "So many things I want to do to you."

"Like what?" I ask, my voice coming out sounding all dreamy.

"I want to fuck you from behind. I want you on your knees, sucking my dick. I want you to sit on my face again. I want to fuck you in the shower, against the wall, on the chair. Everywhere. I want to do everything."

"Tonight?" I ask, eyes going wide. I don't think I'd survive the night, but what a way to go.

His eyes smile, then he lowers his head for a kiss. "I like how you rode me. You'd be surprised how many women are shy to do it, too worried about what they look like from that angle."

"Definitely the worst pillow talk ever," I grumble, closing my eyes. "Quit now, Vinnie, while the amazing sex is still in my head, and my body is sated, my mind all mushy."

"I'm just saying," he says, getting off me and sitting with his feet on the floor. "We better go out there or I'll never hear the end of it. I'm kinda hungry anyway."

"Worked up an appetite, did you?" I ask as I look around the room for my clothes. He's thrown them all over the place in the haste to get me naked.

"Here," he says, picking up my panties and handing them to me. "Red looks good on you, by the way."

"I'm surprised you even noticed," I tease, putting them on, then my matching bra. I turn to see him putting his pants back on.

"Trust me, I notice." He slides his T-shirt back on. "Are you ready? We haven't been gone that long."

I snicker at that. "What? Didn't think you lasted that long, did you?"

He looks at his watch and flashes me a smug look. "We've been gone for two and a half hours."

My eyes widen as I slide my jeans up my thighs. "Really? Shit. They might have finished eating. You heard Faye's evil plan."

Fully dressed, I try to tame my hair. "Ready when you are."

He stands behind me, pressing himself up against me. "I'm always ready."

Holy shit. He is hard. Again.

"I don't know whether to be impressed or scared," I say, making him laugh. With his hand on my lower back, I brace myself to face the crowd. When we step outside, everyone cheers and catcalls, and it makes me want to hide my face from them forever, but instead, I sit down at the table with dignity, while Vinnie goes to get us some food.

"Not bad for Vinnie," Anna says, nudging me with her shoulder.

"Leave her alone," Lana chastises, but then adds, "But I have to agree."

I groan and sag in the chair, making the women laugh.

"So what did I miss?" I ask them, looking from face to face.

"Nothing, we were pretty much just discussing you two," Faye says, shrugging. "Oh, and binge eating."

Clover runs up to me with two other kids by her side, a boy and a girl. "Shay, where did you go?"

Just kill me now.

"I just had a little nap," I lie, ignoring the laughter from the peanut gallery. "Have you been having a fun time with your friends?"

"Yep," she says, bouncing on her feet. "Cara and Rhett are my besties."

"Cool," I say, watching the three of them run inside. "Cute bunch of kids."

"You're telling me," Anna says, pushing her hair out of her face and looking at Tia and Bailey. "Next generation of Wind Dragons right there."

We spend the rest of the night eating, drinking, and just having a good time. By the time it's over, it's late, and I'm exhausted. I help clean up, then head to the bathroom for a shower. Vinnie fills the bath for me though, undresses me, and carries me in there. I grin when he hands me a book, the one I'd left on his side table. So much has happened today, so many things have changed. We left the house, we came here and they let me stay, and now we have to sort things out with Talon and come up with a new plan to save me.

I just hope no one gets hurt in the process, because I'd rather turn myself in.

And if worse comes to worse—maybe I'll have to.

TWENTY

Vinnie

"TALON called," Sin says so only I can hear. "I told him you'll meet him at Rift tonight."

I nod. "About time. He probably only just realized she was missing."

"I think Talon is a lot smarter than we give him credit for," Sin says, sinking two balls on the pool table. "Don't underestimate him. I have a feeling there's something about this whole situation that we're missing."

It was highly likely.

I play my shot and sink the red ball, then take a sip of my beer. "It's been so quiet, nothing's fuckin' happened around here. I don't get it."

"You upset someone isn't pounding on our compound's door?" Sin asks, raising an eyebrow in amusement.

"'Course not," I say, sitting down on one of the stools by the bar. "I just don't understand it. I know the Kings are involved somehow, I just don't know how they fit into this, and it bothers the fuck out of me. I don't want to get too comfortable, you know? Forget why we're here in the first place. Shay's hungover from drinking with the girls last night. This place has turned into a huge party. Don't get me wrong, I want her to enjoy herself, but I can't enjoy anything until I know that she's going to be safe and the threat is eliminated."

"Talk to Talon. I have a feeling he knows exactly what's going on here," Sin says, playing his shot, then glancing up at me. "The compound is at highest security. Even Lana's fuckin' dog is here. No one is going to get in without us knowing about it. Until then, we just need to figure out what's really going on, because no offense, but the story sounds like bullshit to me."

I honestly didn't know what to think at this point. If they really wanted Shay, they'd have found her by now. It's been a week, and not even a threatening call. Nothing. Talon didn't even return my calls until today. If they have something planned, something big, maybe something we're missing, then we're going to be fucked. I don't think they've just forgotten about Shay. That shit is way too easy—and nothing ever comes easy to me.

"Talon better shed light on the situation tonight." I pause and grin wolfishly. "And hopefully we both don't end up beating the shit out of each other."

Yes, he told me not to touch her, but Sin's right, something here doesn't add up. Do I feel guilty for touching her? Yes and no. Yes, I feel shitty that I went against my word, because a man's word is everything. But the fucked-up thing is that I'd do it again and again if I had the chance.

"You better kick his ass." Sin smirks, laying the pool cue against the wall. "Can't have a Wind Dragon losing to someone from the Wild Men."

I make a scoffing noise and pretend to punch Sin in the face a few times. "Dragons are made of tougher substance than any wild men."

Shay walks in, looking like hell, a bottle of water in her hands.

"Good morning." I grin, even though it is about two o'clock. "How are you feeling?"

"Like Faye hit me in the head a million times with those nunchakus she keeps carrying around," she grumbles, coming to stand by me.

"Want to play?" I ask her, racking up the balls.

"Yeah, okay," she says, but winces at the thought. I hide my grin, then tell her, "I'm meeting with Talon tonight. You'll be staying here with the men."

"Why can't I come?" she asks, putting her water down on the bar counter. "I want to know what's going on too."

"And I'll tell you."

"I want to come."

"No."

"Controlling jerk," she mutters, scowling at me, which only makes me laugh. "I want to know everything he says, don't keep anything from me."

"I won't," I assure her, then ask, "Do you want to break?"

"No, you can," she says, grabbing a cue and putting some chalk on the tip. "I suck at breaking."

I break, sinking one ball in the process.

"Do you get horny when you're hungover, or is it just me?" she blurts out, making my head snap to her. We've been fucking like rabbits, usually about three times a day, every day since she got here. We can't seem to keep our hands off each other. I have no fuckin' idea what we're doing, and what's going to happen, but I decided to just not think about it and live in the present. Who gives a fuck what the future holds when all we have is now?

I step behind her and run my thumb across the little bit of skin showing on her flat stomach. "Want to play with a different kind of ball, do you?"

"How do you even get laid with those lines?"

"You tell me," I say, smiling as I move her hair away from her neck and kiss her there. She shivers.

"It annoys me that you know all my weaknesses now," she says, her breath hitching as I kiss her there again.

"Why? You should be happy I know just what to do to turn you on, and how to pleasure you and satisfy you." I bite down on her neck. "Over and over again."

She puts the pool cue down, grabs my wrist, and practically pulls me to the bedroom, or at least tries. I purposely take my time, going slower, causing her to spin around and pin me with a glare that I happen to find fuckin' adorable. When we get to our room, she locks the door behind us and pulls off her pants and top. She's not wearing a bra or panties, and I slowly peruse her body from her breasts to her bare pussy. "Easy access?"

She smirks and cups her breasts with her hands. "Stop fucking around or I'll start without you."

"Perhaps that's something I'd like to witness," I say, reaching behind me to pull my T-shirt off. She lays back on the white sheets and spreads her legs, the little vixen. I love how comfortable she is with her body; she owns it, and her confidence is the biggest turn-on.

"Show me what you like," I command, hardening as she starts to pinch her nipples then slowly trail her fingers farther down south. I remove my jeans and boxers, then start to stroke myself as I watch her. "Come here."

She sits up on her knees and crawls to the end of the bed, glancing up at me, waiting.

"Open," I tell her.

She opens her lips, and I slide the tip between them, then let go and let her take over. She grabs the base with her hand and slides it into her mouth, taking as much in as she can, which is a pretty impressive amount. I look down at her, a groan slipping from my mouth as I take in the picture before me. She always tells me I make a noise like a low growl that turns her on like crazy, but I never realized I did it until she pointed it out to me.

"Where do you want me to come?" I ask her, feeling myself on the edge, her talented mouth driving me crazy.

She pulls back and says, "Inside me."

"Bend over for me," I say, slapping her ass when she goes to do as I told her. I stand behind her, sliding in with one smooth thrust. I love how wet she is, how turned on she gets simply from giving me head. Not all women enjoy it, and the fact that she does makes it so much better. She likes to please and be pleased, and I like giving her exactly what she needs and knowing I can satisfy her. I play with her clit as I slide in and out of her, stopping to kiss her mouth with my hand at her jaw, turning her head to me, before continuing.

"Yes, Vinnie," she moans, pushing back on my dick. "Fuck me harder."

I give her what she wants until she comes, biting down on the pillow in front of her. Only then do I come, even though I've been fighting against it ever since she had me in her mouth. I pull out of her and straightaway pull her body against mine. I kiss her brow and watch her lips as they turn upward, her eyes as they close. She sighs in contentment and kisses my chest.

Not for the first time, I wonder how she does it, how she got me to let her in. I don't know why I'm so different with her than I've been with other women in the past. I've never allowed myself to get attached to a woman before. With Eliza, I really was just in it for the sex, same with the other women I've let into my life.

My own mother didn't want me, and neither did any other woman.

Now that I've grown up, I never allow myself to really rely on a woman, not solely. Sure, I treat them well, and I love them in bed, but no one has ever really made an impact on me besides the other old ladies, and that's in a completely different way from how I feel about Shay. I respect and care for the other women; with Shay, I've actually let her in. I lowered my guard, took her under my wing. Made her my problem when I didn't have to, and went out on a limb to protect her, when I wasn't sure what to do with her. I'm not a person who believes in marriage and true love and all that other shit—I don't ever want to get married—but Shay just fits. She's here, and it feels like it's where she belongs. If she isn't who I'm meant to be with, then I don't know who is, because thinking of moving any other woman into the clubhouse would make me run for the hills.

"What are you thinking about?" she asks, now studying me. "You have the weirdest expression on your face."

"Just thinking it's weird how things turn out."

"It really is," she says, taking a deep breath. "I never really thanked you for bringing me here, Vinnie. I know it wasn't an easy choice to make, but thank you. I'd much rather be here with you than locked away somewhere, and I like it. Both you, and everything about living here."

"You like me, do you?" I ask, lips twitching upward.

"You're growing on me," she says flippantly, rolling her eyes. "It definitely feels like I've known you longer than I have. And you've done more for me than people I've known my whole life have. It's true what they say, time means nothing, only character does."

"Never has a woman complimented my character before," I say, amusement filling me.

She is just . . . cute. I don't know how anyone could want to hurt her.

"Let's nap," she suggests, yawning. "And then we can take a shower and get dressed to go and meet Talon. Also, eating will be thrown somewhere into that plan too."

"Sounds perfect, except the part about you coming with me to meet him," I say, spooning her from behind and shoving all her hair out of my face.

"The two of you aren't going to fight, are you?" she asks, starting to sound a little worried, or maybe concerned.

"No," I say, peppering kisses on the back of her neck. "No fighting. Now go to sleep."

She falls asleep before me, and I replay her words in my head.

I didn't *think* Talon and I were going to end up in a fight.

Maybe.

Okay, we probably were.

TWENTY-ONE

"WHO the fuck do you think you are, taking her to your fuckin' clubhouse?" he yells, throwing a punch that I avoid by moving back.

"Took you long enough to figure that out. I think the real question is, why didn't you take her to yours? Don't want her to see the real bastard you are?" I fire back, throwing my own punch that hits him right in the gut. Yeah, that would have hurt.

He gets me square in the mouth before I slam him back into the wall. "You didn't even call to check on her for over a week. Tell me what the fuck is going on right now, or I swear to God, Talon, you will never see your cousin again, because I'll protect her from anyone, even you."

"I'm the only one protecting her!" he yells, his face contorting in anger. "Look, her father is the one who made it look like she knew everything, had everything they wanted, when she doesn't. And now her father is fuckin' dead. Someone got to him in prison. I didn't want to tell her. How the fuck do I tell her that he's dead? And that he wasn't the man she thought he was to begin with?"

I let him go and take a step back.

Well, fuck.

What do we do now? This news will devastate Shay, and it looks like I am going to be the one who has to deliver it to her.

"When was he killed?" I ask, sitting down at the desk. We are alone in one of the offices at Rift, loud music in the background.

"Three days ago," he says, shoulders sagging. "Look, I can't bring her back to my clubhouse because I have my own shit going on there, and it's not safe for her right now. If it was the best place for her I would have taken her there."

"Why has it been so quiet?" I ask, a muscle ticking in my jaw. "There's been nothing, we've checked the cameras, everything. Nothing suspicious has happened."

Talon scratches the stubble on his jaw. "A member of the Kings of Hell MC killed Shay's father."

My head snaps to him. "I know the Kings are involved in all this bullshit, and I want to know why."

The Kings were an MC we've had trouble with recently. Rake fucked their president's old lady, but even before that we've had run-ins with them. We once thought they were clean, but it doesn't look that way anymore. In fact, it looks like we may have to deal with them sooner than later.

Talon grits his teeth. "Shayla's father was an accountant, and Shay worked with him, which you probably already know. He taught her everything she needed to know, and she's very good with numbers, always has been."

I didn't know that, actually.

"And?" I growl, wanting to know what he's getting at. "You said Shay doesn't know anything."

"I don't think she does," Talon says, looking me in the eye. "She has dealt with the Kings MC accounts though."

"So I need to worry about them too? They aren't just doing the Mafia's bidding?" I ask, jaw tense. I can tell the body count is going to be high. And what did it mean, she did their accounts? To me, that means she does know something. I am going to ask her that though, not Talon. I want to hear that information from her lips.

"I don't know, but the likely answer is that the Mafia and Kings are working together on this. Everyone has their hands full right now. They are still looking for the ledger, so they're killing each other off. Lists of names of people who betrayed others, who made deals with who, who is funding who, it's all fucked-up right now. I don't know who the real threat to Shay is anymore."

"So if her father is dead, what do they still want with Shay?" I ask, a dash of hope filling me.

"They think she has the ledger," he says, pulling the chair next to me and taking a seat. "I don't know what's going to happen, to be honest. I'm hoping they forget about her, but these bastards never do. They bide their time until an opportunity comes up." He pulls out a piece of paper and hands it to me. "Top three people who would have reason to want revenge. These are who I'm keeping an eye on right now, watching their movements. You want to be in the know, well here you fuckin' go, Vinnie."

I scan the list and memorize the three names. "So you're on top of this, then?"

He nods. "You just do what you're doing and keep her safe. And it pains me to say this, but don't tell me what you're doing with her. I have a leak and I have no idea where it's coming from."

"The fuck?" I growl, hands clenching. "You need to handle that shit, Talon."

"I'm on it," he replies, then lowers his voice. "And tell her about her father."

"I'm not telling her that he tried to use her as a cop-out," I tell him. "She doesn't need to know that shit, it will kill her."

There's no way she's going to find out. Let her think her father died loving her more than anything, trying to protect her from the shit he caused in the first place.

"I agree," Talon says, sitting down in the chair next to me. "Just keep that part to yourself, and I'll do the same."

"We done here, then? Or is there anything else I need to know?" I ask him, my gaze going back to the piece of paper in front of me.

"I think for now, we're done." He stands up, and I eye him curiously.

"You aren't going to say anything about me and Shay?" I ask, standing and bracing myself for another fight. "You told me to keep my hands off her, and I didn't. I'm surprised you didn't start with that."

He walks to the door, turns, and flashes me a grin. "Shay now has the protection of the Wind Dragons. Why would I be angry at that?"

He leaves and I stare at the door.

Motherfucker.

He wanted this to happen.

No, he'd counted on it.

I consider finding him and punching him in the face for playing with us, but does it really matter how I got Shay? The important thing is that I have her.

Sin was right though—Talon is more of a smart, manipulative bastard than we give him credit for.

"What are you doing?" I ask Shay when I return to the room and find her standing on a chair, dusting the windows.

"Cleaning your room," she says, not looking at me.

"Our room," I correct, approaching her. She turns around, sees my cut lip and scowls.

"No fighting, my ass. What happened?"

The concern in her voice is palpable. Little does she know she's about to have more important things on her mind than Talon getting in one hit on me. I don't want to tell her, but I know I have to. How the fuck do I bring this up though? By the way, your father is dead? I'm sure he loved her, he did care for her and apparently dote on her; maybe toward the end he just got desperate. People do anything when they're trying to save themselves. Anything. They don't care about other people when they're that low, struggling to get up. How am I supposed to ask her about the work she did for him, when I have to tell her that he's dead? Fuck, I don't know at all how to handle this in a gentle way.

"There was a punch or two, that's all," I say, lifting her off the chair by her waist and placing her on the floor. She reaches up and touches my split lip, making me wince. "It's fine."

"What happened?" she asks, wrapping her tiny arms around my hips. I sit down on the bed and lift her onto my lap.

"I have some bad news," I start, clearing my throat. Who am I kidding? I don't have the fuckin' tact for this. I'm just going to blurt it out and she's probably going to go into shock.

"What is it?" she asks, cupping my face with her hands when I stay silent. "Is Talon okay? Oh my god, did you knock him out or something? Is he in the hospital?"

She really can be dramatic at times.

"Talon is fine." For now. "He did tell me some bad news about your father though."

Bad news?

I could kill myself.

"Bad news" was her father having to stay an extra year in prison or something, not that he was dead as a doornail.

"What is it?" she asks, warily, her brow furrowing.

Fuck.

I just need to say it, not drag it out.

"He's uhhh . . ." Fuck. "He's dead, Shay. I'm sorry. He was killed in prison."

She freezes and stares at me in confusion as if she doesn't understand what I'm saying.

"He's dead?"

I nod.

Her bottom lip trembles.

"Oh my god," she whispers.

And then she cries.

I hold on to her as she cries on my shoulder. I know there's nothing I can say or do to make this better, to fix this for her, so I just hold her and let her cry. I rub her back and make little sounds one would use to soothe a baby or a puppy.

Fuck, I'm really terrible at comforting someone, but for her, I want to try. I don't want her to go to someone else for comfort, I want to be able to fulfill all her needs, even ones I'm not quite comfortable with. I don't think her father really deserves her tears, but then again he did raise her. And Shay loves him, there's no question about it.

"I'm sorry," I say over and over again.

Soon, she stops making any noise, but the tears still fall.

Somehow I think the silent crying is worse.

I lay her down in bed and wrap her in my arms. She cries herself to sleep, and all I do is feel helpless, wishing I could take away her pain.

But I can't.

She'll need to fix the hole inside her on her own. Afterward though, she'll be stronger than she was.

And she needs to be strong, because no matter how hard I'm going to try to save her, it seems the world isn't done fucking her over yet.

TWENTY-TWO

Shayla

DON'T leave bed for three days, except to use the bathroom. I don't eat much, although Vinnie tries to make me. I just don't feel very hungry.

I feel exhausted.

Mentally and physically drained.

My father was all I had left, really, besides Talon, and now he's gone too. At least when he was in prison, I knew eventually I'd see him again. But now. Never again. I don't know what to do to make the pain go away.

I don't want to be like this. I know I can't be sad forever—the world waits for no one—but how do I go on every day with this pain in my gut? Nothing means anything anymore. I just want to sleep, hide under these sheets for the rest of my life. Talon calls me, but I don't feel like talking to anyone. Faye and the girls drop by to check on me, and I thank them but tell them that I'm okay, I just want to sleep.

On day four, Vinnie walks into the room with a determined

look on his face. He opens the blinds, pulls the blanket off me, and says, "Get up, now."

I roll over and ignore him. I hear him running water in the bathroom. Filling the bath? The next second, I'm being dragged down the bed by my feet. I start kicking my legs but there's no way I can overpower him. He lifts me in the air and over his shoulder, then pulls down my shorts. Putting me down on my feet, he removes my top, then carries me into the bathtub, like he's done before.

"I don't want to do anything," I say, my voice weak and pathetic. "I don't want to leave this room."

"You don't have to," he replies, handing me my body wash, shampoo, and conditioner. "Just have a bath, brush your teeth, then you can get back in bed. I'm going to change the sheets and bring some food in for you. If you eat it, I'll even let you go back to sleep without annoying you."

It sounds fair, so I nod and dunk my head back in the water so I can shampoo my hair. It's really knotty, and I wonder if Vinnie will help me brush it out after the bath. The Weeknd starts to play, Vinnie knows he's my favorite artist right now, and I close my eyes and just allow myself to enjoy the warm water on my skin. When I'm all done, I dry myself and walk naked to the room, where Vinnie has indeed changed the sheets. I dress in the black T-shirt he left out, then lie back down. He comes in a few minutes later with some rice and chicken, with another few dishes.

"Did you get this from a Vietnamese restaurant?" I ask him, recognizing the scent of the blended spices used in the dish.

He nods, looking a little sheepish. "You said once that it's comfort food to you, right? So I got you some."

I realize in this moment just how lucky I am.

"Thank you, Vinnie," I say, suddenly feeling emotional. Great, now I'm going to cry over food. No, I'm going to cry because this big, bad biker is so damn thoughtful.

"Did you eat?" I ask him, taking the first bite.

"Don't worry about me," he says, watching me closely as I chew and swallow. "Just eat. There's more if you want, and there's also a variety of desserts and shit that Faye picked up. There's cheesecake—I know how you feel about cheesecake."

I did like cheesecake.

"Will you sit down, at least?" I ask him as he continues to stand there and supervise me. He nods and sits down. I finish half the food, feeling really full.

"Can I finish the rest later?" I ask, not wanting to waste the food, or to act ungrateful when he brought it to me.

"Sure, you did well," he says, taking the tray from me. I yawn, and he grins. "Don't go to sleep yet. I have something for you that I think you're going to like."

"What?" I ask, wondering what he could be up to now. "Does it require me to leave the room?"

"No," he says, exiting the door. "Don't move a muscle."

When he opens the door about a few minutes later, my jaw drops.

He didn't?

"Oh my god, Vinnie!"

My mood instantly lifts.

In his hands are three puppies.

Cuteness overload.

A Great Dane, a German shepherd, and what looks like a Neapolitan mastiff.

He places them all on the bed, and I die. In a good way.

I smile.

I pick them up one by one and hug them.

"I remember how happy taking you to the pet store made you," he says, picking up the mastiff and holding him. "It was the only thing I could think of to try to make you smile again."

He brought me puppies, to the bed, to make me smile.

My eyes start to well up.

"Fuck, don't cry," he says, looking alarmed. He hands me the mastiff as if that will help.

I make a sniffling sound, attempting to curb the tears. "Thank you. Who do they belong to?"

"Well, one belongs to you," he says, smiling. "If you want one. They're all boys. I kind of rented them for two days."

"You rented them?" I ask, laughing. "How did you manage that?"

"I talked them into a two-day trial period," he admits, shrugging. "And money talks."

This man.

"I don't even know what to say," I whisper, hugging the Great Dane against my chest.

"You don't need to," he replies, leaning forward to place a kiss on my lips. "Your smile says enough. Also, you're cleaning all their shit."

A therapy dog.

Not really, but the pup is going to distract me from everything else going on. I don't know if bringing me three was a good idea, although I'm happy he chose three big breeds, because I love big dogs.

"Well," he says, standing up. "I'll leave you to it then. I'll bet the women will be in here soon, wanting a cuddle, they've been fussing over them like crazy all morning." He pauses. "They're going to fuckin' baby that puppy so much."

I was going to too.

He scrubs his hand down his face, but then says, "As long as you're happy again, I don't fuckin' care."

I wouldn't be happy again, but I do feel the cloud of misery move away a little. Not because of the puppies, although I'm already in love with all of them, but because of Vinnie himself. He is so good to me, and even though I don't have a father anymore, I do have him, and that's something to be joyful about.

He leaves the room, and I lie back, three adorable puppies jumping all over me.

And I smile again.

"You know," I say to Faye, watching the pups play with Clover on the grass. "They're all pretty cute, aren't they? And Clover loves them. The compound is big enough for them all, don't you think? And I'm sure we could use the extra guards."

Faye raises an eyebrow and says, "Not very subtle, are you?"

"The only way I'm going to get my way in this situation is to get the queen and the princess on my side."

She throws her head back and laughs at that. "So what are you suggesting exactly?"

"We could raise them all here. One could be Clover's, one could be mine, and one could be yours . . . if you wanted one."

Faye stays quiet for a moment, but then says, "I call the shepherd."

I grin, pressing my fingers together like Mr. Burns from *The*

Simpsons. "Colt is mine." Colt was the harlequin Great Dane that had grown attached to me over the last few days.

"You named him Colt after Lana's character?" Faye asks, laughing even harder than before, tears forming in her hazel eyes. "Basically you named the dog after Tracker's alter ego."

"It suits him," I say, lifting my shoulders in a shrug. "He's going to be as big as a horse too, so it goes."

When Clover picks up the Neo and says, "Mom can we keep this one?" Faye and I share a scheming glance. Yes, our plan was going to work out just fine.

"Should we do an evil laugh too?" Faye asks, copying my Mr. Burns hand moves.

"I feel like it's appropriate."

"Mwahahahahahahaha," Faye laughs, making it sound pretty damn evil.

I copy her, and then she does it again, and then so do I.

Sin walks out and gives us a suspicious look. "What the hell are the two of you up to?"

"What gave us away?" Faye asks, tone full of mock innocence. She then starts giggling. "How great is my evil laugh, babe? I should be in a Disney movie."

Sin blinks slowly, then turns his eyes to his daughter. "We're not keeping all those dogs."

"Of course not, honey," Faye replies, waving her hand flippantly. Under her breath she mutters, "Just two of them."

In that moment, I realize that when I grow up, I want to be Faye.

TWENTY-THREE

Vinnie

HIT the punching bag for the last time and then step back, sweat dripping down my face.

"Do you fight in the ring?" Shay asks, looking at the place the guys usually spar with one another.

"Yeah, we usually do," I say, moving to the weights. "Once a month we'll all get together, make sure our fighting skills are on par."

"Do the women fight?"

"Faye and Anna do. They teach the rest of the women some self-defense moves. Faye is pregnant, so she can't teach you now, but you should ask Anna. It's important to know, and it could save your life one day."

Just in case I wasn't there to save her.

"I like that idea," she says before moving to the treadmill. I watch her ass as she starts to walk, her headphones in her ears, then moves into a jog. The yoga pants she's wearing are sexy as hell, showing off every curve she owns. When I start to get hard, I realize us working out together isn't going to work. I lift the weights a few times, trying not to look in her direction and fail. Eventually I put them down and sit on one of the benches, watching her.

"Working hard, I can see," Tracker says, chuckling. "You look like the seediest bastard right now, you should see yourself."

Not bothering to deny it, I shrug and say, "Best ass I've ever seen. I can't help it. Did you hear about the puppies?"

"No, what about them?" he asks, then adds, "By the way, that was my move, you asshole. You stole it and made it even better by getting three of them, different breeds too. Overachiever."

My body shakes, I laugh that hard. "Shay loves animals. Her happy place is a fuckin' pet store, so I wanted to bring her happy place to her. I didn't mean to steal your thunder, brother."

"Well it seems to work, doesn't it?" he says, tying up his hair in that fuckin' man bun thing the women are always raving on about. "So what were you saying about the pups?"

"Shay talked Faye into keeping the rest of them," I tell him, smirking. "She's crafty, I give her that. Faye and Clover are both going to take one each."

She probably got it from her asshole of a cousin.

"Best move she could've made," Tracker agrees, pulling off his T-shirt. "How's Sin taking it?"

"He said the dogs weren't staying."

"What did Faye do?"

My lip twitches as I say, "She went out and bought three dog kennels, each with the dog's name on the front. Then she somehow bribed Sin into being okay with it. Who knows what creative shit she came up with to sway him."

"I don't even want to know." Tracker laughs. "Maybe she played the pregnancy card."

"Maybe," I agree, my eyes zoning back onto Shay.

"So, is she staying here, then?" Tracker asks, following my line of sight. "The two of you seem fuckin' inseparable. I know you claimed her, but you haven't really spoken about making her your old lady."

"It's still early," I reply, standing up. "We're still getting to know each other."

"Seems a little more than that," Tracker comments before walking off to start his workout.

I don't know why everyone wants me to explain what's going on with Shay and me, because I don't even fuckin' know how to explain it without sounding like a dickhead. I'm just enjoying her right now, while trying to save her ass at the same time, so I do have the option of making her my old lady. If I'm being honest with myself, it's something I definitely plan on doing. But everyone else doesn't have to know that. Shay gets off the treadmill, pulling her earphones out and closing the space between us.

"I know only twenty minutes of cardio is shit, but I'm hungry," she says, looking sheepish. "And I miss Colt."

I shake my head. "I'm gonna stay here and do some weights. I was getting distracted by your ass."

She turns and does a little booty shake, making me growl.

"Get out of here, you little temptress."

She drops her towel and picks it up, taking her own cool time with her ass in the air.

"Seriously?"

She straightens and flashes me a seductive look over her shoulder. "I'll see you later."

I look down at the tent in my shorts and sigh.

"What did you buy me for my birthday?" Faye asks me as she fries some eggs. "I just want to know how big it is, you know, so I know what to get you for your birthday. So from a scale of cheeseburger to a car, how extravagant is my gift?"

I look at Sin with a *How the fuck do you deal with her?* expression, but he just smirks and drinks his coffee. I haven't bought Faye anything yet, one, because I didn't even know her birthday was coming up, and two, I haven't exactly been to a shopping mall in a while.

"It's somewhere in the middle," I tell her, scowling at Sin as he chuckles. "What are you buying your lovely wife, brother?"

"It's a surprise," Sin says, keeping a straight face.

"I love surprises," Faye says, serving the eggs onto plates.

I look at Sin, who mouths, "I have no fuckin' idea."

"When is her birthday?" I mouth back.

"Next Wednesday," he replies, smiling as Faye puts his plate in front of him and then another one in front of me.

"Thanks."

"Thanks, babe," Sin says, grabbing her and kissing her stomach.

"You're welcome. I'm not making dinner though, so someone else will have to tackle that. I have to head to work. Don't forget to pick up Clover from school today." She kisses his lips. "I'll see you at home tonight."

Faye and Sin have their own private house, although they are here most of the time. I owned a house too, but I was currently renting it out. I like living at the clubhouse and don't plan on moving out anytime soon.

"Vinnie, Shay's breakfast is in the frying pan," she says, kissing me on the cheek, then hustling out of the kitchen to get to her law job.

"What are you and Shay doing today?"

"Apparently buying your wife a gift . . . something in between a cheeseburger and a car."

Sin barks out a laugh. "She's something else, isn't she? Never a dull moment."

"She's like a fuckin' superhero. Makes us breakfast; goes to her law job, where she dominates that field too; a great mother; and she also carries around nunchakus in her purse." I pause. "That she can actually kill someone with."

"Not to mention what she's like in the bedroom," Sin adds, lip twitching.

"I'd rather not hear about that," I say, cringing.

Shay walks into the kitchen, freshly showered. "'Morning, Sin."

"Good mornin'," Sin says, nodding his head to the stove. "Hungry? Grab a plate."

She serves herself, then sits down next to me.

"Guess where we're going today?"

"Where?" she asks, biting into her toast.

"To the mall to buy Faye a birthday gift." I look back at Sin. "We having a party here or what?"

"We should throw her a surprise party," Shay suggests, a gleam entering her eyes. "She's always doing everything for everyone, I think it would be fun."

"Faye would find out," Sin and I say at the same time.

Shay laughs and rolls her eyes. "What if we did it before her actual birthday? I don't think she'd be too suspicious then."

"Are you offering to organize this?" Sin asks her, contemplating.

"I am, yes." She looks at me. "You'll have to take me around to get everything we need though."

"Not a problem."

We could do it all today, as a matter of fact. Get Faye's present, decorations, and whatever other shit we need. Then the day before the party go and do a huge grocery store run.

"When are we going to do this, then?" I ask them both.

"I think the more people we tell, the more likely Faye is to find out. We could organize the whole thing ourselves, just tell everyone to come by here, say this Saturday night. That won't be out of the ordinary, and it's only a few days before her actual birthday," Shay suggests.

"I think it's perfect," Sin says, blue eyes on Shay. He looks impressed, and for the first time I actually see him soften a little toward her. I know he was unsure about her from the start—what with her ties to Talon and her story that doesn't quite add up, but also because he looks after his own and wouldn't want to see me get tangled up in something unless it was worth it.

But he didn't have to worry, because she is definitely worth it.

TWENTY-FOUR

Shayla

CHET Faker's "I'm Into You" plays in the car as we're on the way to the mall. Excitement filling me, I glance down at the quick list I made for all the supplies we're going to need for the weekend.

"Remember, stick by me at all times; don't fuckin' go wandering off," Vinnie lectures me, not for the first time.

"I won't. I'm not stupid, Vinnie. I won't leave your sight, and we won't linger, just go in and out and get what we need to. What do you want to buy her for her birthday though?"

"I was kind of hoping you'd have that under control," Vinnie admits, glancing at me, then back at the road. "You're a woman, she's a woman, do you see where I'm going with this?"

I raise my eyebrow at him. "What do you normally get her?"

"Last year I got her a gift voucher for that makeup store she's always spending all her money at."

"How about a gold bracelet or something?" I suggest. "I guess it depends how much you want to spend. I can use my credit card, unless they've figured out my fake name by now and can trace me from it."

"Why the fuck would I ask you to use your money?" Vinnie asks, sounding annoyed. "You don't need your cards, or your father's money. I can give you everything you need."

"I have money," I say, a little defensively. I don't want him having to pay for everything for me, when I do have money put away. I don't really like the idea of having a man look after me in that way. I prefer to be a little more independent, especially since my father passed away, there are shitloads of it sitting in the bank. His accounts are under his shell corporation, in my name in case something were to happen to him. I plan on giving away most of it to charity but to keep enough to buy myself a house and to support me until I can find a full-time job.

"I know you have money, Shay," he says in exasperation. "But I want to take care of you, and I can. I have money too, you know. Not fuckin' millions like you, but more than enough for us to live a good life."

Sometimes he says things like he plans on us being together forever, and sometimes he acts like he has no idea what's going on between us. To be honest, I don't think he really knows what the hell the future will bring, and neither do I. I want him, more than anything, but it's almost stupid to admit after such a short period of time, isn't it? I'm keeping my thoughts to myself, but eventually we're going to have to talk about this. Actions speak louder than words though, and he treats me like I'm his woman. I *am* his woman.

"You don't have to take care of me," I say, gentling my tone. "If I can access the money, I'm more than happy to contribute money toward everything. I don't like the idea of you having to pay for everything; it just doesn't sit right with me."

He surprises me by chuckling.

"What's so funny?"

"Just thinking about how spoiled and selfish I thought you'd be, but you're nothing like that at all, as you keep proving to me over and over again. I'll tell you what, let me take care of everything for now. When everything is a hundred percent safe, you do what you want with your money, but for right now, I'm going to take care of you. I'll give you one of my cards, and you use it as you wish. You don't have to ask me for shit; it's yours— do whatever you want with it."

That was actually really sweet. I can't think of anything worse than having to ask him for money, so having my own card without any explanations is very thoughtful of him. Either way, I will be paying him back for every cent that I use.

"Okay," I agree hesitantly.

"Spend whatever on Faye's present, I don't mind," he continues, reaching his hand over to place the card on my thigh, rubbing his thumb in circular strokes. "Do tell me what's on this list of yours."

I glance down. "The present. Balloons. Birthday sign. Order a cake. I thought it would be easier just to get plastic plates, forks, cups, etcetera. And alcohol. I'm going to make some mocktails for Faye, since she can't drink. The food we can get on Friday, or even Saturday morning."

"We could get one of the DJs from Rift to come," I suggest, knowing how much Faye loves to dance. "I think she'll like that."

"Excellent idea!" I beam at him. "That sounds awesome, Vinnie. So we'll all hide out in the back, get Sin to lead her in." I pause. "And hopefully she actually will be surprised."

"Don't underestimate her," Vinnie says in a dry tone. "She's a fuckin' ninja."

"I believe it," I say, smiling. "So first stop . . . how about a jewelry store? Tiffany's? Or maybe we can get her a designer bag, what woman wouldn't love one of those?"

Vinnie cringes but nods his head in agreement. "I can't even wait in the car while you run in because of those fuckin' assholes looking for you. I swear, I'm going to kill them just because of this."

I roll my eyes at how dramatic he's being and lean over to press a kiss into his rough cheek. "You'll survive, Vinnie. I'll be as quick as I can."

TWENTY-FIVE

Vinnie

I WAIT outside the store, watching everyone who enters and leaves. There's only one entrance/exit so there's nowhere else she could leave from, just in case someone decided to try something. Chances are slim, of course, but better to be safe than sorry.

My mind wanders to Shay, who is happily making an effort to give a woman she only just met a birthday surprise. I don't think I've met anyone like her before. She's always present, always eager to help. Usually upbeat, even though if I'm being honest, her life is in shambles right now.

When I check the time and see that she's been in there for twenty minutes, I decide to go and check on her, just in case. She said she'd just be in and out, but she is a woman after all. When I glance around the shop and can't see her, my heart starts to race.

Where the hell could she be?

I dial her number, but she doesn't pick up. Did someone take her? How? Unless there's a staff back door that they were able to leave through. I'm about to call for backup when I see her standing in the corner, talking to a woman.

"Shay," I growl, ready to take all my worry out on her. She sees me, eyes widening, and says something to the woman before meeting me halfway across the room. I grip her upper arm and all but drag her out of the store. "I thought I lost you."

"I was right in there," she says, brow furrowing. "Sorry I took so long." She holds a little bag up in her hand. "There was a lot to choose from. I think I found her the perfect one though."

"I almost had a heart attack," I say, exhaling deeply, trying to slow down my heartbeat. My hand lets go of her arm and moves up to her nape.

"You thought someone got to me inside a store that only has one exit at which you were standing?" she asks, the look on her face telling me that I'm overreacting.

"Well, you were in the fuckin' corner of the store, a blind spot where I couldn't see you, so what else was I supposed to think?"

I let go of her nape, but she reaches up and touches my arm with her hand. "I'm sorry. Nothing happened, as you can see. Next time, I'll be quicker."

My anger all but disappears. "Next time I'm coming in with you."

My fear of losing her is higher than my dislike for shopping, and I feel fuckin' stupid for letting her go in alone in the first place. From now on, she doesn't leave my sight.

"Okay," she says, shrugging her shoulders. "We'll be joined at the hip for all future shopping endeavors."

See? Upbeat.

She's one of those always-look-on-the-bright-side people, and it's contagious.

I open the car door for her, and she flashes me a little smile in return. I wait until she gets in, close the door, and then make my way to the driver's side.

I think Shay's the only woman I've ever opened the car door for.

I don't bother to question why that is, I just get into the car and drive us to the next place on the list.

TWENTY-SIX

Shayla

AFTER changing my mind and finding Faye the most perfect gold bracelet instead of a handbag, we buy the decorations and everything else on the list. It takes about two hours, and then we're back at the clubhouse.

"I really hope she likes chocolate cake," I say as we get out of the car.

"It's universal" is his reply.

"What are we doing for the rest of the day?"

"I have to go into Rift to do some work, along with a few other errands. Tracker and Rake are here, so you'll be safe."

"I know," I reply. In fact, I don't think I've ever felt safer than since I've been at the clubhouse. "I'm going to do some training with Colt. He already knows sit; next I'm going to teach him how to lie down."

"Where are the other two?"

"Faye took them back to her house," I say, grabbing the balloons and banners out of the car while Vinnie takes the large box full of alcohol and plastic utensils.

"I can't believe you got a piñata."

"The kids will enjoy it," I say.

Vinnie opens the door for me, following me inside. "Faye will probably enjoy it too, who are we kidding."

We hide everything away where she won't stumble upon it, which ends up being in Vinnie's room. Vinnie heads off to work while I spend the rest of the day outside, chatting with Tracker and Rake and training Colt. Tracker shows me some techniques he used to train Lana's dog, Evie, who was here last week before the pups came. I cook dinner for us, and some extra for Vinnie or anyone else who happens to be stopping by. I've noticed that I never know who will be here on any given night, but that someone is always here. After a long, hot shower, I read in bed. Vinnie gets back to the clubhouse at around ten, smiling when he sees that I'm still awake.

"Tracker said you cooked dinner," he says, removing his clothes and jumping into bed with me.

"Yeah, steaks, potatoes, and asparagus. How was work?" I bury my face in his neck. "And why the fuck do you smell like cheap perfume?"

I lift my head to glare at him and I catch his grimace. "Shay—"

It hits me right now that we've never actually had "the talk." We've never spoken about his not being with other women; I just assumed he wouldn't. But he is a biker, so I probably shouldn't have. Although the other men in the clubhouse seem to be nothing but loyal, I'm not Vinnie's old lady, and we haven't even been together long. Or whatever we are. Another issue, we have no idea what the fuck we are. If he slept with someone else, however, I'll take my chances with the Mafia.

I'm not sitting around here and putting up with that, no way, no how.

"Tell me what you did tonight, and think *very* carefully before you try and lie," I say slowly, the threat clear.

"I have no reason to lie," he says, staying calm. He sits up and looks me directly in the eye. "I told you I had to go check on a few of the businesses, and one of those happens to be a strip club."

I grind my teeth together. "You were at a strip club? So what, were you out testing the merchandise, or something?"

His jaw goes tight. I don't know why he's suddenly getting angry. It's not like I spent the night around a bunch of naked men thrusting their bits and pieces in my face.

"I didn't sit there and enjoy a free lap dance, if that's what you're asking. I was mainly in the office, looking over some figures, chatting with the bouncers—we just hired three new ones, and a few of the women came and said hello, and gave me a hug, that's it."

"Really?" I say, dragging the word out, the disbelief in my voice palpable. "Just an innocent little hug? That's it? They didn't try and proposition you in any way? Or rub their tits against you? Is that what you're saying?"

I knew I was acting like a psycho girlfriend, but I was feeling a lot of emotions, none of them good, and didn't know how to control them.

He grabs me and pins me underneath him. "Of course they rubbed their tits on me, but I didn't give a fuck because I knew the only tits I wanted to see would be waiting for me in my bed. Did I look onstage? Yes. I'm a man. Did I do anything wrong? No. I didn't, and I wouldn't. You think I'd bring you here to be with my family, to be with me in my bed, in my world, and then go out and cheat on you? If I wanted other pussy, then I wouldn't have stepped up and claimed you as mine."

We're both breathing heavily at this point, eyes locked. His say that I should've known better, and mine say that he didn't even tell me they owned a strip club, so his visit was kind of sprung on me. If he explained it beforehand, I wouldn't have freaked out like this. His lips slam down on mine before I can finish processing my last thought, and his hands are touching me all over my body. Our clothes land on the floor, and I soon find out one thing.

I really love makeup sex.

Or was it angry sex?

Either way—it was fucking amazing.

TWENTY-SEVEN

"**S**URPRISE!" we all yell as Faye walks outside.

She looks around, her eyes wide and her jaw dropping open. "Oh my god!"

We all cheer, hug her, and wish her an early happy birthday. "How the hell did you manage to pull this off without me finding out? No one can keep a secret around here."

"We didn't tell anyone until they arrived here today," Sin says, glancing up at me over her head. "It was Shay's idea, actually. She's the one who organized it all for you."

"Way to make us look bad," Tracker teases, hugging Faye and kissing the top of her head. "You're going to love our present best."

"I'm sure I'll love them all; thank you so much," she says, her eyes starting to water. "Stupid hormones!"

"Now she's all humble," Sin adds, laughing. "In the car she was saying how annoying it is couples give presents together, otherwise she'd have double the amount."

Faye shushes him, then says, "This is really amazing everyone, thank you. And, Shay, thank you for organizing it. I'm so happy Vinnie found someone as great as you."

My face goes bright red as everyone cheers to that. I look behind me at Vinnie, wondering how he is taking that comment, but all he does is wink at me. The DJ starts to play, and everyone dances, including the kids. I sit next to Rake and Bailey with my plate of food, while Vinnie dances with Clover. Seeing the two of them together is so damn adorable. I don't have any experience with children, but the sight makes me a little clucky, so I decide to look away and concentrate on the delicious food on my plate instead. I pick up a mini quiche and take a bite.

"This quiche is the best I've ever had," Rake groans, shoving a whole one in his mouth.

"Thanks." I grin, taking a bite of my own. It's actually the only thing I made, everything else I ordered in. The sandwiches, homemade sausage rolls, and platters were catered by a local bakery Vinnie and I came across.

"You made this?" he asks, already devouring another one. "It's the shit, Shay."

"I'm glad you like it," I say, my smile turning sad. My father used to love them too. It's nice that other people can enjoy them now, but it still hurts that he's not here, and will never be again.

"Your turn," Vinnie says, offering me his hand. "All My Friends" by Snakehips, Tinashe, and Chance the Rapper plays. "May I have this dance?"

I blush and accept his hand, putting my plate down on my chair. "Yes, you may."

He brings me right up against his body with his hand on the

small of my back, my breasts against the top of his abs. I roll my body against his in a sensual way, grinding my hips. He moves against me, in time with the music. I had no idea he could dance, but he's actually pretty good. To me, a man who dances terribly is a bit of a turnoff, so I'm glad he can handle his own on the dance floor.

"I forgot you could move like that," he says into my ear, making me shiver. "I'm pretty sure I told you that you shouldn't dance like that in public."

"Yet here we are," I reply, flashing him a seductive look.

"But this time you're mine," he says, kissing behind my ear. "So you can dance like that all you want. If other men look though, just know that you'll be causing a fight."

"I'll make sure to remember that," I say.

He grins and spins me around so my ass is pressed against him. He's hard, he knows it and I know it, I just hope no one else does. With his mouth at my neck, we dance together, probably a little too raunchily given that there are children present. I gyrate my hips in a circle, then shake my ass. Irish and Tina dance next to us, and the two of us share a smile. She's a beautiful woman, with all that red hair, and I can understand why Irish can't take his eyes off her.

"Can we leave the party for a little while?" Vinnie asks in my ear. "I want you, right now."

I'd never admit this out loud, but I kind of want to eat the rest of my dinner. We can have sex tonight after the party, so I literally want to have my cake and eat it too.

"Can you wait an hour or so?" I ask, spinning to face him and wrapping my arms around his neck. "We can't miss her cutting the cake."

His eyes narrow and then fill with amusement. "You don't care about her cutting the cake, you just want cake, don't you?"

"You were there when we ordered it! It's going to be the best cake anyone has ever eaten; I can't miss it," I say, pouting. "Can't we please wait until after cake?"

"Well my hard-on has gone," he says, kissing my forehead. "With all this fuckin' food talk, so yes, you enjoy your cake, babe, but after that you're all mine."

"I'm always all yours," I say, pulling him back to where I was sitting, where my plate of food is just waiting for me. I turn to look at him, just in time to catch a glimpse of his expression at my comment. His eyes light up possessively, and I see him adjust himself. Is he still hard?

"Faye, can we cut the cake?" Vinnie calls out to her, making me laugh.

"What's the rush?" Faye asks, walking by hand in hand with Clover. She looks between Vinnie and me and scowls. "It's my birthday, can you two control yourselves for one night? The only person getting birthday se—" She looks down at her daughter. "I mean, birthday *fun* should be me."

"Just cut the cake, woman," Vinnie growls playfully. It makes me think of the growling noises he makes in bed, and suddenly I do wish Faye would cut the cake right now. Maybe we could eat the cake in bed, naked.

"Fine," Faye says, giving in and smiling at me. "Only because you did all this for me."

We sing "Happy Birthday," and Faye cuts into the giant chocolate mud cake.

I have two pieces.

Shortly after that, it's me who drags Vinnie to the bedroom.

However, after eating so much we were both in food comas and weren't in the mood to do anything except sleep naked, holding each other.

In the middle of the night though, we make up for it.

And in the morning.

I have cake for breakfast.

I help clean up and then jump in the shower. Vinnie is meeting with Talon again today, and although I tried to get him to tell me what it was all about, I didn't really get any answers. Vinnie just said that Talon is going to give him an update. Trace and Jess are in the kitchen, and I don't know them too well, so I stay in my room with Colt, writing an essay for my online class. With everything going on, studying seems pointless, but it keeps my mind active, and I actually like learning. I really want to get my business degree, for myself, no one else. I studied accounting for my father, and while I'm good at it, I don't really enjoy it.

When lunchtime comes around, I'm surprised when Tracker and Rake come into my room.

"Hey," I say, closing Vinnie's laptop. "Is everything okay?"

Tracker just smiles at me and says, "Want to go on an adventure?"

I arch my brow and clasp my hands together. "What did you have in mind?"

"I think my first question is going to be, why?" I say, looking out the car window. They've brought me to the woods. The fucking woods. "Or what? Oh my god, are you going to kill me? I thought we were all getting along great. Is this because I ate the last piece of cake? Or because I showed Bailey my Chanel bag and now she wants one?"

They both ignore me and get out of the car. I sit there, wondering why the hell we are in the woods. This didn't sound like an adventure to me. I was a victim of a severe case of false advertising. Rake opens my door and says, "Come on."

I get out.

Tracker pulls out a gun and hands it to me. I hold it like it's a bag of poop, away from my body, stretching my arm out as far as it can go. "A gun lesson?"

"Yep," Tracker says, flashing me a lopsided smile. "Followed by ice cream."

"Well, that softens the blow a little," I admit, holding the gun properly, stepping away from the two of them, and pointing it toward the trees. "What do I aim at? I don't want to hurt any animals that might get in the way. Don't you have some cans or something?"

"Follow us," Tracker says, leading the way. We walk through the woods for about five minutes until we come to a clearing. There's a wooden fence running along it, with about ten cans tied to the fence, so when they fall you can put them back up, I'm guessing.

"This is cool," I have to admit.

"It is," Rake says, then goes into teacher mode. "Now, safety first. We don't want you accidentally shooting us in the nuts or something."

He shows me how to put the safety on and off, how to hold the gun properly, and how to aim.

He takes one shot at the first can, not missing.

Then he hands the gun back to me and says, "Your turn."

I raise the gun, aiming it at the second can, fire, and miss. I feel nervous about using the gun, but also strangely empowered. I feel like a badass—or at least I will when I learn how to use it better.

"We're not leaving until you hit at least five out of the ten," Tracker announces, nodding toward the can. "We've got all day."

Two hours later, I get my ice cream.

TWENTY-EIGHT

Vinnie

STAND over the dead body, impressed. "That was a good shot."

"I know," Talon replies, not sounding smug, just stating a fact. "Shayla know what we're out doing today?"

"Told her I was meeting you for an update," I say, looking around the mansion we are in. The man now lying dead on the floor, Tony Addario, was a threat to Shay. Talon recorded a conversation between him and another man, Tony's cousin Abe, who is a member of the Kings MC. The two of them were talking about raping and killing her in revenge for all the shit her father caused them since the feds have some information and were breathing down their necks. And now they had to watch their backs even among their own family members, since everyone was out for themselves. I felt no pleasure in his death, but I felt no remorse either. This man would have hurt Shay without a second thought, and the world is better off without him.

"Let's go," Talon says, heading toward the back door. "He has so many enemies no one will know who killed him. No one will suspect us."

"What about the cousin?" I ask. After hearing the voice message, and the word *rape* coming out of their mouths, I wanted them both in the ground.

"We'll take care of him next," Talon says as we walk through the woods behind his house. "I have no issues with the Kings, and I will handle them. If this starts a fuckin' war, then so be it. No one has any idea that Shayla is under your protection. They think she's just fallen off the grid. That's why no one has even tried to fuck with the club yet. What do you think is the best plan of action?"

I'd actually been thinking about this for a while now. With her father having so many fuckin' enemies, I didn't see how Shay was going to get out of this. We'd have to spend the rest of our lives watching our backs. While I'm used to living that way, I don't want her to have to.

"For now, I think we should let everyone think she's deep in hiding." I pause, looking Talon in the eye. "And then I have another idea, but I don't think anyone is going to like it."

I thrust my hips forward, loving the feel of her. I'm on top, her legs over my shoulders, as I pump away, finding the perfect rhythm and angle. I lean forward to taste her lips, and she moans into my mouth. Finding her sweet spot with my thumb, it's not long before she comes, and I join her. I pull out of her, kissing her once more, then collapse onto the bed. It's the third time tonight that we've fucked, and I'm exhausted.

Shay had offered to babysit Clover, Cara, and Rhett for the day, so she had to be up in about five hours.

"You're going to be tired tomorrow," I say against her temple.

"I know," she whispers in reply. "But sometimes you just have to take one for your vagina."

I laugh at that, my chest shaking. "The shit you come up with, Shay. Get some sleep, temptress."

"Okay," she says, yawning, already half-asleep. "Love you, Vinnie," she whispers, just before falling into a deep slumber. I, on the other hand, was suddenly more awake than ever, like someone had thrown a bucket of cold water on my face. She loved me? But it was too soon. Will she remember saying it in the morning? For a second, I find myself wishing that she won't, because I won't know what to say back. I'm not ready to say those words to her; to be honest, I don't really know what love is. Yes, I've seen it in the others, but I've never felt it, so how would I know? I'd never say it unless I knew that I meant it, and right now I'm not sure how I feel. More than I have for any other woman—sure, but love? That was a whole new playing field. I try to relax, holding her in my arms, her head on my chest, her soft breath tickling my skin. Before I fall asleep, one last thought crosses my mind.

If she really does love me—I'm the luckiest man in the world.

"So how is he?"

"How is who?" I ask distractedly as I look over the guest list at Rift several days later. There is an event tonight, and the club is going to be full. Luckily I get to leave before the doors open and people barge in, but Rake, Bailey, Shay, and I are stuck doing the day shift, making sure everything is ready for tonight. I didn't want to bring Shay, but she practically begged me, obviously sick of being stuck inside, so I relented.

"Did someone do stocktaking?" I ask Sian, our bar supervisor.

"Yes, I did it," she replies, looking toward the back. "I made a new order sheet for next week, but we're good for now."

"Talon," Shay continues, looking at me and waiting for my attention. "You saw him the other day but never told me how he was doing."

I put down the list and look into her beautiful brown eyes. "He's fine. Don't worry about him, we need to worry about you instead."

She rolls her eyes and sticks her straw in her mouth.

Bailey sits down next to Shay and looks between us. "I hope I'm not interrupting anything."

"No," Shay says instantly, I guess wanting Bailey to feel welcome. "I was just about to ask Vinnie what I can do to help. If he tells me to sit here and look pretty again though, I might scream."

I laugh at that. "I'm almost done, you just relax."

"All I do is relax," she grumbles.

"Shark will be here soon to take over from me, so we can go do something if you like."

I was taking a gamble, of course, but I fuckin' hated it when she was sad.

"Who is Shark?" she asks me, scrunching her nose up.

Bailey laughs, touching Shay's arm and answering the question for me. "That's Ronan's road name."

"How come you don't have a road name?" she asks me, looking curious.

"I do," I reply, smirking. "No one really uses it though, probably because Vinnie itself is a nickname. My first name is Tyler."

"I didn't even know that. So why do they call you Vinnie then?" she asks, tilting her head to the side. "And what's your road name?"

"Vincent is my middle name," I explain to her. "And it's Wolf."

"Wolf?" she asks, sounding surprised.

I shrug and try to explain. "I guess you can say I'm kind of a loner. Before I walked into the MC, I had no one. No family or friends, no attachments. A lone wolf. That's me."

I watch Shay process this, buying me silence for a few moments.

Then she blurts out, "I think Wolf suits you."

"Thanks," I say, smiling.

Even though I wasn't exactly a lone wolf anymore.

Because I had her.

And I'm never going to give her up.

Is this what it's like for the other men? How do they even go on runs? I wouldn't want to leave Shay behind to go anywhere, although I guess knowing some of the men stay behind to watch over her would help. It's nice having something that's all mine. I mean, I know she's a person and not a thing, but she's mine all the same, and no one else's. I've never had that before.

I've also never had a reason to go home before, but now I do, and now that I have it, I'm going to do anything to protect it.

Anything.

TWENTY-NINE

Shayla

"N OT bad for your first session," Anna praises, pushing her hair out of her face. "You're tiny but fast. And you're pretty flexible, aren't you?"

"Pilates and yoga," I say, resting my hands on my knees. "I don't have much strength though."

"We can work on that," Anna says, sitting down on the mat and stretching. "You just need to be able to use whatever advantage you have. It's not always the strongest who wins the fight, sometimes it's the most analytical—the quickest thinker."

"I like learning this," I say, smiling at her. "It feels powerful."

"It is empowering, yes," she replies, lying back on the mat. "The truth is there are times when shit goes down, and it's better to know how to protect yourself any way you can. The men will always do their best to save us, but sometimes you need to save yourself, you know? No one wants to be a victim."

"No, they don't," I agree, copying her and lying back. "A few more of these and a few more gun lessons will be good for me."

"A few more? Try one every week for the rest of your life," she says, laughing. "We try to get in here, keep fit, and learn new moves. Sometimes we get the men to pretend to attack us and see if we manage to get out of the situations."

"You guys are so awesome," I say, rolling over onto my stomach. "I've been around the Wild Men only a few times, but they're nothing like this. Their clubhouse has men and club hos, that's it. There's no family environment, or nice old ladies, or anything like that. It's like a bachelor pad."

Anna makes a sound of amusement. "I know, I've been there before."

"You have?" I ask, surprise filling me.

"Yeah, and I dragged Bailey with me, we both got into shit," she says, sitting up and watching me. "Did you ever meet the man Talon's mother married?"

I nod my head. "Yes, I did."

"He was our biological father," Anna says, quickly explaining the story to me. "Talon sees me as his family, in a weird way. Honestly I think he feels guilty that our father raised him instead of Rake and me, and was good to him, while abandoning his own children."

"I had no idea," I say, my eyes wide. "I didn't even know he had other children. I'm so sorry that happened to you, Anna."

How could I know so little? Talon never told me this. He's never mentioned Anna to me before at all, and he apparently considered her family. I think I needed to have a talk with my elusive cousin.

She waves her hand in the air. "Shit happens, yeah? I had my brother, and that's all that matters. Everyone has pain in their life, everyone. It just comes in different forms, but you need to look at what you do have and be grateful for it. My father might not have wanted us, but he still gave me Rake."

"That's such a beautiful thing to say, Anna," I say, emotion hitting me. She really is an amazing woman, strong—inside and out.

"Don't get all mushy on me," she says, but her green eyes soften. "So are you still public enemy number one?"

I accept the subject change with a laugh. "I think it's cooling down now, I don't know. Vinnie doesn't seem to want to tell me all the details, but security seems to have relaxed a little. The day I can go to a movie by myself, I'm going to celebrate."

"It's temporary," she says, shrugging her shoulders. "Whenever shit was going down with me, I'd always tell myself it's temporary. You just have to push through for now."

"I know. I always think about how much worse it would be if Vinnie hadn't brought me here," I admit. "If I didn't have him in my life . . . He just makes everything better, you know? Gives me something to fight for."

Anna grins, showing her teeth. "You've got it bad, don't you?"

I duck my face. "He's just . . . everything. I don't know. I know it's new, and we pretty much started living together from the second we met, but it just feels right. That's the only way I can explain it."

I never thought I'd end up with a biker, but Vinnie is everything I could wish for in a man. He's rough around the edges, but I kind of like that. He's strong and takes charge, dominant, but also a total sweetheart. He can be stubborn, but so can I. He knows how to handle me, in and out of the bedroom, and doesn't get distant when I show emotion of any kind.

He sets my blood on fire.

Anna makes a sound of amusement. "You have been living together since you first met, that's pretty hilarious when you think about it."

"I know."

She pushes off the ground and offers me her hand. "Let's work on more punches. You kind of suck."

I grin and place my hand in hers. I really do suck. "Can't I just slap whoever it is?"

She turns and laughs. "No, definitely no."

Well, fine.

I guess I was going to learn how to fight like a man.

Or like a biker chick.

"Colt, sit," I say, pointing with my index finger.

He sits.

"Good boy. Colt, down."

He lies down.

I look to my audience and say, "Okay, he's still working on stay, so that's all for now."

Vinnie, Tracker, Rake, and Lana clap.

"I still can't believe you named your dog after one of my book characters," Lana says, laughing. "That's crazy."

"She practically named him after me," Tracker says for the millionth time.

Everyone ignores him.

"He's going to be massive," Rake says, patting Colt. "The kids can probably ride him."

"I need to get him leash trained before he gets big enough

to drag me," I say, wincing. "Which will probably be very soon."

"Should have got her a pug, or something," Rake jokes to Vinnie.

"I'm sure a pug will protect her," Lana says, sitting down on Tracker's lap. "A pug with small-man syndrome. Those small dogs can be pretty vicious."

Everyone heads back inside, but Vinnie grabs my arm. "Two things I want to talk to you about."

"Yeah?" I ask, brow furrowing.

"The accounts you did for your dad, you didn't mention that you did work for the Kings MC."

He's right, I didn't mention that, and I'm pretty surprised that Talon mentioned it to him.

"Vinnie, when they say accounts, it isn't some code word for dodgy shit. I legitimately did their accounting. I helped Dad with the numbers; I don't know about anything else that went on with them."

"Why didn't you mention it?"

I sigh and try to explain it to him. "I just don't want anything to do with all of that anymore. I didn't do anything wrong, and I didn't know my father was doing anything wrong until it was too late and men wanted me dead." I tilt my head to the side and study him. "You knew all this, yet you didn't say anything, and you accuse *me* of being a liar?"

To a man like Vinnie, loyalty is everything. Although I didn't do anything wrong, I also didn't tell him small details like that. I kept everything to myself, even though I wouldn't have lied about it if I was asked. Keeping things to yourself protects people. I don't want any more people to get hurt because of me. I just want everything to be over with.

"I go with my gut, Shay," he says, eyes gentling. "I don't think you have it in you to deceive me."

We look into each other's eyes, something passing between us.

"What else did you want to talk about?"

"Talon said you should go to your father's house to sort out the estate and shit, figure out if you want to sell it or what. I told him I can take you out there next week. Is that all right?"

"Yeah, sounds good," I say, my heart feeling heavy. The thought of going there . . . but it has to be done. What did I want to do with the house though? I definitely didn't want to live there; I guess I'll just have to put it on the market.

"Is it safe for me to go there though, won't everyone be expecting it?"

"I'll make it safe," Vinnie assures me, pulling me by my hand toward him, so our bodies touch. He grabs my hair in his hand and uses it to lift my head back. "Now give me a kiss."

He leans down and catches my lips with his, his tongue delving into my mouth and making me feel weak in the knees. When he pulls away, I grip his T-shirt for balance. He kisses my nose and then my forehead. "I have to go to Rift. Do you want to come with me?"

"Yes," I say quickly, making his eyes smile. I look down at my shorts and T-shirt. "Let me go get changed though and do my hair and makeup."

"It's not like we're actually going clubbing," he say, eyes dancing. "You can look around, have a drink, but no one is there except staff."

"Yeah but I still need to look decent," I say, patting Colt and then heading inside. "Just give me fifteen minutes."

"It better be an actual fifteen minutes," he grumbles from behind me. "Oh, and we're taking my bike, so keep that in mind."

"Will do," I say, excited to be going on the back of his bike with him. "I think I want to learn how to ride one day."

"Really?" he asks, brows almost hitting his hairline. "I can teach you if you like."

"Yes, please," I say, walking into our room and pulling out a pair of jeans and a tight black top. I start to undress, throwing the clothes I was wearing into the laundry basket. Vinnie sits on the bed, enjoying the show. "You just going to sit there and watch, are you?"

"Yep," he replies, lying back with his hands behind his head. "Can't help it when the view is so amazing."

"Not sick of it yet, huh?" I tease, sliding my top on and then my jeans.

"Never."

I put on my new biker boots, brush and tie up my hair, and apply some foundation, brow powder, and bronzer on my cheeks. "See, all done. Didn't even take me fifteen minutes."

He checks me out from head to toe, then looks down at his crotch, where his cock is straining against his jeans. "I think we have another problem that might need attending to before we can leave."

"If I attended that problem every time it came up, we'd never leave this bed," I fire back, laughing.

He groans, covering his eyes with his arm. "It's not my fault you wiggle that ass so much, trying to get it into your tight-ass jeans."

"That's what I have to do to get them on," I reply, going to stand next to the bed and offering him my hand. "Come on, badass motorcycle time."

That makes him smile and get out of bed. "All right, but for the record, Rift has a private VIP room we could always use. . . ."

I ignore him and walk outside to his bike.

And that's when I hear the gunshots.

THIRTY

Vinnie

"**G**ET down!" I yell at Shay, grabbing her and pinning her beneath my body. I hear her cry of pain as she hits the ground, but I'd rather her be scraped up a little than have bullets through her. The car speeds off, and I wait, covering her for a few more moments, just to make sure it's safe. Tracker and Rake run outside, guns in their hands, ready for backup, but the cowards just shot and sped away. They were aiming right for Shay, and probably don't know whether they hit her. I'm fuckin' pissed that they figured out where she was and who was protecting her. Fuck, Talon was the only other person who knew she was here. Now it's time to regroup and come up with a new plan.

"Are you both okay?" Tracker asks, racing to us, while Rake stands there, ready to shoot in case they decide to come back.

"Shay?" I ask, getting off her and helping her up. I scan her from head to toe, but she looks fine, no injuries that I can see.

"I'm fine," she says, running into my arms and hugging me. "Holy shit, that was scary."

She's shaking, and I run my hands up and down her arms, looking at Tracker.

"Take her inside," he demands, putting his gun away. "Someone might have called the cops if they heard the gunshots, which means they'll probably drive around here at best, come visit us at worst."

I nod, lift Shay in my arms like she's a new bride, and carry her inside. I lay her down on my bed and just hold her in my arms.

Fuck.

That bullet just missed her.

I almost lost her.

I lift up her T-shirt, and she does have some scratches on her from when I pushed her to the ground, but other than that she's fine. "Are you sure you're okay? Fuck, Shay, they almost got you. I don't think I've been so scared in my fuckin' life. Fuck!"

I want to rage, break shit, and ride on after them.

I want to beat Talon's ass. 'Cause her location did not come from any of us.

But more than anything, I want to make sure she's okay.

"I'm fine, thanks to you," she says, rubbing my back. Great. She almost gets shot, and now she's the one comforting me. I close my eyes and just feel her in my arms.

So. Fucking. Close.

Things can change in an instant, but we're lucky this time. Still, I could have lost her. The pain that slices through me at that thought tells me I was right the whole time about her— she's mine. I don't care what anyone has to say, or how long we've known each other, or any other fuckin' minor details, the woman in my arms belongs to me. I've never followed any rules, and I'm not going to start now; I want Shay, and so I'll have her.

I know she wants me too. I know that she follows her heart, unlike me, who always listens to his head—this time though I'm listening to both.

"Those bastards are going to die," I announce, stilling her hands. The fear and anger firing through my veins are a dangerous, heady mix.

"Vinnie—"

"No," I say, not wanting to bother with her trying to talk me out of it and all that shit. I don't care about the danger, I don't care if I get hurt, as long as she's safe. I can handle myself; she can't. I can protect myself, but all she has is me.

And the men who just tried to shoot her—they will pay with their lives.

"I'm fine, Vinnie," she says, over and over again, from where she's lying in our bed. I, on the other hand, am pacing up and down while trying to call Talon, and of course the bastard isn't answering. We can't just sit here anymore, idly, waiting for them to make their moves. Talon and I have taken out two people who wanted to hurt her, but we need to do more, and we need to do it faster. I don't care how high the death count goes, one innocent woman is worth more than any amount of corrupt, dirty men.

"Vinnie, will you come and sit down, please?" she asks, worry dripping from her tone.

For her, I stop, squeezing the phone tightly in my hand before coming to sit on the edge of the bed. She intertwines her fingers with mine and brings my hand to her lips to kiss my knuckles.

"I'm a little shaken, but I'm okay. It's not like I didn't suspect something like this would happen, Vinnie. I'm extremely lucky this is only the first time, or that they didn't get me. I feel lucky right now, more than scared. I'm here, breathing, you by my side, and I for one am happy about it." She looks down at her hands and takes a deep breath. "Do you think it's time I left here? They know where I am, and I don't want anyone here to get hurt, I'll never forgive myself. What if Clover was out front when they decided to do the drive-by? Or Faye, or one of the other women? I wouldn't be able to live with myself, and as much as I love it here, I can't stay. I need to talk to Talon, he can set me up somewhere else."

I wait for her to mention what she thinks I'll be doing, going with her or staying, but she doesn't. Obviously, I go where she does, but I want her to know that too. Her line about Clover hits me hard, because if anything happened to that little girl, the whole club would die with her. I don't know what to do, how to keep everyone safe, but I do have an idea that might work.

"Don't worry about all that," I tell her, kissing her forehead. "All the necessary security measures will be taken now, no one will get hurt. I messaged Sin, and he's on his way here, along with all of the other men.

"Either the clubhouse will go into lockdown, or everyone will stay at their private residences—I think in this case that will be the best option, because it's you they're after, but that's Sin's call, not mine."

No one would bother going to Sin's or anyone else's private residence. Even though the Kings MC are involved, I don't think they'd be stupid enough to come at the Wind Dragons head-on, although I'm sure they don't give a fuck who gets hurt in the cross fire. I hope they realize just what kind of enemies they're making though, because we're known to hold grudges.

"I hate that this happened," she says, sighing sadly. "I really thought for a while that they'd just gotten over it, with my father's death, maybe forgotten about their stupid revenge for everything he did, especially since I had nothing to do with it, but I guess their pride or whatever wins out over logic."

"No one was hurt," I remind her, lifting her chin in my fingers. "That's the main thing. They struck at us and missed, but when the Dragons strike, we never miss, so they just made a huge fuckin' mistake. We'll identify them from the surveillance cameras and go from there."

And by that I mean get rid of them.

I'm not usually so bloodthirsty, but for Shay, I'd do anything.

After I find out some information, like how they knew where Shay was and who else is after her.

Tracker is right—I've never been this cold before.

But I've never had anything to lose before either.

"There were two in the car," Sin tells the table, then slides two pieces of paper to Arrow. "We managed to print out still shots of their faces. Tracker, you and Arrow will find them." He waits for them to nod in agreement before looking to me. "What do you want to do next, Vinnie? The clubhouse isn't safe until we take care of these two men."

"I can take her away somewhere," I say, leaning back in my chair and studying each man. "But they might think she's still here and attack anyway. I don't think the women and children should be here until I sort this shit out."

"I agree," Sin says, sitting back in his chair, a contemplative look on his face. "We need to see what information we can get from these men, and if the Kings are directly involved. Vinnie, I'm leaving that up to you. Trace, I want you to make sure our weapon supplies are ready, in case shit goes down. I want men protecting the women and children at all times—no one goes anywhere alone, just in case. Everyone can just stay at their houses and avoid the clubhouse until this shit is sorted. I don't think they'll bother hurting anyone unless Shay is with them. They're not stupid enough to want a war with us, but that's exactly what the motherfuckers are going to get." His blue eyes narrow to slits. "No one shoots up our clubhouse and gets away with it."

Murmurs of agreement.

"Anyone have anything else to say?" he asks, glancing around the room.

Silence.

"Let's do what we have to then."

Everyone leaves the room except me and Sin.

Then I tell him exactly what's been on my mind.

THIRTY-ONE

Shayla

"I HATE that everyone has to leave because of me," I tell Sin, looking down at the floor. "This is your home. I never should have come here. We should've known it wouldn't end well."

"Shay," Sin starts, patting Colt but his eyes are locked on me. "We're bikers. We live our life a certain way, and with that comes danger. This isn't the first time and it won't be the last time shit like this happens. More than anything, we're family, and we all look after one another. The women will understand, trust me. They've all been in some kind of shit at one point or another, and we always saved them, just like we're gonna save you. You just need to be patient and trust that your man is doing his best to bring all this shit to an end."

"I do trust him," I try to explain. "I guess I just wish he didn't have to do all this, you know? Why couldn't I just be normal?"

"Then you probably wouldn't have met Vinnie," Sin points out, sounding amused. "There's no point wishing for shit; the only thing you can do is work toward your goal of getting what it is you want. I've seen the way you and Vinnie are together. I know you care for him. I've seen how you look after him." Colt runs off, and he watches him. "Love the man, love the club. We're a package deal, and you fit in here, Shay. Maybe that makes you fuckin' crazy too, but you do. The women love you. The men go out of their way to teach you how to shoot guns, and shit; hell, even Clover talks about her aunty Shay now. I wasn't sure about you at the start, but Vinnie was right. He never makes decisions lightly. Everything with him is thought out. The fact that he brought you here spoke volumes and surprised us all, to be honest, but Vinnie knows what he wants."

His words mean everything.

"Thanks, Sin," I say, smiling at him. "I really needed to hear that right now, because I'm second-guessing everything, just because I feel the exact same way about everyone here, and it breaks my heart that you're all getting dragged into my shit. I even thought about leaving—"

"We'll find you," Sin cuts me off. "And it just wastes our time, and it will stress Vinnie out; you don't want to do that, do you?"

"No," I say on a sigh. "I don't know what's more selfish, me staying or me leaving."

"You're not selfish. You're in a bad situation—you didn't ask for it, and you didn't do anything wrong. There's no point concentrating on all the details, Shay. Everyone pays for their family's mistakes in some way, your price just happens to be high." He pauses and smirks. "Like people-wanting-to-kill-you high."

I roll my eyes at his badly timed joke. I have no idea how he can find anything funny about this situation. "If anything happens to Vinnie . . ."

"It won't," Sin says, sounding confident enough for the two of us. "Because I won't let it."

He sounds so sure, even though we both don't know what the future will bring.

"Okay, no more feeling sorry for myself," I decide, choosing to be more optimistic like him.

"That's it," he says, nodding. "You have to fight for your happiness; everyone has a different war, but you need to tell yourself that you're going to win. Who's going to believe in you if you don't?"

Vinnie will, I think to myself.

Sin smiles, as if he knows exactly what I'm thinking. "You're a good egg, Shay."

"About time you realized that," I tease.

He barks out a deep laugh. "I didn't get where I am today by trusting everyone I meet. My trust is earned, not freely given. I observe; I analyze." He pauses and grins slyly. "I consult my know-it-all wife."

I laugh with him over that one. "So now we plan for war?"

"Something like that," he says, standing up. "We were hoping you'd make us dinner, since you're the only woman left in the clubhouse."

It's then that I give the president of the Wind Dragons the finger.

He throws his head back and laughs, then disappears inside.

I end up making them dinner. After all, it's the least I can do. Plus, like Sin said, love the man, love the club.

And I sure as hell love both.

Several days later, I'm packed and ready to deal with my father's house. Vinnie and Sin are coming with me, and although I feel like this is an unsafe trip, the two of them assured me that it's going to be fine, that they've covered every angle. Faye and Clover are staying with Tracker and Lana until we get back—we decided it would be easier to just spend the night there. The thought of going through all my father's belongings and putting them into storage makes me feel sick, but it needs to be done. I need to start facing things head-on, and I'm going to start with this. It's a six-hour drive to get there, and although I offer, for some reason Vinnie is adamant that he drive the whole way there and back.

"I can drive, you know," I say, wanting to prop my feet up on the dash, but I don't, because we're in Vinnie's four-wheel drive, not my car. "You're going to get tired if we drive the whole way."

"I'm sure I'll survive," he says, then mutters, "Unlike if you were driving."

I gasp, my head turning to him in an instant. "What is that supposed to mean? I'm a great driver, thank you very much. I'll have you know that I passed my test on the first try."

Vinnie doesn't look impressed. "I rode behind you on the way here, remember? Babe, you suck. You swerve all over the road, probably because you're singing along to some terrible song and not paying attention to what you're doing. I saw you dancing too, and the car was flying all over the place. Don't even get me started on the way you slam your foot on the brakes." He glances at me and says, "I don't know what the brakes ever did to you, but there's no reason to kick the shit out of them."

I roll my eyes at his exaggeration. "I've had only one accident, and that wasn't even my fault. No one else has ever complained about my driving." I pause and add, "I'm such a good driver that I get to sing and add in little dance moves when I see fit."

"Sing and dance all you want on this trip, because I'm driving the whole fuckin' way," he says, softening the blow with a cheeky grin. "You can even listen to any music you want. I have a great skill of being able to block shit out when I don't want to deal with it."

"Charming," I mutter, pursing my lips. Still, I turn on the radio, letting the music fill the car. Twenty minutes into the drive, I sigh heavily. "I'm hungry."

"We planned to stop in about half an hour, so can you wait? If not there's some snacks in the back. I got chips, chocolate, and bottled water."

I turn around and see a plastic bag on the car seat that I didn't notice before. I go through it and pull out a packet of chips. "You're the best."

"Can't have my woman hungry, can I?" he says, reaching over to squeeze my thigh. I'm about to tell him how sweet he is when he continues talking. "Then I'd have to deal with you being grumpy the whole night. What's it called? Hangry?"

"Hangry?"

"Yeah, when your hunger makes you angry."

"I don't get angry," I say, scowling at him, then forcing my lips to soften to prove my point. "See? All smiles." I shove a chip in my mouth. "Do you want one?"

"No, thank you," he says, mouth twitching. "I don't know how you can eat those."

It's the habanero ones I always get from the store; they're my favorite, but after a while my mouth does start to burn a little. I must like it though, because I keep going back for more.

"They're addictive," I say, crunching into another one. "You've never even tried one, yet you don't like them."

"I can barely eat pepper, Shay," he says, making me laugh. It's true, he couldn't really handle much of any spice.

"You think that's funny, huh?"

"I do, it's like we're opposites."

"Opposites attract," he says, running his hand down my thigh.

"That they do. Are you sure you don't want me to drive? Just let me know if you get tired. I won't kill us, okay? I promise. Wouldn't want to do the mobsters' work for them."

Vinnie smirks and says, "Shay, you'll be asleep in an hour. Trust me. Especially if you play your Sam Smith CD."

"You don't know that."

He puts in my Sam Smith CD.

I sleep for the rest of the drive.

THIRTY-TWO

"**Y**OU wanted me to sleep so you could have a peaceful drive, didn't you?" I ask him as we walk toward the house.

I pull out my key and hand it to him. The real estate agent will be here tomorrow morning, so I have all of tonight to take what I want. Vinnie said he'll hire people to pack the rest of the stuff, so I don't have to do it myself. I don't really need anything from here—other than some clothes and belongings, everything is replaceable. The only thing I do want to take is my mom's jewelry, something to remember my father by, and our old family photo albums.

"I wanted you to rest because I know that being back at your father's house is going to be hard for you—both physically and mentally draining," he says, looking out toward the road, probably waiting for the rumble of Sin's bike.

"I'll be fine," I say gently, wrapping my arm around his waist. "But thank you for looking out for me."

"That's what I'm here for," he says, eyes softening on me before he goes back to paying attention to his surroundings. He's on alert, I notice, and probably with good reason. It would go without saying that people would be watching this house, and probably have been for a very long time. I look around myself but see nothing. Then again, what do I know? I hear Sin's bike before I see it. He parks next to Vinnie's four-wheel drive, dust filling the air.

"It's so weird being here," I say to Vinnie, shifting on my feet.

"This is probably the biggest house I've ever seen in my life," he says, arm tightening around me.

So much has changed since I called this house home. Being back here is like stepping into the past, and bringing Vinnie with me is like mixing past, present, and future. Sin walks up to us, removing his leather jacket as he looks around.

"How was the ride?" Vinnie asks, with a tinge of longing in his voice. I know he couldn't take his bike because we need to bring my stuff back, even though I told him that I could easily drive alone like last time.

"Pretty good," Sin replies, lifting his chin to the door. "Shall we?"

"Yeah," Vinnie says, pushing the key into the lock and turning it. The door opens, making a creaky sound. "Stay between us, Shay."

With Vinnie in front and Sin at the back, I play the meat in a Wind Dragon sandwich, as we enter the house and look around.

"This place is fuckin' insane," Sin comments, whistling. "Our clubhouse must be like a shack to you."

I turn and give him a dirty look, which only makes him grin.

When they decide the place looks safe enough, I head to my

room and start to take the things I want. Vinnie carries every-thing down to the SUV, packing it in the back. I walk into my parents' room, my fingers trailing along the wall. I remember when I used to hide inside my dad's walk-in closet as a child, playing with my dolls and trying to jump out and scare him when I could hear him. I remember my mom brushing my hair while I sat on their bed, and telling me that I was her favorite girl. When she died from cancer, it was just my father and me.

I sit on his bed and make a list of everything I want to do, donate his expensive designer clothes and suits, sell the house already furnished so I didn't have to worry about the furniture. Who knows what could be found in this house though, what things my father tried to hide or keep away from everyone?

"You okay?" Vinnie asks, standing in the doorway in his black V-neck T-shirt and jeans, pulling me out of my thoughts. I check him out from head to toe, admiring him for a moment, before getting off the bed and closing the space between us.

"Yeah," I tell him. "I'm just making a list of what I want done with everything."

"Good idea," he says, placing his hands on my hips. "Do you need any help?"

"No, I'm good," I tell him. "I'm just going to finish up in my room and then I'll be done."

"Okay," he says, hand on my nape. "You know I'm here if you need anything, but if you want to do it alone, I get it too, all right?"

I nod and place a kiss on his chest, then head to my bed-room.

The quicker I get this over with, the better.

＊　　＊　　＊

A few hours later, I'm downstairs, sitting in the den with Vinnie and Sin. Both of them seem on edge, and it's making me nervous. The sun has just gone down, leaving an almost eerie feeling, like we were all just waiting for something to go wrong.

"What is it?" I ask softly, looking between the two men.

When I hear a noise coming from the front door, I instantly stand. Vinnie grabs my hand and pulls me toward the kitchen, where he looks out the back door.

"They're here," Sin announces, pulling his gun out. "You ready for this, brother?"

"I was born ready," Vinnie replies, pulling out his phone and barking into it, "Now."

Irish suddenly appears at the back door out of nowhere, and Vinnie quickly lets him in.

"There are six men," he says, looking at me. "The back exit is secure. I can get her out, and then I'll come back for you."

"Wait, what?" I ask, looking straight to Vinnie. "What are you going to do?"

"No time, Shay," he says, gripping my face and giving me a hard kiss. "Go with Irish, and do as he says, now."

Irish grabs my wrist, but my eyes are still pleading with Vinnie. "I don't like not knowing what you're planning. If anything happens to you . . . to any of you . . . Vinnie, just leave with me, now."

He doesn't even look at me this time, just says, "Irish, take her. They're going to be inside any second."

Irish grabs me, and I let him. I don't need to make this any harder on them, but at the same time I want to rage and scream.

He didn't tell me anything! He left me in the dark, and in this moment, I hate him for it. I just hope he doesn't get hurt, I pray that he doesn't. And Sin—he can't get hurt. He's a father, with another baby on the way. I wish I knew how they planned to get out of this safely.

Irish takes me outside, where a car I've never seen before is parked in back. I have to say though, when he puts me in the trunk, that's not exactly how I expected his saving me to go.

He opens the trunk about ten minutes later, but still, it was fucking terrifying in there.

"I'm going to kill you," I tell him, gasping for air. Luckily I'm not claustrophobic, but still, holy shit.

"Sorry, darlin'," he says, checking over me. "We didn't have any other choice. I had to make sure anyone watching only saw me in the car. You all right?"

"I'm alive," I say, wrapping my arms around myself. "Where are we?"

I look around. We were parked in front of a large, old-looking house. Irish leads me to the front yard, which overlooks streets of houses. The house was high up on a hill, so you can easily see everything below. He points, and I instantly know what he's pointing at.

"My house," I say, squinting to try to see. "You need to tell me what the plan is, Irish, please, because I'm freaking the fuck out here."

I hate the sympathetic look that flashes across his face. No, it wasn't sympathy—it was pity, which is a million times worse.

A flash of red catches my eye.

I turn back to my house and watch in absolute shock and horror as it explodes.

All I see is fire and smoke, all I feel is my heart racing, fear and shock.

"Where're Vinnie and Sin?" I ask, sounding hysterical.

I can't breathe, feeling like I was stuck down there, in the smoke and burning rubble.

"Shay, calm down, they're both fine," Irish says, his accent becoming more pronounced. "Breathe, woman, you're hyperventilating."

Breathe?

I can't breathe.

Then all I see is black.

THIRTY-THREE

"**S**HAY?" I hear Vinnie say over and over again, gently tapping my cheek. I open my eyes, feeling groggy, like one would after a weekend of binge drinking and waking up after only an hour's sleep.

"Yeah?"

"Wake up, babe," he says, sounding worried. "Look at me."

I look into concerned, familiar brown eyes.

"There you are," he whispers, pushing my hair out of my face. "Irish said you fainted on him . . . that doesn't sound like something my stubborn woman would do."

I force myself to sit up and glance around. We're in a moving car, with Irish driving.

"What happened?" I ask as everything hits me. "My house blew up." I slap his shoulder. "You didn't tell me anything! You had everything planned, didn't you?"

He continues to play with my hair, soothing me while I rant at him.

"If I told you the plan, you wouldn't have let me go ahead

with it," he says, not sounding sorry in the least. "I'd rather ask for forgiveness than permission."

"Tell me what you did."

He cringes a little, so I brace for the worst, knowing I wasn't going to like the words that come out of his mouth.

"Your house was under surveillance. They knew you'd have to come back eventually, so instead of chasing you, they were just being patient," he starts to explain. "Irish and Tracker scoped out your house last week so we knew what we were dealing with. They also set up the explosives. I needed them to see you arrive with me, because after it blew up, I want everyone to think that you were in the house."

"You're faking my death?" I ask, eyes widening.

"Faking your death and killing those bastards at the same time. Two birds, one stone."

"They'll check for a body," I say, knowing it isn't that easy.

"There will be a body," Vinnie says quietly. "Don't worry, it's all taken care of."

I open my mouth and close it. Wait, what?

"Vinnie—"

"You don't want to know, Shay. Trust me," he says, warning in his tone.

I gulp and rest my head on his lap, my head suddenly hurting. Where did he get a woman's body from? Holy shit. I think he's right, I probably don't want to know.

"Where's Sin?"

"Riding in front of us," Vinnie replies, now rubbing my back. "Go to sleep if you want, we have a few hours left."

"What about your SUV?" I ask him.

"Rake drove it back while we were all still in the house. Don't worry, everything is fine, Shay. No loose ends."

No loose ends? How can he even say that? Men died, in my house, from explosives they set up. Sure, those men wanted to kill me, but still. And a woman's body is in there, pretending to be mine, her bones probably burned to charcoal. How long was she dead before they placed her body in the house? Was she there when I was there? Vinnie is right—I don't want to know. I push it all from my mind and try to focus on the good things. The men are all safe, no one I care about was hurt, and although I'm a little traumatized from the ride in Irish's trunk, I'm okay too.

I close my eyes and let myself fall asleep, knowing that I am safe in Vinnie's arms.

Shayla Anderson's body was found among the rubble, along with the bodies of . . .

I listen to the news lady talk about me and my dead body, then turn to see everyone watching me, maybe checking for my reaction.

"So . . . I'm dead," I blurt out, not knowing what else to say. It's been three days since everything happened, and I'm still not sure how to process it, it all feels so surreal, like something that would happen in a movie—but this is my life.

"No, you're safe," Vinnie says, tugging on my ponytail. "It looks like they're confident it's you and aren't bothering with dental checks, which saves us from more bribery."

Bribery?

I look at Faye, who just gives me the thumbs-up.

"How do we know they won't come back to the clubhouse?" I ask Vinnie.

"Because the men who did that are dead," Sin answers as he hands Faye a drink. "We identified them; Tracker found them. They were two of the men who blew up in the house. And now that you're dead, the Kings will want to lie low to minimize their involvement. You're safe now."

I study Vinnie's face, but it shows nothing. Was he the mastermind behind the ruthlessness of the plan? Did it even matter? He did it to protect me, and no innocent people were harmed. Or is that just me making excuses and justifying it?

I lived in a world with only shades of gray, and now I was leading into blackness, but I still don't know if I'd change anything. I rest my head on Vinnie's chest and watch the news as they talk about my father and the other men who died. I listen to Vinnie's heartbeat in one ear, the news of the men's death in the other, and I know in this moment that I don't care how many men died, as long as everyone in this room's heart still beats.

Especially Vinnie's.

Talon almost doesn't recognize me with my lighter, shorter hair. Tina cut it in a blunt, shoulder-length bob, and I'm in love with it.

"Nice to see you alive and well," he says, pulling me in for a warm hug. "You look amazing, baby cuz."

"Thanks, Talon," I say as he takes the seat next to me at Rift.

"How have you been?"

"Good," I say, enjoying just being in his presence. "Does this mean you're going to see me more often now, instead of being MIA?"

"Sorry," he says, green eyes gentling. "I was looking out for you from the sidelines. I knew Vinnie was taking good care of you." He looks down at my almost empty glass. "Can I get you another drink?"

"No, I'm good."

"I'm going to take all the money out of your accounts for you," he tells me, ordering a drink from the bartender. "Luckily your father took precautions and gave us both access to the shell company accounts. I'll open a new account with a fake name, or I'll send it to Vinnie's account."

"I guess he put both of us on there in case one of us ended up dead," I say, bitterness lacing my tone. I sigh.

"I don't want all of it," I tell him. "Just enough for a house and to keep me going until I get a job, you can give the rest to charity."

His eyebrows rise. "You want only one mil?"

My eyes widen. "Is that how much a house is these days? I don't need that much."

"I'm not sending you anything less than that," he grumbles, looking unhappy about it. "You choose the charities you want me to put the money into, and I'll handle it."

I tilt my head to the side and say, "Actually, give some to the Wind Dragons too. They can do whatever they want with it."

Talon suddenly looks amused. "They have plenty of money, but if you insist."

"I do."

"Consider it done," he says, sipping on his drink.

"How come you didn't have to pay?" I ask.

"I have a tab here," he explains, glancing around the bar. "Where is Vinnie anyway? I thought he'd be loitering around you."

"He's in the VIP room, thought he'd let us catch up," I say, smirking. "Not like he can't see us through the cameras anyway."

Talon looks toward the cameras and gives them the finger.

"Mature," I chide, my twitching lip contesting my words. "I think we should plan to catch up every other week at least. Anna tells me the two of you are close."

He rubs the back of his neck. "Yeah, we are. She'll take good care of you. I know you didn't know the story about her father, and you had enough on your plate. Plus it was better for you that you went in without knowing my history with everyone. Not everyone loves me as much as you do, Shayla."

"Trust me, I know," I tease, resting my hand on his arm. "Did you sort out the shit going on in your club?"

"Working on it," he says, grimacing.

"You sure you're all right though?" I ask, squeezing his arm before letting go. "We could always fake your death. That seems to be the way to get out of things these days."

He barks out a laugh. "My problems aren't that big, Shayla. Nothing I can't handle, just need some time to figure out a few things, you know?"

I study my cousin. He's handsome, funny and kind, and also very intelligent, much more so than the average person, although you probably wouldn't guess that about him. In fact, in primary school, he was put in all the classes for gifted children. The thing about Talon though is that his mind is usually working overtime, and that's not always a good thing. He analyzes everything, and he sees things in an almost clinical way. He loves—yes, I know he loves me—but I've never seen him love a woman. Although he seems stressed out, he does seem a little lighter for some reason. I wonder if maybe he met someone.

"You know I'm always here for you if you need me," I say softly. "You helped save me, now let me save you for once."

"I'm the man here, Shayla," he gently reprimands. "It's my job to protect you. It's your job to be happy and annoy the shit out of that man of yours."

"Sexist pig," I grumble, rolling my eyes. "Some things never change, do they, Talon?"

"You tell me," he says, putting his hand over his chest. "You ended up with a Wind Dragon. What? None of the Wild Men were good enough for you?"

"You didn't let any of your men even breathe in my direction," I say, eyes narrowing to slits. "I remember you told Ranger off for even looking at me for more than a few seconds. Quite a jump from that to letting another biker from another MC watch over me, don't you think?"

Vinnie told me that he thinks Talon set us up on purpose, so that Vinnie and his club would protect me. I wouldn't put it past him. And while I should be angry at his meddling and his schemes, I can't be, because without it I wouldn't have Vinnie.

"Desperate times, baby cuz, desperate times."

He smirks into his drink.

"I'll bet," I reply, shaking my head at him. "Your scheming really knows no bounds, does it?"

"I do what I have to, Shayla, to protect the ones I love. There aren't many of them, so I have to keep you all safe."

"Are you seeing anyone?" I blurt out, voicing the feeling I have about him.

He grins and asks, "Why do you ask?"

"Why don't you answer?"

"Nosy," he says, lip twitching.

"I'm going to take that as a yes," I say, about to bombard him with questions when he says, "I'll tell you everything soon, all right? Just not now. Today is about you."

So he *is* dating someone.

Who?

I want to ask, but I decide to wait and let him tell me when he's ready.

I change the subject, lightening the mood. "Want to do a shot?"

We share a grin.

THIRTY-FOUR

Vinnie

WITH all the drama over for now, we decide to lay low for a little while, as the last thing we need is someone to recognize Shay after her photo was shown all over the media when they spoke of her death.

"What if someone's watching the clubhouse?" she asks, looking between Tracker and me. "Does that mean I can never leave or go out the front? I'll be stuck in here forever." She pauses, arching her brow at me. "Someone will have to dig a secret tunnel for me."

"Is she always this dramatic?" Tracker asks, not looking away from the TV.

"Yes," I reply at the same time she says, "No."

"Sound like an old married couple already," Tracker says, opening a can of beer. Lana walks into the room and sits down next to him.

"Can we watch something else?" she asks, taking Tracker's beer from him, helping herself to a sip, and then making a face.

Rake, Arrow, and Anna walk in next, all squeezing in on the couches. Anna sits on Arrow's lap.

"You can change it," Tracker says.

"Lana, put Netflix on," Anna calls out.

"Okay, but I'm not choosing what we watch," Lana says, grabbing the remote. "It's too much pressure."

"Pressure?" Rake asks, sounding amused. "Choosing something to watch is too much pressure? But writing bestselling novels isn't?"

"Yes."

I catch Shay mouthing something to Anna.

"What are the two of you scheming?" I ask.

Everyone's heads turn to them. Anna looks at me and says, "We're bored. Can we take Shay to Rift to have a few drinks and a dance? She's never been at night before—that's pretty sad."

I reply with one word: "No."

"What if we all go?" Lana suggests, ever the peacemaker. "Nothing can go wrong, surely. Close the place to the public if you have to, we haven't been out in ages!"

"Since when are you such a diva?" Tracker asks her, chuckling.

"Since Shay looks all sad and bored and hasn't done anything fun, and Irish threw her in the trunk of his car, and her house was blown up, and she has to pretend to be dead," Lana says, ticking each off on her fingers.

I look at all the men, seeing what they thought.

"We can't close it tonight, but we could close it tomorrow if you want to have your own party there," Arrow says, looking to me. "Your call though, Vinnie. Your woman."

Shay looks up at me, pouting.

"Yeah, all right, if we're closing the club, then there's no harm. We have to be careful getting you there though. I know you changed your hair but just to be safe. I'd rather not have faked your death in vain." Shay smiles widely and does a little happy dance.

"So cool that you can shut down a club just so we can have a little fun," she says, blowing kisses to Anna and Lana.

"I'll message everyone and let them know," Anna says, pulling out her phone.

"I'm going home now, so I'll tell Bailey," Rake says, standing up. "I'll stay home with Cara and Rhett so she and Tia can go out and have some fun."

"Do you want me to come and pick them up?" I ask him, so they don't have to go to Rift alone.

"That will be great, brother," he says, touching my shoulder, and he leaves the room, calling good-bye to everyone.

Shay stands up and says to the women, "Let's go plan what I'm going to wear tomorrow."

They all leave the room in a hurry, like that's a fun thing to do.

"She fits in with them so well," Tracker comments, staring at the door the women disappeared through. "What are you guys gonna do now that all the drama is almost at an end?"

To be honest, I have no fuckin' idea, but I need to talk to Shay about it.

"No clue," I say, peeling the label off my beer bottle. "We haven't spoken about it, but I want her to stay here."

Sure, I owned my own house and land, but this clubhouse was my home. I also need to tell her that I can never offer her marriage or children, because that's just not something I've ever wanted in life. I don't think I'd be a good father, and I think marriage isn't something that's necessary to prove my commitment to her.

"We better tell management to put up a sign about tomorrow, otherwise people are going to be pissed when they rock up and find out Rift is closed for a private function," Arrow says, changing the subject.

"Yeah, just let them know; they'll post it on social media," Tracker tells him, putting his beer down and lifting his feet up on the couch. "Private function? More like biker chicks gone wild."

"I'm sure they'll be on their best behavior," I say, unable to keep a straight face. "Mainly because we'll be there, so they have no option."

"Controlled environment," Tracker adds, chuckling to himself. "They'll find a way, they always do."

We all hear them laughing from Shay's and my room, then share a look.

Yeah, they'd definitely come up with something.

"No, Talon and his fucking Wild Men are not fuckin' invited," I growl, ignoring the pleading looks on Shay's, Anna's, and Bailey's faces. "Why are you all annoying the shit out of me? Go and ask Rake and Arrow, see what they have to say about it."

"Okay, fine, not the MC," Anna says, putting her hands out. "Just Talon. He comes to Rift anyway, you even meet him there! So what's the big deal?"

I cross my arms over my chest. "The biggest deal will be Rake, who will want to kill him, especially after a few drinks, then would probably be Arrow, who also isn't a fan. . . ."

"Rake won't be there, but okay, we get the point," she grumbles, her green eyes—so like her brother's—going all sad. They didn't work on me though, so she'd better save them for Arrow or her brother.

"I tell you what, Arrow and Rake say yes, then I'll be cool with it."

Anna groans, probably because she knows they'll never agree, just as I do, which is the reason I suggested that they take it to him. The thing is, even if Rake does say yes, no one can guarantee that a fight won't break out. I don't think the women will want to see that, especially Shayla and Anna.

"He's family," she says quietly. "Shay's his cousin, don't forget."

"How could I?" I mutter, sighing and looking at each of their three faces. "Don't you all have shit to plan? Clothes, makeup? Whatever else you've been talking about all day. You're all acting like you go out once a year."

"I pretty much do," Shay says, shrugging. "In fact, I think it's been longer than that since I've been to a club."

"You're the exception," I tell her, and she is. To every rule. I look at the women. "Now can you all please leave my bedroom? This isn't your home base to congregate and chat all day, there's a living room, a game room, a kitchen, and the backyard for that."

"When did you get so grumpy, Vinnie?" Anna asks, glancing up at him with a glint in her eye. "Saving all your fun vibes and energy to bust out your dance moves tonight?"

"Yeah, I saw you dancing at Faye's birthday," Bailey adds, fanning herself. "Hooooot."

Faye walks into the room and glances at all of us. "So this is where the party's at. What are we talking about?"

"Vinnie's sexy dance moves," Shay tells her, laughing behind her hand.

Faye starts thrusting her hips and grinding, practically fucking the air, and says, "Yeah, who knew Vinnie could dance? Certainly not me."

"I hope you don't dance like that in front of the princess," I say, cringing. "You'll scar her for life."

Faye rolls her hazel eyes, grinning at me. "Lighten up, Wolf. I'll save the moves to embarrass my son when he arrives."

"Wolf?" Anna smirks, looking at me. "It's still weird hearing anyone call you that."

"It's the best road name too," Faye says, sitting down and making herself comfortable on my bed. "Although the lone wolf has found a mate, hasn't he?"

I reach my limit. "Okay, that's enough. Everyone out. Now."

"But—"

"Now," I growl.

They all grumble but leave, Shay grinning and giving me a kiss before she leaves. I sit down on the bed and enjoy the silence.

THIRTY-FIVE

Shayla

"**F**UCK me," Vinnie mutters as I walk out of the bathroom, dressed and ready to go. We'd decided on an all-black theme, so I'd chosen a high-waisted leather skirt and crop top, showing off the expanse of my stomach. A bright red lip, winged eyeliner, and chunky heels complete the look. I'd ironed my hair dead straight and framing my face, and Vinnie was currently staring at me like a virgin in a strip club. He stalks over to me, running his hands down the side of my body. "You look fuckin' amazing."

"Thank you," I reply quietly, the intensity in his gaze making me feel dazed. He reaches down to cup my ass, squeezing with both hands. "Are you sure you want to go out tonight? Or maybe we could show up late."

"You have to pick up Bailey and Tia, remember?" I say, licking my lips. "You'll have to wait until we get home."

He groans and rubs his thumb along my bottom lip. "I'm going to be walking around with a fuckin' boner all night. Only good thing is that I won't have to get into any fights, because there won't be any random men there to look at you."

I roll my eyes and lift up on my tiptoes, wanting a kiss. He gives me what I want, kissing me deeply. Luckily I wore my long-stay, smudge-proof lipstick tonight, otherwise it would be all over my face right now.

"Are you drinking tonight?" I ask him when he pulls away, resting my arm on his chest.

He shakes his head.

"Why not?" I ask, sitting down on the bed and tightening the strap on my shoe. "You deserve to have a little fun. I won't drink if someone has to be designated driver, I don't mind. I'd rather you have a good time, Vinnie."

"There's no problem with designated drivers," he explains. "We have the prospects, and Shark's not drinking either."

"Shark?"

"Ronan."

"Oh," I say, my eyes widening in realization. "Right, I keep forgetting."

I know he's not drinking because he's paranoid something might happen, and it kind of makes me sad. I want him to have a good night and not have to be on guard all the time; he's always expecting the worst. Then again, with what we've experienced, it's a very valid feeling. This life isn't all bad though, and nights like tonight, when you get to let loose with great people, it's something to treasure.

"I just want you to have a good time," I say, running my hand down his biceps. "I know this was our idea, and you didn't even want to do it, but everyone is going to be together, and it's going to be fun, like Faye's birthday."

"I know, babe," he says, his eyes softening. "Tonight is for you though, to get dressed up and dance with the girls. . . . Like a girls' night, but not, because we'll all be there watching you like hawks."

"It makes it even more fun that you'll be there," I say, heading into the bathroom to check my makeup once more. "I'm ready when you are."

"Why don't you message Bailey and Tia and see if they're ready," he suggests, sliding his feet in his shoes. "What's the bet I end up sitting in the fuckin' car while they ask you your opinion on shoes, or some shit?"

I send a quick text to the both of them, asking if we should leave now. Bailey replies straightaway, saying they're both ready and having some wine.

"We can leave now," I say, wondering how drunk they'll be by the time we get there. "It was so nice of Rake to watch the three kids tonight. I had no idea he was such a nice guy."

"He is to Bailey," Vinnie says, standing and offering me his hand. "Let's go."

He waits for me to walk in front of him. I turn and flash him an amused, knowing look. "You just want to stare at my ass, don't you?"

"I don't think I've ever seen you dressed in anything so short and tight. Fuck yeah, I want to watch your ass jiggle as you walk," he says in a low husky tone.

"My ass doesn't jiggle, thank you very much."

At least it better not with all the squats that I do.

"Hmmmm," he murmurs, not even paying attention to what I'm saying. "If you bend over tonight, I'm taking you to the VIP room and fucking you."

I stop in my tracks. "Why the hell would I be bending over?"

"To do some dance move . . . or maybe you drop your little bag or something, I don't know, but this is your warning."

He slaps my ass, making me rub my right ass cheek. "Ouch. It's different doing it in bed and in the daytime, you know. That hurt."

He just grins and shakes his head.

I keep walking, swaying my hips exaggeratedly just to torture him.

Shots are lined up, and we throw them back, except Faye, who is sipping on some orange juice. Loud music is playing, and the only time we stop dancing is to drink, or go to the bathroom. I'm tipsy for the first time since I can remember, my head buzzing, but in a good way. I don't worry about anything, just enjoying the moment, the music and the company. Tia grabs my arm and pulls me back to the dance floor. "Sorry Not Sorry" by Bryson Tiller plays. It's so cool having basically your own DJ in a club, playing all of everyone's requests, and I find myself wondering who chose this song. I dance in between Tia, Tina, and Bailey, closing my eyes and letting my body take control, chasing the rhythm of the music. I don't know how long we stay like that, but song after song passes, and soon I need another drink. I'm return to the bar when Vinnie pulls me back against his chest, kissing my neck. "Watching you dance like that, dressed like this, is fuckin' torture. Can we leave now? Faye is tired and leaving, so can we."

Faye is pregnant and has an excuse to leave early, but I don't bother to point that out.

"Are you going to dance with me?" I ask, spinning around and dancing against him. "Please?"

He kisses me, probably tasting the tequila on my lips, cupping the back of my neck and bringing me closer to him. I hold on to his T-shirt, touching my tongue with his, turning the kiss from something sensual to one filled with hunger and lust. I don't think about everyone watching, because in this moment I don't really care. All I can think about is Vinnie, how he tastes and how he makes me feel—which right now is pretty damn turned on. He's the one who pulls away, the look in his eyes making my knees buckle.

"How drunk are you?" he asks me, lifting my chin up and turning my face from left to right.

"A little," I say. "Why? I'm not drunk enough that my judgment is clouded. For example, if we have sex in the VIP room right now, it's not like I'd regret it tomorrow morning."

Vinnie's eyes darken at that, and I know that I have him. He's been stalking me with his eyes all night, like a wolf with its prey. I grin at the wolf pun and remind myself to tell him about it tomorrow. Apparently tipsy me is witty as fuck. With his hand in mine, he leads me to the VIP room.

The door pushes open and he ushers me inside. I don't look behind me, because I don't want to see any knowing glances, I'll deal with those on the way out. Vinnie locks the door as I look around the room, then turn to face him. He takes a step forward, so I take one back, teasing him. He smirks and nods toward the red couch, silently commanding me. I shake my head and move in the opposite direction. The second I turn my back, he grips my waist and pulls me against his hard chest, then pushes my hair off my neck and starts to kiss me there. His hand reaches around and gently holds my throat as he kisses up to my ear, nibbling on the lobe. I reach my hand behind me and run it over his hardness, which I can feel straining against his jeans. I turn and lower myself to my knees, glancing up at him as I undo his button and try to tug his jeans down. With his assistance, they fall to his knees with his boxers, his thick cock springing free. I lick my lips and take it into my hand, stroking gently, then suck the head into my mouth. I lick him from tip to base and back up again, before taking him fully into my mouth, hollowing my cheeks with the suction I know drives him crazy. His hand tangles in my hair as he gently encourages me, and he starts to make those low growling noises that instantly make me wet. When he pulls his cock out of my mouth, lifts me off the ground, hikes my skirt up and pulls my panties down, all I can think about is having him inside of me. I kick my panties off so they're not around my ankles, and squeal as he lifts me in the air.

He's inside me before my back hits the wall.

THIRTY-SIX

Vinnie

I PUSH into her, burying my face in her neck and gritting my teeth as she squeezes herself around my dick. She tugs on my hair, her sharp little nails digging into my back, but I don't mind one bit. I thrust into her harder when I feel she's about to come, the noises she makes and the way her thighs always tremble is a sure sign.

"Vinnie," she moans, panting, closing her eyes and saying "Fuck."

I come just after her, kissing her mouth and letting it catch my moans and grunts of pleasure. I pull back and look at her face after we're done: her sultry yet sated gaze, her swollen lips from my rough kisses, and her messy "just been fucked" hair. She's never looked more beautiful.

"Hi," she whispers, grinning.

I smile and kiss her lips, softly and sweetly this time, then rest my forehead against hers. I pull out of her, and put her back on the ground. We both make ourselves decent, then sit down on the couch, her head on my chest.

"We should probably go back out," she says, cringing. "Everyone is going to give us shit, again. We really need to stop doing this. We have no control."

I laugh and rest my hand on her thigh. "Don't worry about it. There's no judgment here, Shay. Yes, they'll give us shit, but just own it. We're not doing anything wrong. Trust me, if you saw the clubhouse before the women took over . . ." I shake my head as I remember the wild parties, the women, and the public sex . . . the threesomes. . . . We've had some crazy-ass times over the years. A little private fucking is nothing. Everyone here has seen a lot more, but Shay wouldn't know that. I'll bet everyone has fucked in this room at one point or another, it's not even a big deal.

"I'd rather not know," she says, nudging me with her elbow. "All right, let's go be social. Although I have a lot less energy now than I did before we walked in here."

We leave the room hand in hand, and head to the bathrooms to clean up. I walk out before her, and assume she's chatting with Lana, who I saw go in there just before her. Back at the bar, I order two bottles of water and glance around the place. Everyone is drinking and having a good time. Shark must have left, along with Trace and Jess, because they're missing.

The reason I don't want to drink tonight is because I want to be ready, just in case. You never know what can happen on any given night, and I don't want to be drunk and out of control if something goes wrong. I want to be on alert and keep an eye on everything and everyone, especially Shay. I'd rather her have a good time, with me watching over her—it's safer that way. The night has gone smoothly so far, and I know I'm being a little paranoid, but I'm also being realistic. We don't really have the luxury of all of us being able to let loose when shit can go down at any second. It's happened before, and it will happen again. It's a part of the lifestyle, and it's a part of our need to protect everyone we love and care about.

Shay and Lana walk out of the bathroom, then head to the dance floor together. Tracker walks up to me, blue eyes bright with amusement. "You two need a room twenty-four-mother-fuckin'-seven, don't you?"

"As if you can talk," I reply, grinning at him. "How long do you think these women are going to want to stay?"

Tracker looks at his watch. "It's only one a.m., I say until at least four."

"Fuck me dead," I utter, opening my bottle of water and taking a long sip.

"You just got laid, don't know what the fuck you're complaining about."

"Room is free now," I tell him, nodding my head toward it. "Don't act like you haven't used it before."

Tracker laughs at that, because we all know that he has, and when he pulls Lana into the room, I make sure Shay sees it, so she can give them shit if they say anything to her. She crooks her finger at me from the dance floor, since her dance partner is now missing. I approach her and hand over the bottle of water.

"Thank you," she says over the music.

I thought her mouth might be dry, after all the fuckin' amazing head she gave me, but I don't say that to her, I just smile. She finishes half the bottle, puts it down on the closest table, and makes me dance with her. She's so cute when she dances, she gets lost in the music, in her own world. Like she's in her element.

We dance for two more hours before she decides it's time to go home. I'm fuckin' thankful for that, but I never complain, because I know she's having a good time, and this night is for her. We close up the club and leave. I drop Bailey and Tia home, making sure they get inside safely before driving back to the clubhouse. Irish and Tina are in the kitchen when we get there, but I just want a shower and bed, so we don't stay around long to socialize. After a quick shower together, we dry ourselves and get into bed naked, wrapped in each other's arms.

I sleep like a fuckin' baby.

"Are you happy here?" I ask Shay, as we're outside with Colt, playing fetch. She picks up the ball and throws it before answering. "In the clubhouse? Yeah, why?"

"I mean," I say, trying to word this the best way, "would you be happy living here permanently?"

"Are you asking me to move in with you?" She pauses. "We never really spoke about what will happen after the danger is over—is that what this talk is?"

I was already messing this up.

"What I'm trying to say is, I want you with me, but the clubhouse is my home, and I'm asking if you're okay with living here, or did you want to move into a house somewhere else, like everyone else. I do own a house and land, which I'm renting out right now."

"But you'd prefer to live here?"

I nod. "Yeah, I would. But what do you want?"

She throws the ball, then turns and gives me all of her attention. "If you want to live here, then I'm happy living here, Vinnie. We never really spoke about us though, and like we've said before, we've kind of always lived together because of our unusual circumstances."

She looks unsure for a moment, but I have no fuckin' idea why, or where she's going with this.

"What are you saying?"

She looks down at Colt now and pats his head. "I guess I just don't know where your head is at with us. You've never really talked about the future, and now that everything has calmed down, we have the opportunity to make more decisions and find out what we want to do."

I still have no idea what she's getting at.

"Do you want me?" I ask her, staring her down.

"Yes."

"And you're happy living at the clubhouse?"

"Yes," she replies. "But—"

"Then that's all I need to know."

I cup her face with my hands and kiss her lips. "Don't overthink everything. It's still just you and me against the world, all right?"

"All right," she whispers, puckering her lips for another kiss, which I give her. "I just think we need to have some talks about the future. I want to finish college and get my degree."

"Then do it," I tell her. "You don't have to work if you don't want to, but if you do, then that's up to you. I'm not going to control your life, Shay, unless it comes to your safety. I agree that there's a few things we need to discuss."

I was putting off telling her that I didn't want marriage or children, because women don't react well to hearing that kind of shit. Maybe she really wanted children, and she'd leave me to find a man who would give that to her. I'd do anything to make her happy, but having a child with her isn't something one just does for the other person. Being a father is a full-time gig that I'm not qualified for. We haven't been together long, but she should know that, even in the future, I don't plan on ever having children or walking down that aisle. What will I do if she leaves? Maybe that means she isn't the one for me. My mind rejects that thought instantly, knowing that it isn't true. I guess I can only tell her and see how she reacts.

But not today.

THIRTY-SEVEN

Shayla

I SPEND the rest of the day with Faye and Clover, while Vinnie goes to Rift to do some work. I wonder if he's going to drop by Toxic to do some work there too.

"Do all the men go to Toxic?" I ask Faye as I help fold the new baby clothes she bought.

"At one point or another, I'd say yes," she replies, looking up from the baby-blue onesie in her hand. "You need to trust your man, Shay. Do they go to Toxic and have a look at the women? I'm sure they do—as a matter of fact, I know that they do." She grins. "I've been there before with them. You should ask Vinnie to take you there, you can go see for yourself. They look but don't touch, unless they're single."

"I don't think Vinnie would cheat," I admit, sighing. "But you know, in the back of my head is always a part of my brain saying never to completely trust a man."

"That part of your brain is called your common sense," she surprises me by saying. "You can't trust all men, and sometimes even good men mess up. You just have to go with your gut, honey. I think Vinnie is a great man. I've known him for many years." She lowers her voice. "But you have to handle men in a way they don't know they're being handled."

I laugh at that. "You're amazing, you know that?"

"I do okay," she replies, looking over to where Clover is asleep on the bed. "She's so excited to be a big sister."

"She's such a great kid," I say, smiling at her sleeping form. "You've done such an amazing job. I'm going to come to you for advice if I ever have children."

"Aunty Faye will be more than happy to help," she says, grinning, then studying me. "Now what do you want to talk to me about?"

I open my mouth, then close it. "How did you know that I—"

"I wasn't born yesterday," she says, cutting me off. "Is everything okay? Tell me."

So I tell her everything that's been on my mind.

"What on earth are you doing?" I ask Rake, who is looking into the oven like there's a monster in there.

"I'm hungry, so I put something in the oven and now it's burned. And Bailey is at work and isn't here to make me something."

Seriously?

I blink slowly. "You're spoiled, you know that?"

"What I am is hungry," he groans, rubbing his abs. How he stays that muscular with the amount he eats I have no idea.

"Do you want to do a food run?" I ask, feeling a little hungry myself.

"Are you allowed to leave the house?" he asks, closing the oven with a slam. "I could go for a burger and fries. Or some fried chicken."

"I mean, I'm not *not* allowed to leave the house," I hedge, shrugging and flashing him my best puppy-dog eyes. "I'm just meant to stay hidden a little. I'm sure no one will spot me going through a drive-through."

"True. Yeah, all right, let's go then."

"I'll even drive, so you can eat in peace," I offer, being the kind person that I am, but all he does is laugh.

"Fuck no. I heard how you drive, and I'd like to survive to see my daughter grow up, thank you very much."

I found it adorable how he calls Cara his daughter, even though she isn't his biologically.

"Fine, you drive then," I say, rolling my eyes. I'm not that bad a driver, these men are the biggest exaggerators. "Maybe we can go do some shooting practice when we're done?"

"Dying to get out of the house, are we?"

"I'm going to kill someone," I admit, shoulders sagging. "I've studied, cleaned, and taught Colt every trick I can think of. I also baked cupcakes."

I continue before he can even open his mouth to ask. "Everyone already ate them."

"You could save me some next time," he grumbles, lifting his chin. "Let's go. I'm starting to get hangry."

I follow him out to the four-wheel drive, sliding in when he open the doors. "Chicken or burgers?"

"Let's get both," he says, putting his seat belt on. I do the same, realizing that I've never really been alone with Rake before, and I have no idea what to talk to him about. He takes care of that though, making me feel comfortable. Sometimes I forget that not everyone is as awkward as me.

"Well, we can't go shooting," he says, looking straight ahead.

"Why not?"

"Because I forgot to bring a gun, unless you have one stashed away in that purse of yours." He pauses. "Why did you even bring a purse? If you try to pay, I'm throwing you out that window. You'd probably fit through it too."

"You don't have a gun in the car?" I ask, opening the glove box. "What kind of criminal are you?"

He gasps, pretending to be hurt. "Is that what you think of me?"

"There's no gun in there but there's a shitload of condoms," I say, pursing my lips.

Rake chuckles, glancing at me for a second before returning his eye to the road. "Priorities, Shay."

"Are they yours? They're extra-small ones," I joke, pulling one out and throwing it at him.

"Definitely not mine then. Maybe they're Vinnie's?"

"Trust me when I say that they're not."

They weren't even small condoms, they were extra-large, I just wanted to annoy him. We go through one drive-through, then another, getting way too much food for two people. Rake eyes his food, then me, and says, "I'm wondering what I care about more right now. Eating this food, or possibly getting into a car crash if I let you drive." He grabs a piece of chicken, and I do the same. We look at each other, and then slap the pieces of chicken together. "Cheers!" I say, making him laugh.

"Cheers. Luckily, when it comes to food, I can multitask," he mutters as he takes a giant bite.

When we get back to the clubhouse, Vinnie is standing by his bike, texting on his phone. He rushes to the car, opening my door and scowling. "Jesus, fuck! I tried calling you, I had no idea where you were."

I rub my mouth with the back of my hand. "I just went to get food."

"I can see that," he says quietly, as I grab the bag and exit the car.

"I didn't think you'd be back so early, that's why I didn't bother messaging you."

"You could have anyway," he grumbles, rubbing his hand over his head. "I freaked the fuck out for a second. And no one else was here, so it made it even worse. I wasn't sure what had happened."

"Everything all right?" Rake asks, coming over with double the amount of food in his hands. "Sorry, Vinnie, I didn't know you'd freak out. We were gone only thirty minutes."

"No problem, brother," Vinnie replies, helping me carry the food.

We walk into the clubhouse and sit at the kitchen table, sharing our food with Vinnie. There's something I need to talk to him about, but I know it's going to be a very awkward conversation, so I've been avoiding it since yesterday. I figure that I'll tell him tonight in bed, and try not to spend the rest of the day worrying about it. Rake and Vinnie talk about some run that the men are going to on the weekend, but I find out that Vinnie and Tracker will be staying behind this time. I wonder what they do on these runs, or what they're even for. When I ask, they both answer at the exact same time, saying, "Club business."

So I just bite into my chicken, not bothering to ask them any more questions on that subject.

"Save some for me," Rake grumbles, making me laugh as I point out his pile.

"You're so greedy!"

"You're so tiny, how much food can you possibly need?" he fires back, checking over me.

"Let her eat, it all goes to her ass," Vinnie adds, chuckling at my outraged gasp.

I put down the piece of chicken. In a moment of immaturity, I pick up Rake's last piece and lick it. He shoots Vinnie a look that says, "Control your woman."

Vinnie just laughs. I for one am glad he's in a good mood. I push my burger toward Rake to make up for it, which he accepts with narrowed eyes. Guess I was now on his shit list, all over a piece of chicken.

"Are we still going to shoot?" I ask him.

"No."

My lip twitches.

I look to Vinnie. "Want to take me shooting?"

Vinnie's never taken me before, it's always been something I do with Tracker and Rake, kind of like our little bonding moment.

"Okay," Vinnie replies, and I can see his mind working behind his eyes. "Let's see what you've got, Shay."

I'm going to show him.

Right after I emerge from this food coma.

THIRTY-EIGHT

Vinnie

"NOT bad," I comment as she hits six out of the ten cans. "I'm actually pretty fuckin' impressed."

She smiles widely, and aims for one of the cans left standing. I ask her if I can take a shot, then hit down the remaining cans.

"Team effort," she says, moving to stand next to me. "Vinnie, there's something I want to talk to you about. I was going to tell you tonight, but we're here, all alone so . . ."

I put the safety on the gun and ask distractedly, "Is this the future talk?"

She nods.

To be honest, I don't really want to have this talk right now, mainly because I'm terrible at being open about my feelings and shit, but if she really wants some reassurance about us, I'll try my best to give it to her.

"I want to be with you, Shay," I tell her. "I know we haven't been together long, but I don't give a fuck. I've never wanted a woman like I want you in my life, I've never felt like this before, like I just know you're mine, you know?" She nods, and I take a deep breath, needing to get the words out. "I will give you every-thing in my power to give, do anything to make you happy, but you need to know a few things. A life with me means no mar-riage and no children." Her face falls, but I keep going, wanting her to know that it has nothing to do with her. "I don't really believe in marriage. I don't think two people have to be mar-ried, it's just a piece of paper, and I've always known I'd never get married. You know the childhood I had, in foster care until I was eighteen, and I just never planned on having any children in my life. I don't think I'd be a good role model, I never had a father, so I have no idea how to be one. I want you, Shay, more than anything, so I just really hope you want me back enough to still be with me."

She stays frozen for a few seconds, then schools her expres-sion. It fuckin' kills me that she's hiding her emotions when she hasn't done it since we first met.

"I see," she says, not looking me in the eye. "This is a lot to process, Vinnie."

"I know," I say, rubbing the back of my neck. "And I should have told you sooner. I really think we could be happy, Shay; we don't need kids or a piece of paper for us to have an amazing, fulfilling life together."

"I know," she says, seeming distracted. Needing to touch her, I bring her against my body, hugging her in my arms.

"Let's go home. We can talk about this some more, if you like, or we can discuss it later after you've gathered your thoughts."

I was just 100 percent honest with her.

I don't want to hurt her, I don't want her to leave, but she has to know what I'm thinking and feeling, where my head is at. I want both of us to be happy, and she definitely deserves my honesty. She's quiet as we walk back through the woods to the bike, and it's almost as if I can feel her withdraw from me. I almost wish I could take the words back, but I can't, and I shouldn't have to. I can only hope that she understands and can find it in her to give us a chance. She leans against my back on the ride home, giving me hope that she isn't trying to distance herself, because she doesn't need to hold on to me so closely.

Maybe I'm just looking into things that aren't there though. She's quiet—too quiet as we get off the bike and walk inside the clubhouse. She doesn't even smile or tease Rake when we pass him, and he makes a chicken-licker joke. She just goes straight into our room, gets into bed, and takes Lana's new book from the side table and starts to read it. I decide to give her a little time alone before I try to talk to her again, so I sit in the game room with a beer and think about what the fuck I'm going to do if she decides I'm not worth it. It's a lot to ask of any woman, I know, especially because some dream of being mothers their whole lives. Then again, more and more women are opting not to have children too. Shay never mentioned wanting kids, but that doesn't mean that she doesn't. It probably means I should have brought the topic up a long time ago.

Yeah, I fucked up.

One hour and two beers later, I walk into our room to find her asleep. I remove my shoes and slide in next to her, wrapping my arms around her tightly. "I love you, Shay," I whisper to her. "Please don't leave me."

*   *   *

The next morning, I find her awake early, already showered and dressed and sitting in the kitchen, eating some toast.

"'Morning, you're up early."

She smiles, but it seems forced. "I couldn't sleep. What are your plans for today?"

"Sin wants some help painting his house today," I say, scanning her face. "Do you want to come? Faye will be here though, because the paint smell apparently isn't good for the baby."

Her face brightens when I mention Faye. "No, I'll stay here and hang out with Faye. She's going to show me how to throw knives."

An average day with Faye then.

"That sounds more fun than literally watching paint dry," I say, kissing the top of her head. "I still want to talk to you a little more about yesterday. I don't want things to be strained between us. You know you can say whatever is on your mind, right? I won't hold it against you."

Just like I hope she won't do to me.

"I know, I know," she says, leaning into me. "Why don't we go out to dinner or something tonight? We can talk about everything then."

I breathe a sigh of relief. "Sounds like a plan. I'll be back in a few hours anyway. Now give me a kiss."

She lifts up on her toes and kisses me. I deepen the kiss, wanting our connection back—it's like I can just feel something isn't right, and I need to fix it, now. Today. I will fix it.

"Do you want something to eat before you leave?" she asks, resting her palm on my chest like she always does. "I can make you some bacon and eggs, or some pancakes or something."

"No, I'm fine," I say, running my fingers along her collarbone. "Sin says food is provided. Probably knows it's the only way to get us there."

She grins and says, "Ten bucks says Rake will be the first one there."

"I don't know," I say, loving the fact she was acting more like herself. "He likes his sleep too."

"He's like a giant kid."

"Says the woman who licked his fried chicken yesterday."

She lifts her shoulders in a shrug. "He deserved it."

I kiss her again, unable to stop myself. The truth is, yesterday scared the fuckin' shit out of me, and I can't wait to get all this over with so we can go back to being Vinnie and Shay.

"Probably," I murmur, taking a step away from her. "Faye should already be on her way here, so you won't have to wait long—or do you want me to wait until she gets here?"

She rolls her brown eyes and says, "I'm sure I can manage for ten minutes without you. Besides, I'm not even alone, Irish and Tina are here." She pauses. "And Colt. Will you tell me how the other two puppies are doing? Maybe take some pictures?"

"Yeah, of course," I say, leaving the kitchen. "Sin says they're destroying his garden and ruining his life."

"Dramatic much?"

I grin at her, lingering for a second before leaving for Sin's house.

The sooner I get there, the sooner I can come back and take my woman out to dinner. After we talk, I'm going to bring her home and make love to her all night.

Yes, I fuckin' said it, I'm going to make love to her.

Fuck.

How the mighty have fallen.

And I don't even give a fuck.

When I arrive at Sin's, I'm about to walk inside when my phone rings.

And that's when everything goes to hell.

THIRTY-NINE

Shayla

M Y heart is in my throat.

I check into the hotel using the fake ID Talon had made for me, grateful to have it. If I didn't, I would have been screwed, because without any ID, they wouldn't have given me the room.

So for today, my name is Alexis Osborne. I leave my suitcase in the corner of the room and sit down on the bed, wondering just what the hell I'm doing. I left the clubhouse because I didn't know what else to do. Because for the first time ever, being there didn't feel so comfortable. How can things change so drastically within twenty-four hours? I went from being happy with the man I love and his amazing family, to being alone in a hotel room, my phone off and tears in my eyes. The situation I'm currently in, I don't know how to get out of. There's no fixing it, and there's no happy ending for everyone involved, especially me.

I wonder how I am going to live without everyone I've grown so close to over the last few weeks. I turn my phone on and send Vinnie a message, letting him know I'm safe, because I don't want him to worry that something bad has happened to me. I put my phone on silent, use the bathroom, and then climb into bed. I don't know what's going to happen, or what the future holds for me, but for right now, I'm going to take a nap.

I don't have it in me to do anything else.

I wake up feeling less sorry for myself, and more anger. I check my phone, but ignore everyone's messages and calls except one person's. I don't want to drag him into this, but he's all I have right now.

I need you, I type.

Tell me where you are, I'm coming to get you, he replies instantly. I decide I want tonight to myself, so I reply with, *I'm safe. Can you come and get me tomorrow? Come alone.*

Stubborn.

I grin and put the phone down. He better come alone. The last thing I need is Vinnie showing up demanding to know why I left, and then I'll have to tell him that I've ruined his life by making him a father. Even though it wasn't all my fault. Or maybe it was? I don't remember ever skipping a pill, but with everything going on I guess I must have. My stomach rumbles, and I know I have to get up to get something to eat.

When I told Faye that I was feeling nauseous, and my period still hadn't arrived, she quickly went and bought me two pregnancy tests. They were both positive. Then, when I finally worked up the nerve to tell Vinnie, I find out that he never wants kids. Ever. And now . . . now I don't know what to do. I'm lost, and confused, and all I want to do is stay in bed, cry, and eat junk food.

Will he try to make me get rid of this baby? I don't think I can, I'd lose a part of myself. But, if I have this baby, I've pretty much lost Vinnie. I love Vinnie, but I love myself, and now my child, more. I know I shouldn't have left like I did. I know it was selfish of me, but I just had to go away, and I'm not ready for everything to be out in the open. Maybe Faye told Vinnie I was pregnant, and now I won't have to. Maybe he won't even come after me when he finds out.

Back to feeling sorry for myself then.

I need to go back to the clubhouse at some point to get Colt. I miss him, but I knew I wouldn't be able to take him to a hotel with me. I left out food and water, and a note to please look after him until I get back. I know they'll take good care of him for a few days until I find us a permanent place to live. I'm hoping Talon will let us stay with him until I buy a place. Maybe I should move to another country. Then again, I couldn't really take Colt with me overseas, so it looks like I'm staying. And therefore having to face my problems.

Great.

I sit up in bed, my hands covering my face.

Right now—I'm being a coward.

I guess I just don't want to see Vinnie's face, hear the words pouring from his mouth as he says that he doesn't want him or her . . . doesn't want us.

But what can I really expect from him? He never even told me that he loves me.

Talon picks me up from the hotel in a red sports car I've never seen before. When I raise my eyebrow at the car, he just smirks and says, "You told me to come alone, so I wanted to make sure no one follows me."

"Very inconspicuous," I mutter as he gets out of the car and takes my suitcase for me, kissing me on each cheek.

"You have some explaining to do, baby cuz."

"I know." I sigh, getting into the passenger seat as he loads my case. I put my seat belt on and wait for him to get back into the car, wondering what the best way to say this was.

"Speak," he says softly, after he turns on the engine and exits the parking lot.

"I just want to hide out with you for a few days," I say, looking at his profile. "Please."

"That's no problem, Shayla. What I want to know is: why?"

I clear my throat, then decide to just blurt it out. "Vinnie told me he doesn't believe in marriage and never wants children."

"And that's a reason to run away and hide from him?" Talon asks, confusion marring his brow. "At least he was being honest with you."

Since when was Talon all Team Vinnie?

"Yes, I agree," I say, swallowing hard. "I do appreciate the honesty. However, hearing that he never wants children, and that he'd be a terrible father, just before I was about to tell him that I'm pregnant, wasn't a situation I ever thought I'd find myself in."

Talon mutters one word that sums up this whole situation. "Fuck."

"Exactly."

"Why didn't the two of you fucking use protection?" he growls, making me cringe. The last thing I want to hear is a sex talk from my cousin.

"I'm on the pill," I say, scrubbing my hand down my face. "I don't know, I must have missed one, or something, I don't even know. But it's my fault, he trusted me to have it under control."

I should have just made him wear condoms too. Fucking hell.

"It's not your fault," Talon tells me in a gentle tone. "You didn't do it on purpose. Look there's no point going over the what-ifs, you just need to handle the situation and deal with the now. What do you want to do, Shayla?"

"I don't want to get rid of him or her," I say in a small voice. "I'd hate myself, Talon. I'd think about it every day. It's not an option for me. If Vinnie doesn't want anything to do with our baby, then so be it. It's not like I need money, or anything from him. I can handle everything on my own."

"Being a single mother is hard work."

"I know."

I'm lucky that I don't have to work—I can easily be a full-time mother and live off the money my father left behind, getting a job eventually. I can always do bookkeeping, although accounting didn't really work for me the first time around.

"So what, you told Vinnie, then bailed? He rang me, fucking frantic, wondering where the fuck you are," he says, sounding like he feels sorry for Vinnie.

I wince and look out the window. "I didn't tell him."

"You what?" Talon practically yells now.

"I didn't tell him! I panicked, and I left, okay? I didn't want to watch him get angry or to tell me to kill my fucking baby because he doesn't want it! I don't want to hear it, Talon. Imagine hearing those words from the man I love."

Talon curses under his breath and slams his hands down on the steering wheel.

"Is it safe for me to come to the clubhouse?" I ask him. "I know you had your own shit going on there . . ."

"Vinnie is not going to want you staying at the Wild Men clubhouse," Talon says, green eyes pinning me to my seat. "I'm going to become public enemy number one for bringing you there."

"I can stay at a hotel, but I want to bring my dog with me wherever I am."

"I'm not going to take you to the clubhouse, but that doesn't mean I'm not going to look after you. I have a house you can stay in—consider it yours, all right? I'll move in there with you for however long you need me, but to be honest, I don't think that's going to be very long."

"Why?"

"Because Vinnie is a Wind Dragon, Shay. You're his, and they always come for what's theirs."

I lay my head back and close my eyes. "How did things turn out like this?"

Talon's eyes gentle. "It's all temporary. Things will work out for you, Shayla. I promise."

I'm glad he's so confident, because me?

I'm not so sure.

FORTY

Vinnie

STALK through the clubhouse, phone in my hand, waiting for Talon to call me back. He said that she's fine, and that he will get her to call me ASAP. I got no fuckin' sleep last night, instead I kept calling her and Talon's phones, wanting some damn explanations. We were meant to talk everything out, she said we would, but then she just leaves?

When Faye rang me and asked where Shay was, I felt it in my gut that something wasn't right. And it wasn't. She was gone. Without a word. Fuck, how she played me yesterday morning in the kitchen, letting me think everything was going to be okay between the two of us, when really she knew she was going to leave without giving me any kind of explanation as to why, or without giving us a chance.

Faye leans against the wall, hand on her protruding stomach, watching me as I pace.

"Vinnie, why don't you let me make you something to eat? You haven't eaten or slept."

"I'm fine," I tell her, waving off her concern. I won't sleep until I get to talk to Shay. I'm so angry at how she's handled this whole thing, yet at the same time I'm worried and just want her home.

"Vinnie," Faye says quietly, looking unsure. "Shay confided something in me, and I think it has to do with this whole thing."

I stop, turn to her, and approach. "What are you talking about?"

"Fuck!" she snaps. "This isn't my place to say, it should come from her. I just don't want you to find out that I knew, and then lose your shit at me. She spoke to me, woman-to-woman, and it doesn't feel right telling you when it isn't my thing to tell."

I study her for a moment, and then yell out one word, "Sin!"

Faye mutters something under her breath, I'm pretty sure she called me a snitch, but I'll have to deal with her ass later, because right now all I want to know about is what Shay confided in her.

Sin walks in from outside, shirtless. "What the fuck is going on now?"

I look at his wife. "Faye knows."

"Knows what?" he asks, wiping his forehead with the back of his hand.

"Everything."

"For fuck's sake, someone give me more than that," he growls, losing his patience. "I'm trying to build a higher fence. I don't have time for this shit."

"I think I know why Shay left," Faye tells her husband. "She confided something in me, and after Vinnie told me what their last conversation was about, it all makes sense."

"Faye," Sin says in warning.

She turns to me, her hazel eyes narrowed. She doesn't look very happy with me all of a sudden, and I'd like to know why.

"You said that you told her you never want kids, or marriage, and that you'd be a terrible father, and that you never plan on moving out of the clubhouse. Basically, in a way, you gave her an ultimatum. You set the rules, leaving nothing open for compromise. That's not how a relationship works, Vinnie. You gave her nothing to work with, no hope for the future, except for a life staying exactly how it is now. What about what *she* wants? Did you even ask her that?"

"You said all that to her?" Sin asks, blue eyes going double their size. "Ice-cold, Vinnie. Ice-cold."

"I was honest," I say, defending myself.

"Yeah, well," Faye says, hands now on her hips. "You gave that asshole of a speech to a woman who's already pregnant with your child and was going to tell you that day."

"What?" I ask. I can't have heard correctly.

There is no way.

No.

Pregnant?

But she's on the pill. I know no contraception is 100 percent, but what the fuck?

"So you told a pregnant woman, who is unsure and probably scared, not to mention hormonal, that you don't ever want children?" Sin asks, cringing. "Fucking hell, you're so screwed."

"Thanks for that, prez," I reply, still in a daze.

Shay is pregnant.

I don't really know how to process this, to be honest. I fucked things up with Shay, she's probably really hurt right now, and hating me, but I don't know how to accept that I'm going to have a child, when like I said, I never planned on having one.

Ever.

Under no circumstance.

I run my hand over my head, and turn to walk away from these two, because I need to be alone right now.

"Are you going after her?" Faye asks, hope lacing her tone.

Hope that I soon dash. "No."

How fucked-up is that? My first instinct after hearing this news isn't even to go after her, to tell her everything will be okay, because I don't know if it will be. I've never trusted another woman when she said she was on the pill, I always wore condoms anyway, but with Shay, I trusted her completely. I guess that's not exactly fair, because shit does happen and nothing is foolproof, but fuck, I only just heard the news and my head is fuckin' spinning.

This can't be happening.

I run my fingers over the bridge of my nose and take a deep breath.

Shay.

Pregnant.

A fuckin' baby.

I picture a small baby with her dark hair. A baby of mixed nationalities, raised by two people whose own parents didn't even want them.

I don't know anything about being a good father.

Nothing. I never had one, I never had a good childhood, I never had anything, and that's all I know to give back to a child.

Nothing.

I wouldn't know how to be there emotionally. I wouldn't know how to calm a crying baby, or how to bond with one. What the fuck do you even do with them all day long? A baby would just hog Shay, and I'd be there on the outside, wondering what the fuck happened to my life. Sure, Faye and Sin make it work, but they're different. I'm a different man than Sin is. I'd have to move out of the clubhouse, because that's not exactly a place you can raise a child for its entire life, and live the exact life I always said I never wanted. I'd be living a life I might grow to hate, or maybe I wouldn't, I won't know until it happens.

Maybe Shay was right in leaving. Maybe she knows, just as well as I do, that this child would be better off without me.

"He's not going after her," I hear Faye tell Sin. "You need to make him. You're the president!"

"I can't make him do anything," Sin replies, sounding exasperated with her.

"Then give him a male pep talk, you've been in this situation. Imagine if you'd treated me like this when you found out I was pregnant. I would've thrown it in your face for the rest of your life."

"Well hopefully Shay is a more kind and forgiving woman than you are," Sin says in a dry tone. "Their situation is different than ours, and I can't make Vinnie fix it, it's his decision."

"The longer he waits the harder it's going to be to fix."

"He only just heard she's pregnant, let the man digest it. You can't solve everyone's problems."

"The hell I can't," Faye mutters, and I can just imagine her giving Sin her narrow-eyed, stubborn look. "I love Vinnie, and I really like Shay. Vinnie's kid will be my niece or nephew. This affects us all."

"Well us standing in front of him discussing it isn't really going to help now, is it?" Sin says. "You need to give him time. He's a man. He will do what he wants, when he wants, not because there's a stubborn-ass woman waiting at his door, a woman who's not even his, talking about him where he can hear her."

"Fine," she says, then calls out, "Vinnie, if you don't go and get Shay right now, you're a dumb-ass. That's all I'm going to say about it. Men become fathers the second they hold their baby, women become mothers the second they become pregnant. Don't be a dick and realize too late what you're going to miss out on." She squeals, then yells, "Sin, put me down! I'm not finished yet."

I hear her yelling down the hallway.

Thank fuck he took her away.

Still, her words play in my mind.

The thing about Faye—she's usually right.

FORTY-ONE

Shayla

TALON gets me settled in his house, then leaves and tells me someone will be dropping off groceries and lunch. He says he'll be back in the evening to take me out to dinner. So basically, I'm alone in a new house with nothing else to do but overthink my life and everything that's happened in the last few days, which is the last thing I want to do right now. I wish Colt was here. I put on the TV and try to distract myself. I'm watching *Supernatural* when there's a knock at the door. I open it, coming face-to-face with Ranger.

"Shayla," he says, smiling, his hands full of bags.

"Hey, Ranger," I say, opening the door wider for him. "Do you want some help?"

"Do I need any help from the knocked-up baby cousin of my president? No, thank you," he teases, stepping inside and placing the bags on the kitchen counter.

"News travels fast, then," I grumble, smiling when I see he brought some carrots, celery, and dip.

"Talon told only me," Ranger explains, helping to unload

the food. "Probably 'cause I was being an asshole asking why you can't go to the damn store yourself."

"I could've," I say, opening the fridge to put the juice inside it. "But Talon said he'd sort it out."

He mutters something unintelligible under his breath, then looks at the TV. "*Supernatural*, fuck yeah."

He walks to the couch and makes himself comfortable. I peel and cut some carrots, put them on a plate with the dip, and bring it to the table.

"Thanks," he says, scooping a big dollop onto his piece. I take in his features. Dark, thick hair tied at his nape. The beard he had is now gone, but I think he looks good either way, and he's tall. I mean really tall. He must be at least six foot five. He's just one giant winner-of-the-gene-pool biker. Oh, and he's also very intelligent, just like Talon. Three degrees under his belt, and I won't be surprised if he goes back for more. I remember he once said to me that knowledge is power, and he likes to keep his mind occupied.

"Did Talon tell you to babysit me too?" I ask, raising an eyebrow.

"Nah," he says, chewing thoughtfully. "Talon normally doesn't let me be around you for too long, but now you're knocked up and Wind Dragons' property, so I don't think he'll care if we hang out."

"Property? Nice," I say in a dry tone. "And I wonder why you're still single, Ranger?"

"I'm single because no woman has caught my eye yet."

Talon once told me that Ranger is one of the most complicated men he's ever met. He's laid-back but can be intensely competitive. Usually he never takes anything personally, and nothing can offend him, but sometimes he loses his shit over the most random things, and he can struggle with reading people's emotions. Like if you're sad, he probably won't pick up on that unless you tell him. He's an interesting guy.

"I know a girl—" I start, but he cuts me off with a look.

"One of the crazy Wind Dragon women? No, thank you, I'm going to have to pass."

The look on his face is priceless, almost like he'd rather be doing anything else.

"Hey now," I say, getting a little defensive. "Those women are amazing. And I'm kind of one of them."

Well, I *was*.

It hits me then that I might not be hanging with the women again, and it really sucks. I'll miss them all, especially Faye. I'll miss Rake and Tracker, and our gun practices; I'll miss Sin and his disapproving glares every time Colt does something bad; I'll miss Lana—asking her all about her books and trying to figure out how her amazing mind works. I'll miss Anna and her self-defense lessons. Fuck. I'll miss everyone and everything about being a part of the Wind Dragon family. Most of all, I'll miss Vinnie.

I fell in love with him so quickly, so deeply, and to have to push him away now kills me like nothing else. I just don't see a positive outcome for this situation. There's no quick fix. He can't change who he is and what he wants in life, and if he tries, he'll probably end up resenting me and the baby. It's a disaster waiting to happen, but damn, am I going to miss him.

"Bailey's friend Tia isn't one of the Wind Dragon women," I add, pushing away those thoughts. "She's just guilty by association. Bailey has told me stories and she sounds hilarious." She also mentioned that Tia thinks Talon is hot.

"Tia?" Ranger asks, looking amused. He throws his head

back and laughs. "No, she definitely isn't a Wind Dragon chick, she's now sole property of the Wild Men."

My brow furrows in confusion. "First, women aren't property, asshole, and second, what?"

"You didn't know about her and Talon?"

I open my mouth, then close it. Then, a big smile spreads on my face. "About time he settled down."

I can't wait to hear that story.

"I told Talon he should've let you hang around us more. Maybe we could've kept a good one for ourselves," he says, lifting his feet up on the coffee table.

I roll my eyes, resting my chin on my hand. "I feel like the Wild Men live a more bachelor lifestyle. I've never even met any of their old ladies. To be honest, I've only ever seen a few women there and I'm pretty sure they were groupies."

Maybe things will change now that Tia and Talon are together.

"Groupies? That's a nice name for them."

"I'm a nice person."

"Exactly," he says, studying me. "You are, and Talon didn't tell me why you're here and not with your man, but obviously something is going on. I know you're a Wind Dragon, but you'll always have a place here with us too."

"I thought it didn't work like that," I tease, my eyes gentling as the kind words pour from his mouth.

"Special circumstances," he says, grinning. "You're Talon's family, which means you're ours. It's simple. Plus, you apparently have good taste in TV shows."

I pick up a carrot and dip it. "And you apparently have good taste in snacks and dips."

He chuckles and glances over at me before returning to the TV. "You'll be fine, Shayla. Whatever is it, whatever this asshole has done, you will be fine."

"How do you know?" I ask him, resting my hand on my flat stomach. It won't be flat for much longer.

"Because you're strong," he says simply, like it's a fact.

"You don't know me well enough to make that statement," I say, arching my brow. "You probably only know what Talon has told you."

"I know," he states.

I look into his beautiful, captivating eyes and see that he believes what he's saying. "How long can you hang out?"

"I have nothing better to do today, if that's what you're asking. Why? Is that a hint to leave or to stay?"

"Well, I wouldn't be opposed to some company," I say, shrugging. "It keeps my mind off things, and like you, I have nothing better to do today."

"*Supernatural* marathon is it," he says, stretching his arms above his head. "Let me guess, you're a Dean fan."

"Naturally," I say, smirking.

He stands up and says, "Want some ice cream?"

I nod.

Yeah, Ranger isn't a bad guy at all.

"Are you sure you're okay?" he calls through the door. "I'd love to hold your hair back, but the sounds you're making are making me want to gag too."

I stand up from the toilet, feeling like utter shit, and Ranger is not helping. "I'm fine!"

I wash my face, brush my teeth again, and then sit on the bathtub, just in case I feel like throwing up again. After a few minutes of being okay, I leave the bathroom and sit back down in my chair.

"Are you okay?"

"Yeah," I say, leaning my head back. "If this is what it's going to be like for the next few months, my life is going to be hell."

And it was only my first time getting morning sickness. It wasn't even morning anymore, so that title is obviously false advertising.

"Eat some crackers or toast," he advises, typing on his phone. "Let me search what you need to do to handle the nausea."

He's researching for me? Now that is cute.

"Imagine going through all this while having another child to look after, or having to work or study as well. It would seriously suck."

I have a new respect for Faye and other mothers all over the world. This stuff is no walk in the park, although I know it's going to be worth it, and I know that it's going to make me a stronger person.

"Whatever you do," he murmurs, cringing. "Do *not* look up childbirth."

Great, just great.

"Why are you looking at that? Getting a little far ahead there."

"I just wanted to see what I'd have to do in case in eight months from now you went into labor at the clubhouse or something," he says, eyes still on his phone. "But all I'll be doing is calling the motherfucking ambulance."

"Ranger!" I growl. "You aren't helping right now."

"They should show a childbirth video in high schools. Best contraception ever," he continues, making me want to strangle him.

"You're getting off course now," I say, yawning.

"Take a nap if you're tired," he says, putting his phone away. "I'll stay here until Talon gets back. I don't think you should be alone right now."

I struggle to get comfortable in the single seat, until suddenly I'm lifted into Ranger's arms. He sits down on the larger couch, and places me next to him, pointing to his thigh. "Best pillow in the house."

I smile sleepily and lay my head on his thigh.

I'm out in an instant.

FORTY-TWO

Vinnie

'M a little drunk when Talon calls me back. He says that Shay is safe, and maybe give her a day to herself before I try to talk to her. I thank him and hang up, throwing my phone against the wall. Arrow sits next to me and eyes me drinking straight from the bottle but doesn't say anything. He's been here before. There was a time no one even bothered to pour him anything into a glass.

"So Shay's pregnant," he says, always one to get straight to the point. "And you're here drinking because you never wanted kids and don't know what the fuck to do now?"

"That sums it up, pretty much," I say, twirling the amber liquid in the bottle, then taking another mouthful. I look down at Colt, who is sitting at my feet asleep, probably missing Shay just as much as I am. "I don't know how to be a father. I'm not even sure that I like children, and now I'm going to have one."

"I've seen you with Clover, Cara, and Rhett, so I don't think any of that is true," he murmurs, studying me a little too intensely. "You're amazing with them. Faye always lets you babysit—do you think she'd let you do that if you're not good with her daughter? She's a psycho when it comes to Clover. So why don't you think about that? It's all in your head, Vinnie. You've convinced yourself that you don't want kids and that you'll be a shit father, and that any kid will be better off without you, but it's all bullshit. Everyone else sees it from a whole fuckin' different perspective, because we know how good a man you are. I think you need to get off your ass, put the bottle down, and go and fight for your family."

"It's not as simple as that."

"Nothing ever is," he replies, standing up and resting his hand on my shoulder. "At least nothing ever worth it is. You know where to find me if you need me."

He leaves the game room, and I'm once again alone to feel sorry for myself. Is he right though? Am I being my own worst enemy, is it all in my head? Can I be a father? I rest my forehead on the table, close my eyes, and picture Shay, her stomach big and round, her cheeks flushed. Who will look after her? Who will protect her? Who will keep her off the roads so it's safe for everyone?

And who will help her raise that baby, if not me? Another man? I think fuckin' not. Fuck, what am I doing? This baby is my responsibility too—Shay shouldn't be alone. I've been acting like a total dick, just like Faye said.

Shay is mine, for better or for worse, and I'm hers, so she's just going to have to deal with me. Now I just have to make her forgive me, make her come back home where she belongs. I realize one thing, I can break the cycle and try to become a father to this child, make sure he or she knows that they are loved, or I can be like my own father, the one I've never met or known. The one who decided to give up on me before he even knew me, before he gave me a chance. I don't want to be that guy. I don't want Shay to be a single mother because I wasn't man enough to step up. I don't want this baby to wonder why, for even a second, his father didn't want him.

I need to go to her.

I stand up but then stumble, the alcohol hitting me.

I sit back down.

I'll be going to get what's mine, but first, I need to sober my ass up.

I wake up to water being thrown on my face.

"What the fuck," I growl, wiping my eyes and opening them to look up into Faye's, Anna's, and Lana's angry gazes.

Fuck.

"This is an intervention," Faye states, then looks to me and says, "I always wanted to give someone else one, and this is my chance."

I remember when Faye was pregnant with Clover, the men held an intervention over her OCD.

"I don't need a fuckin' intervention. I'm not breaking into people's rooms to clean them, like you were."

Anna and Lana both snicker at that.

"This isn't about me, this is about you, and the fact that you're asleep on the game room floor, like a drunken bum, while Shay has spent the entire day with Ranger, who, if you didn't know, is one of the hottest men any of us have ever seen."

Wait, what?

I sit up and narrow my eyes. "How do you know this?"

"We spoke to her," Faye says, wrinkling her nose at me. "You need to take a shower, because you smell like alcohol, and go talk to your woman. She's beautiful, brave, and smart, and I'm sure Ranger has noticed all these things. Do you really want your child to be raised by the Wild Men?"

I see red as that image comes to me.

"Exactly," Anna adds, offering me her hand to get up. "If you don't make things right, you'll regret it, Vinnie. And Shay needs you right now. You're meant to be a team, but you've bailed and she's carrying the heavy load."

"Literally," Lana says, making the women giggle in amusement together.

"Where is she?" I ask them, taking Anna's hand and getting off the floor. My head hurts, and I'm pretty sure I'm still a little drunk, but I've waited too long as it is. I need to find Shay and tell her that I love her, and that I'm sorry. Yeah—I'm fuckin' sorry for being so selfish.

"I'm not sure—Talon has put her somewhere. A house, it sounds like. She's not at their clubhouse," Faye says, typing on her phone. "I'll message Shay and ask her if maybe we can come over to see her too. She said she's missing Colt and wants him, so I'm sure if you bring her him, she'd be in a much better mood than if you walked in without him."

She was missing Colt, but no mention of missing me?

It hits me just how badly I've fucked up, how much Shay must be hurting right now because of me. I've been such a dick that she actually left me, without even talking about it first, because she knew exactly how I'd react. And I did react that way; she'd been right. If she'd told me herself, who knew what shit I'd have said in the moment, shit I wouldn't have been able to take back.

"I'm going to take a shower," I say, looking at the three women. "Try to find out where she is, if not I'll call Talon and tell him I'll show up at his fuckin' clubhouse if he doesn't tell me her location."

"What are you going to do?" Faye asks, looking wary. "You can't show up there alone, are you crazy? I know Talon wouldn't hurt you, but what about the others?"

"Take Arrow with you," Anna says, pulling out her phone. "You can't go alone, Vinnie. Otherwise we'll follow you there. I think we'd be great backup, and we always miss out on the action."

"I'm going to bring my new gun," Faye says, rubbing her hands together.

"You're pregnant," Lana reminds her. "You aren't going anywhere."

"None of you are going anywhere," I yell, losing my temper. "I'm going alone, and that's final. I'm not even taking Colt. If she wants him, she can come back here where she belongs to get him."

I leave them standing there staring at me and jump in the shower. I get dressed quickly, then call Talon and tell him I'm coming. He gives me the address, but says that if Shay wants me to go, I have to. I agree, even though I won't be giving up that easily, and get on my bike. The ride takes me twenty minutes, and I think about what I'm going to say the whole way. It isn't something easy to talk about—the things that ran through my mind when I found out she's pregnant aren't things she needs to know or things that I'll ever say out loud.

No, I won't be telling her those thoughts, just the ones after.

I just hope that she will forgive me.

FORTY-THREE

Shayla

THE familiar rumble of a bike has me looking at Talon with narrowed eyes.

"Told you he'd come," he says, standing and walking to the front door. He opens it and we both watch as Vinnie walks up the pathway. "Do you want me to stay or leave the two of you alone?"

"Alone, if you don't mind," I tell my cousin. The things that are going to come out definitely don't need to be heard by a third party.

"Call me if you need me. I'll wait close by," he says, kissing my temple.

"Thanks, Talon," I tell him, truly grateful to have him in my life. "I don't know what I'd do without you."

His green eyes soften, then harden as they land on Vinnie. I step away from the door and walk into the living room, and Vinnie follows me. I hear Talon close the front door as he leaves. Here we are, the moment I knew would come, but one that I've feared the outcome. He came for me, yes, but he sure did take his time. He must have been conflicted. Or maybe he knew what he wanted, he just didn't know how to tell me because it's bad news. Or maybe he's just angry at me for leaving. I don't know, but I'm about to find out.

"How are you?" he asks, gesturing for me to sit down.

I do so and want to tell him we don't need to bother with the small talk, instead reply with a polite, "Fine, thank you."

"You left," he says, voice catching. "Without a word. You acted like you'd be there that night, then just bailed."

I know that he knows about the pregnancy, because Faye admitted she told him so, but it looks like he's working up to the subject.

"I didn't know what else to do," I admit, wringing my hands together. "I panicked. I felt alone, Vinnie, and yes, I just bailed. I honestly didn't know what else to do."

And he didn't come after me. Maybe that's what I was hoping for, but he didn't come after me straightaway. Probably because he heard about the baby and reacted just how I thought he would.

"You left because you didn't want to tell me about the baby, because you thought I'd what . . . tell you to get rid of it?" he asks, brown eyes sad, pain etched across his face. Why was the pain there? Because I was wrong or because I was right?

I decide to be painfully honest and just put everything out there.

"In my mind, I had three options, Vinnie. Have an abortion and not be able to look myself in the mirror; to keep you, stay with you, and have you resent and grow to hate me and possibly even the child; or leave and have this baby on my own. I chose option three."

He looks away from me, and I see his throat work as he swallows. "Fuck, Shay. I've been such an asshole. I want you to know that I'm so sorry, I'm sorry you couldn't come to me with this, I'm sorry you've been dealing with everything alone, and I'm sorry it took me time to figure all this out." He pauses and takes a deep breath. "I've been so fuckin' selfish, and only seeing it from my point of view, but here's what you have to know. I love you. I want to spend the rest of my life with you."

"Why are you saying it now?" I fire back, feeling a spark of anger. He only tells me he loves me now? When he's apologizing? He should have told me the moment he knew, or maybe he only just realized when I left.

He comes over to me, sits down, and takes my hand in his. "I've never loved a woman before, Shay. Never been in love with one, until you. I wanted to make sure it was love, I didn't even know how to tell if that's what it was. But I don't want to live without you, you consume my every thought, and I'd fuckin' do anything for you. I know that's what love is, and I should have told you sooner. I should have done a lot of things sooner, and differently. All I'm asking is for a chance to make things right."

"You said you never ever want children, Vinnie, and now I'm having one. You can't just change your mind. You made your views on that very clear. I don't know if there's any way we can fix this. I'll always think in the back of my mind that this isn't what you wanted, and fear that you'll grow to resent me." I try to explain what's going on in my head. It wasn't as simple as just saying "I forgive you; let's work on it." To be happiest, he said he wanted to live at the clubhouse, not have any children, and not be married. There was no room for compromise.

"Would I have ever wanted you to get pregnant? No," he

admits, wincing as the honest words leave his mouth. "But you are, and Faye said something to me when she was yelling at me yesterday—she said a man becomes a father the moment he holds his baby for the first time. I want that, I want to be there for that, I want to see the beautiful baby we made together. Most of all, Shay, I want to try. Losing you isn't an option, living without you sure as hell isn't an option, and I've been so stubborn, so sure about what I think will make me happy, I've been fuckin' stupid. *You* make me happy, and this baby, I want the baby to know that he or she is loved. I never want our kid to have to ask where her father is. Arrow said I'm great with Clover, and that Faye thinks so, so maybe I could try to be the father that I never had."

My heart breaks at his words, at the childhood insecurities appearing when he talks about being a father. His parents abandoned him, and he didn't have a good life growing up. He never even talks about it, besides saying he was moved from house to house, and no one adopted him. He must genuinely think he wouldn't be a good father, maybe until he heard Arrow say Faye's words. He needed to hear reassurance, and I hadn't given him any of that. Instead, I just left, assuming the worst, which probably made him feel as if he was right—he wasn't father material.

"I think you'd be an amazing father, Vinnie," I tell him, squeezing his hand. "Faye is right: Clover adores you, and I've seen the two of you together. I just don't want you to feel like you're trapped, like one day you wake up and think that this isn't the life you wanted. I think you need to make sure that this is what you want, that you're willing to be more open-minded about the future. I'm happy with only having one child, I'm not asking for any more, what I'm asking for is for you to be willing to give this child everything, your love and your attention, and not once look at him or her and think that the baby isn't what you wanted."

"I'd never make my child, or any child for that matter, feel not wanted," he says, looking me in the eye. "I fucked up, I admit it. I freaked out, okay? I was in shock, and I needed to think real fuckin' deeply about a few things. But please don't hold it against me, Shay. I'm going to try to be the best man for you and the best father to our child." He puts his hand on my stomach. "I know nothing about babies, I don't know how to change one, or feed one, or anything else, but I'll learn. I know nothing about children of any age. My only experience has been with Clover, Cara, and Rhett, and they're all about the same age, so it's almost like you're getting two children here, because you're going to have to teach me what to do too."

His words give me hope, although there's still concern lingering in the back of my mind. I want to give him a chance though, everyone deserves a chance to prove themselves. I know Vinnie is a good man, and I really hope we can be a family, and that he can be happy. I want him to be happy, not just for him to do what he thinks is right—and then hate it.

I wrap my arms around him, sitting on his lap. I take his face in my hands and look into his eyes. "What if you change your mind?"

"I won't," he murmurs, turning his face to kiss my fingers. "I'd never do that to you."

I lean forward and kiss his mouth. "Do you need more time to think about it?"

"No," he replies instantly. "I've taken more than enough time to think about it when I should have been rushing over here straightaway, taking what's mine. Can we go home now? Colt misses you."

"Just Colt, huh?" I tease, burying my face in his neck. "Are you sure it's only him who misses me?"

"I'm sure the others miss you too. I know Faye does; she's been your number one champion."

"Well, remind me to thank her, then."

"Shay?"

"Yes.

"I need you to promise me that you won't run again, okay? You have a problem, we deal with it. You need space, you go to Faye's, or somewhere where I know you're safe. You don't just leave and turn to another man, even if it's Talon."

I swallow hard. "I promise."

No more running.

"Shay?"

"Yes."

"Let's go home."

FORTY-FOUR

Vinnie

I RIDE home on the bike, then return with the car, not wanting her to ride now that she's pregnant. I even bring Colt in the car with me, and the smile that appears on her perfect lips is worth the barking I had to listen to the whole way here. Shay hugs Talon good-bye, and I give him a chin lift, a silent thank-you. He nods in return, his eyes telling me that he'll always be here to save her, he doesn't care who it's from or who he has to cross to do so. I respect that. Talon isn't so bad after all. I'd never admit it, but I get a little jealous as Shay kisses Colt on top of his head, telling him over and over how much she missed him.

"Can you stop kissing the dog, please?" I grumble. "How am I supposed to kiss you after that?"

"It's not like I'm kissing his mouth," she says, amusement dancing in her eyes.

"Still."

She pats Colt's head and tells him she'll never leave him again.

"Faye wanted to come and see you. I told her you're mine for tonight, so she said she'll come see you tomorrow, and take you out for lunch or something, if you want to do that."

"I'd love that."

It seems she and Faye have gotten close, more so than she and any of the other women. Faye must like her a lot to take her under her wing. Even though Faye does take care of everyone, she and Shay seem to really get on well together. Shay told her about the pregnancy before telling anyone else, even me, and Faye was really on my ass to go and fix things. I don't think I've seen her that worked up in a long time.

"How have you been feeling?" I ask her, placing my hand on her thigh. Colt bites at my hand until I remove it. I'm really regretting getting her that dog right now.

"I was sick today," she says, turning to me. "I threw up a few times, so the morning sickness has officially started."

Fuck.

She was sick, while I was drinking, or sleeping off being drunk.

"I'm sorry," I say, squeezing the steering wheel. "I should have been there to look after you."

She smiles sadly, then says, "Ranger was there. Although he wasn't really helping much by standing and yelling through the door while I was being sick."

I try to keep my tone even. "Why was he there?"

"He brought me groceries and stuff," she says, watching me. "Then we watched some TV and hung out for a bit, I didn't really feel like being alone."

I feel my eye twitch, but luckily it's the one that she can't see. "I see."

I can feel her staring at me, but I look straight ahead. "Are you jealous?" she asks, sounding amused. "What, you think I'm going to find a new man while I'm pregnant, and after I just left you, like, two days ago?"

"Well the women keep talking about Ranger, and how good-looking the fucker apparently is, so what the fuck am I supposed to think?"

She laughs now, and although it's at my expense, the sound of it makes me happy and gives me hope. Not all is lost. What happened between us is just a bump in the motherfuckin' road.

"He is good-looking, yes," she agrees, making my jaw go tight. "And he's actually a really nice guy."

I wait for the but . . . but it doesn't come.

"Well, he's just perfect then, isn't he?" I seethe, wishing I could punch this guy in the face. Then, I remember something. "Aside from the fact that he kidnapped Anna and hit her over the head, but hey, if you're into men who hit women, then by all means."

Shay starts laughing so hard that the dog jumps off her lap and gets into the backseat. "There's only one biker for me, Vinnie. And it isn't Ranger."

"There's only one woman for me too," I say softly.

Only she can calm me with her words.

Fuck.

I can't believe my stupidity almost caused me to lose this woman.

When we get home, all I want to do is take Shay to my bedroom, but Sin has other ideas.

"We need to talk," he says to me, then walks away. I can tell that something isn't right just by the tone of his voice, and I'm instantly on alert. I walk Shay to our room and kiss her deeply. "I'll be right back."

"Is everything okay?" she asks, concern etched across her beautiful face.

"I don't know, I'm going to find out," I say, kissing her forehead. "Wait for me in bed."

She rolls her eyes at my demand, but I know she'll be waiting for me naked, wrapped in my sheets, when I return to our room.

"They know she's alive," Sin says as I walk into the room and take a seat.

"How?" I ask, gritting my teeth together. I put so much effort into that fuckin' plan. How do they know it was a setup? I blew up Shay's childhood house for nothing? That plan was meant to be fuckin' foolproof, and I'm pissed it didn't turn out that way.

Sin rubs the back of his neck. "Talon has a fuckin' mole. He's spoken to me about it. One of his members is working with the Kings, and now the Kings know everything. We need to handle this, Vinnie. Talon needs to sort his fuckin' club out, because he's dragging us down with him."

Fuck.

So Talon was right: he does have a mole. Sin is right: he really does need to sort his shit out, because this is affecting everyone.

"What now?" I ask, my head spinning, trying to think of ideas to keep Shay safe.

"I don't know," Sin says, scrubbing his hand down his face. "No one says shit to Talon. We need to come up with a plan. And then we take down the Kings."

I nod.

If they want a war, we'll give them one.

One they have no chance in hell of winning.

I push inside her gently, looking into her eyes the whole time, loving her with everything I have. I kiss her already-swollen lips, my skin warm against hers, the feel of her so fuckin' amazing. She moans into my mouth as I increase the pace, sliding deeper and a little harder. She's so wet, and so tight, it's like heaven being inside her, nothing else compares. She wraps her legs around my waist and lifts her hips in time with my thrusts. I don't stop kissing her until she starts to come, and then I pull back to watch her face as she does so. I love watching her as she comes around my dick, the way her eyes glaze over, the panting noises she makes have my dick so hard it's about to explode, and it does, just a few thrusts later.

"Fuck, Shay," I grit out as I finish inside of her. I roll over, still inside her, so she's now on top, lying on my chest.

"That was amazing," she says, kissing my chest. "I missed you, Vinnie."

"I missed you too." Even though it was only for two days, it felt wrong having things messed up between us. I don't want to fight with her like that ever again, to be in a place where I don't know if I've lost her or not—it was hell.

"You have this freckle, just here," she says, touching my collarbone. "Every time I see it, I just want to kiss it or lick it."

She touches it with her tongue.

"That's what you pay attention to? A freckle?"

Women are weird.

"Well it's not like I don't notice your big cock," she says, lifting her head and smirking. "Just that this freckle catches my eye, and I always want to kiss it."

"Kiss away, babe," I say, kissing her lips. She kisses me back hungrily, and I can feel myself hardening again. I don't think I've ever got hard so fast with any other woman, it's only Shay who does this to me. She moves to kiss down my neck, as I let my hands wander down her back and over her ass. I squeeze each globe in my hands, then slap them. Now fully hard again, Shay sits up and slowly begins to ride me. I watch her breasts bounce as she lifts up and down, taking me all the way inside her before rising up. I hope we make up like this after every fight, although hopefully the fights won't be as bad as this one was.

I cup her face, look her in the eyes, and tell her that I love her. My hand moves farther down to her throat, and then down to play with her breasts, pinching her nipples just how I know she likes it. She mutters a curse under her breath, then starts to ride me faster, more urgently. When I feel myself on the verge of coming again, I lick my thumb, then reach down to play with her clit. Her body jerks, and I can tell she's almost there, she just needs a little push to take her over the edge. I rub her clit, adding more pressure, and when I feel her come, I join her a second later, gripping her thighs and making noises I'd rather never hear again. She practically collapses against my body, as I cup the back of her head, my other hand on her back. Will we have to stop having sex soon because of the baby? I need to do some research, maybe ask Faye for one of the baby books I've seen her reading. I need to know what to expect; I can't go into this blind—I want to help Shay, not be added stress for her. When I hear Shay's soft snore, I realize she's fallen asleep on top of me. The poor thing must be exhausted, it must take a lot out of her to create life within her. Understatement of the year. I make a mental note to not let her do anything except eat and rest, and yes, make love if she wants to. Running my hand down her back, I kiss the top of her head and close my eyes, just allowing myself to be thankful for what I have in my arms. I never thought I'd have this, I didn't really think that I deserved it.

"I'm going to be a father," I say out loud, testing the words on my tongue.

Me, a father.

I kiss her head again.

Yes, I'm still terrified, but I'm going to be here.

Right where I belong, with my family.

FORTY-FIVE

Shayla

"I DIDN'T know if you'd be angry that I told him about the baby or not," Faye says, taking a sip of her juice. "He needed to know, but it wasn't my place, but then Sin got involved and they were all ganging up on me."

I smile at her as she explains what happened that day.

"I'm not angry you told him, Faye," I say, wincing slightly when I admit, "I'm kind of glad it wasn't me who had to tell him. If I was there to see how he reacted, I don't know if I'd have been able to forgive him."

"I totally understand," she says, nodding. "He was being a dick, but I'm so happy the two of you managed to work things out. I love Vinnie, and I want him to be happy, and it was so frustrating to see that what would make him happy was right in front of him, everyone could see it, but he couldn't. I had to shake some sense into the man."

"Thank you for talking to him," I tell her earnestly. "Your and Arrow's words made him realize he could be a good father, that it's all about his choices, not his past."

"I'm so happy for the two of you," she says, beaming and looking at the restaurant menu. "And now we'll have another baby in the house. So exciting!"

The waitress asks us what we'd like, so we place our orders.

"Imagine you with a big baby bump," she says, her hazel eyes amused. "You're so tiny, you'll probably fall over."

I laugh and unconsciously touch my stomach. "I guess we'll soon find out. For now I just have to deal with the morning sickness. Luckily today it stopped before lunchtime, or I'd be running to the bathroom right now."

"Morning sickness sucks ass," she agrees ever so eloquently. "So did you and Vinnie decide where you'll be living when the baby comes? I know he said he wants to stay in the clubhouse, but I think you'll both find it's nice to have your own private retreat when things get hectic."

"One thing at a time," I tell her, making her laugh. "He's just getting used to the baby, so I think I'll wait and let him bring up the living situation. I don't want him to think I'm trying to push him, you know? I'm fine with not getting married, to be honest, but yeah I think I'd like a house. Talon gave me the house that I stayed in the other night, he said it's mine to do with as I please, but I don't think Vinnie will want to live there."

"I wish I had a cousin who gave me houses," Faye says, sighing longingly.

"I know that Vinnie has his own house and land, so I'm not sure why he bought it if he never intends to move into it," I say, stomach rumbling as I look at the people next to us, who are currently getting served their food.

"All the men have investments," Faye explains to me. "And

stocks, and land. They're all well set-up. Another reason why so many women want them. Good-looking, badass, and they're well off."

"I can see the appeal," I admit. "I never thought I'd end up with a biker though. Vinnie literally came to my doorstep and just changed everything for me."

"Yeah, I remember when Sin told me he was bringing his marker home," she says, laughing. "You should have seen my face. I've never seen Vinnie really pay attention to a woman, except once, but he was young and she's dead, so it doesn't count."

My eyes widen at that.

Faye cringes. "Long story, don't ask. But yeah, I was surprised, and very intrigued. It's funny, watching the men fall in love, one by one, and seeing what kind of women they end up with. I have to say, they've all chosen well. I don't know what I'd do if I didn't like one of their women."

"Not teach her how to throw knives?"

"Definitely not."

We share a smile.

Our food arrives, and we stuff our faces like the two hungry, pregnant women we are.

When I see Vinnie lying in bed, reading a pregnancy book, my heart melts. He's trying, and that's all I ask. I think he'll be a great father, I really do, he just needs to feel more confident about himself and his future parenting skills.

"Interesting book?" I ask, smiling and crawling under the sheets with him.

"Did you know your cervix will stretch to ten centimeters?" he asks, eyes going double their size. "I hope you decide to have some kind of drugs, maybe an epidural?"

I peer over his shoulder at the page he's reading. "Jesus."

"I know."

"I think I should read this book after you. Everyone's just telling me how amazing everything is going to be, no one mentioned ten centimeters. Although it does explain how the baby gets out. I always thought it sounded like pushing a watermelon out of a tap."

Vinnie winces and mutters "Ouch" under his breath.

"Tell me about it. I'm going to let future me worry about the pain of the delivery though. I have a lot more time to go before that."

"True. We have a doctor's appointment in an hour, so we can ask him any questions we want to know. How was lunch?"

"Food was amazing, company was even better," I say, snuggling up to him. "We ate more than any one person should, and then Faye wanted to go look at new throwing knives."

"Typical day with Faye, then," he says, turning the page over, which shows a woman with her legs apart, the baby's head crowning. I slam the book shut. Vinnie laughs. I don't.

"I'll just ask Faye how her labor with Clover went," I say, not wanting to see that book ever again. "I'm sure she'll have plenty of advice."

Vinnie starts laughing so hard, and I have no idea why, so I jump on him and demand that he explains.

"Do not ask Faye about her labor story," he says, then starts laughing again.

"Why not?"

"Because I've heard what she has to say, and it's something no pregnant woman should ever hear," he explains.

Well that decides it.

Now I can't not ask her.

"Just imagine getting stabbed in the stomach, repeatedly," she says, rather cheerfully, considering. "Just as the pain from one knife ebbs, another fresh one pierces you right in the gut, and then it starts to happen more regularly and more painfully. That's what contractions feel like."

I open my mouth, then slam it shut.

"All while your man, who got you pregnant in the first place, stands by, just watching, pain-free. You wish some of the knives will point in his direction, but no, they're aimed only at you. He just gets to stand there and pretend he knows what you're going through, probably thinking, 'Oh, it can't hurt that much, it's part of nature' or some other stupid shit men say. Then, when you think nothing could be more painful, you have to start pushing the baby out of your vagina, because it doesn't come out by itself, no, you have to do all the work. Your vag is stretching, you're being yelled at to push, it kind of feels like you need to go to the toilet. It's all very traumatic."

Vinnie walks into the kitchen and sees my expression. He looks between Faye and me, then says, "You asked her, didn't you?"

I give him a look that clearly says to shut up, but instead he starts laughing. Sin comes in and asks what the fuck is so funny.

"Faye is telling Shay Clover's birth story. I told her not to ask." He smirks, throwing me a smug look.

Sin chuckles, kissing the top of Faye's head. "Looking forward to doing all of that again, are you?"

Faye's eyes narrow. "Ready to take my abuse again?"

"Yep," Sin replies instantly, taking the seat next to her. "It's the least I can do, right? You take the pain, I take your abuse."

"I'm sure I'll come up with some excellent insults to throw at you this time around. My vocabulary has grown since Clover was born."

"I'm sure you will," Sin says in a dry tone, then throws Vinnie a look that clearly says, *Good luck. Pregnant women are fuckin' crazy.*

"Don't let her take her throwing knives with her," I suggest, wincing. "She might decide to make you share the pain."

Faye grins, kissing Sin on his jawline. "Now why didn't I think of that?"

"We need to talk about something," Vinnie says, rubbing the back of his neck. "You're pregnant, and I don't want to stress you out, but you need to know that the Kings know you're alive."

"How?" I ask, standing up from our bed. "How do they know?"

"Talon has a mole," he says, looking pissed off. "Whoever he told in his MC is involved with the Kings and told them shit. Now we have to deal with this shit again, because the Wild Men don't know fuck about loyalty."

Harsh words, but I can't even defend them. Who would betray Talon? I think about what we could do now, and only one thing comes to mind. However, it's going to involve me having a little explaining to do.

"I could go to the feds," I blurt out, looking Vinnie in the eye.

"The fuckin' feds? How would that help?" he asks, narrowing his brown eyes.

I remain silent, not knowing how to start this conversation.

"Shay?"

I cringe and sit back down. "The feds were in contact with me. Well, they tried to be in contact with me, but I'd been avoiding them. When they called, I'd send it to voice mail. Remember that day in the jewelry store when I went to buy Faye's present? The woman I was speaking to was a federal agent. She cornered me, wanting me to go with her to talk, but I said no. I didn't want to work with them or have anything to do with them. I didn't think they could help in the situation, but maybe they can now?"

I don't trust the feds, mainly because I knew my father was working with them, and look what happened to him. I just don't see another way out of this now though.

Vinnie searches my eyes, then says, "How can they help, Shay?"

I swallow hard. "I think I might know where the ledger is. I mean, I know of a place where my father kept some of his important documents. I've been thinking, racking my brain, and if it is anywhere, it has to be the place where he left it. It's worth the shot, don't you think?"

His expression hardens. "And you didn't think this is something that I should know?"

I stand up and walk to him, resting my hand on his chest. "I didn't lie or betray you in any way, Vinnie, and I would never. I just didn't want to be involved in all of this, I didn't want the feds contacting me, or coming here. I don't physically have any-thing. I didn't touch it or look at it, I just know where it is."

"We need to get it, now," Vinnie says, pacing up and down his room. "Tell me, Shay."

So I tell him exactly where the ledger is. My father hid it in one of the investment properties he owned, in the attic, in a locked chest. He told me about it before he went to prison, just in case. The only issue is, the property is rented out, so tenants are living there. We'll need to wait until they're not home, then break in to retrieve it.

I just hope this is the right move.

"Where did you even get that outfit from?" Vinnie asks Faye, grimacing. Sin brought Faye with him for the retrieval, appar-ently she's good at improvising in difficult situations. What we didn't expect though, is her showing up dressed like a nun.

Yes, a nun.

"I like to dress up now and again," she says, turning to Sin and winking. "And come on, everyone likes nuns. They can't not let me in their house."

"Hopefully no one's home," I mutter, rubbing my forehead with my palm. We park around the corner, and Faye gets out, holding a Bible in her hand.

"I'll go suss out the situation, then I'll message you," she says to Sin, kissing him on the lips. "Let's do this, team!"

She walks off, leaving us all looking after her.

"What the fuck is the plan again?" Vinnie asks, turning to Sin with a quizzical expression on his face.

"Faye is gonna see if anyone is home, and if they are, she's going to distract them while you break in," Sin says calmly, like he does this shit every day.

"What am I doing?" I ask, looking between the two men, realizing that Sin just said *while* you *break in*, not *while* we *break in*.

"You're going to come with me," Vinnie says. "You know what this fuckin' ledger looks like, right?"

"I'm going to sit here and wait for you guys to jump in and speed the fuck away," Sin says, gripping the wheel. His phone beeps. He reads the message, then turns to Vinnie. "There's a woman home. Faye is having tea with her in the kitchen, she said she left the front door unlocked, so run in, turn left then go up the stairs."

I swallow hard. Fuck, I'm about to rob a house while an innocent woman sits there talking to Faye, the nun.

We get out of the car and Vinnie grabs my hand. "Don't panic, okay? We're just going to go in and out."

"And if she sees us?"

"We'll worry about it then."

Great.

Vinnie opens the door, and we both tiptoe inside. The first thing I hear is Faye's louder-than-usual laugh. We turn left, and head up the stairs, looking around frantically for the attic entrance. We find it to the right, an opening with a handle on the ceiling. Vinnie pulls the handle, and stairs appear, reaching the floor. It makes a bit of a noise, and I'm scared the lady heard, but then I hear Faye singing some sort of church song, probably trying to cover any sounds. We climb the stairs into the attic, and I look around for the chest. When I find it, I tap Vinnie on the shoulder. He opens the chest, grabs the box inside, and we get the hell out of there.

*   *   *

When Vinnie hands me an envelope addressed to me, I run my finger over my name, written in my father's handwriting. He found it inside the box with the ledger. My father left a letter for me, and I don't know what to think about it. Alone, I sit down on our bed and rip it open.

> *Shayla,*
> *If you're reading this, it means that things got out of hand. I'm sorry, my beautiful girl, that you were dragged into this, and that you will have to pay for my mistakes. Just know that I love you, and you are without a doubt the best thing that ever happened to me.*
>
> > *Stay strong,*
> > *Love, Dad.*

I place the letter on the bed and close my eyes. He knew this would happen to me; he knew they would come after me, but I guess there's nothing he could have done about it—or maybe there was, I don't know. Either way, he's gone now, and I need to remember him for the good things he did for me, not the bad. It's hard to stay angry at the dead. Vinnie comes into the room, wraps me in his arms, and I know that I'm safe.

I don't have to hide anymore.

The agent walks into the interview room, looking over at Vinnie, Sin, Faye, and me.

"Agent Higgs," I say, nodding my head in welcome.

"Here's a group of people I never thought I'd see in here," she says in a dry tone, then looks to me. "Thank you all for coming. I hear you have something for me, Shayla."

Faye shows her the ledger but doesn't hand it over. "There are some things we want discussed and signed by you before we hand this over."

The ledger contains a lot of information that any criminal could use to his or her advantage. Names. Dates. Information on members of the Mafia. Basically if you wanted to blackmail someone, everything you need is in these documents, along with enough evidence to put a lot of people behind bars. It's like a little black book of criminal activity.

"Faye Black, your reputation precedes you," the agent says, her dark eyes revealing nothing. "This is going to be painful, isn't it?"

"You have no idea," Faye says, placing a piece of paper down on the table. "Let's begin."

FORTY-SIX

Vinnie

I LOOK at the SOLD sign on the two-story house and feel a sense of pride. Shay is going to love this house, I know it. It's only a five-minute drive from the clubhouse and has four big rooms and two bathrooms. She never asked to move out of the clubhouse, and I know if I wanted to stay there, she would have without complaint. Just another reason that I love her. She never guilts me into anything, or tries to get her way—she just lets me make my own decisions and lets me know that she will be here by my side no matter what. After thinking it over for the last few months, I realized that a baby can't grow up in the clubhouse. The baby needs their own home, a quiet place with just his or her mother and father. Don't get me wrong, we'll still be at the clubhouse a lot, just like everyone else, but this way we also have our own private sanctuary, a place that is ours and only ours. I ride back to the clubhouse, finding Shay outside with Colt.

"I have a surprise for you," I tell her, smiling. "You have to come with me."

"What is it?" she asks, glancing around. "Where is it?"

I simply smile and take her hand, leading her out the front, where I tie a blindfold around her eyes, then put her in the car. She asks me a million questions on the drive to the house, but I tell her nothing except that she needs to be patient. I park in our new driveway, walk around to her door, and help her out, making sure she can't peek. I walk her to the front of the house, then stand in front of her. Just before I take the blindfold off, I say, "I've thought about this for a few months now, and this is what I want too. Okay? So don't question it. I love you, Shay."

She opens her eyes and looks at the huge house in front of her, and then the SOLD sign.

"Oh my god," she whispers, tears filling her eyes. Everything makes her cry nowadays with all the hormones. "But, Vinnie, I thought—"

"Things change," I say, resting my hand on her stomach. My tattooed knuckles look out of place against her pink floral dress.

"You bought this for us?" she asks, looking shocked. "Vinnie, I don't even know what to say."

I take her hand, palm up, and place the key in it. "Should we go have a look at our new house?"

She nods and kisses me, a tear dripping down her cheek.

"Don't cry, Shay," I tell her, kissing away the tear. She's crying because I bought her a house; I'm sure she's happy, but it makes me a little sad, because she probably wasn't sure this day would come, that we'd probably live in the clubhouse forever because that's the place that I considered home. Home is wherever she is though, and it's not like I'll lose the clubhouse. I'll just have two homes now, and I'm perfectly content with that. Making her happy makes me happy, because she does everything in her power to make me happy too. That's what love is. We explore the house from bottom to top, and just watching the way her eyes are lit up lets me know I made the right choice. Sure, I'd stay in the clubhouse forever and be happy about it, but I know she wouldn't be. I'm not going to be that selfish, and being so close to the clubhouse is having the best of both worlds.

"When do we move in?" she asks, hugging me from behind.

"Whenever you want to," I tell her, turning and wrapping her in my arms. "We can go furniture shopping tomorrow if you want, so maybe think about what you need, what colors and stuff, and then we can go have a look."

"That sounds perfect, Vinnie," she says, looking up at me. "I know you did this for me and the baby, and thank you."

A kiss, and then she's gone to see what exactly we'll need for the place. I watch her, remembering this moment. With members of the Kings arrested, Shay is safe once again.

And I just know that everything is going to be okay.

Two weeks later, we have a housewarming party. Everyone comes to see the new place, including Talon and Tia, bringing presents even though I told the women not to bother. Shay cooked a huge meal for everyone—my favorite of course, lasagna and chicken, but also ribs, garlic bread, and salad. She did some fancy platter as well, with cheese, salami, crackers, carrots, celery, pickles, and different dips.

"The house is beautiful," Faye says to me, looking around animatedly.

"Why are you pretending you haven't been here already?" I ask, lips twitching in amusement.

"Because everyone else hasn't been here yet," she whispers to me. "I don't want them to feel left out."

"Why? It's not like we invited you, you just showed up."

We hadn't told anyone where the house was, we were waiting to surprise them all, so imagine our surprise when Faye rocks up at the front door. The woman has no boundaries whatsoever. She's lucky we love her, and that she's the president's wife, or I wouldn't put up with half her shit. Who am I kidding—yes, I would. The woman is worth her weight in gold, but there are times she can be frustrating as fuck.

She elbows me playfully in the ribs. "I wanted to help Shay choose the colors for the house. So yes, I followed you back to the house, what's the big deal? If you can't stalk your family, then who can you stalk?"

"Preferably no one."

She waves her hand in the air. "Where's the fun in that?"

"You're insane."

"You love it."

"I hear you want to work with the feds to bring down more bad guys," I say to her, after Sin had a talk to me about it yesterday.

He's not happy.

"I do," she says, nodding. "I think it will be a good experience, and I can help bring down the real corrupt assholes. The world needs people like me."

"You realize we kind of are the bad guys, right?" I say, raising my brows.

She waves her hand again. "You're all the best men I know. And with me working with the feds, I will make sure nothing ever touches you."

"That sounds a bit corrupt," I tease, making her shrug.

"Loyalty and family first."

"Always," I reply, my tone sobering.

"Remember when you had a thing for Allie?" she blurts out, wincing. "I accidentally brought that up with Shay once, but I didn't say her name. Isn't that an awkward story?"

I stare at her, blink, then say one word. "Sin!"

After dinner, I stand, getting everyone's attention.

"Just wanted to say thank you to everyone for coming. You know you're all the family I never had, and yeah . . . fuck, I'm not going to get all mushy and shit, but I'm thankful for each and every one of you."

"Uncle Vinnie swore," I hear Clover whisper to Faye.

"I know," Faye whispers back.

I turn to Shay and pull the box out of my pocket. My hands start to shake. Fuck. Am I doing this? Proposing? Another thing I never thought I'd do. Fuck. Fuck. Fuck.

Say the fuckin' words, Vinnie.

"Shay, will you marry me?" I ask, opening the box, showing her the giant diamond.

Eyes wide, she looks at the ring, then back up to me. She then looks around at everyone at the table.

"Vinnie," she says quietly, clearing her throat. "No, I won't marry you."

Wait, what?

The table has gone deathly silent.

She quickly explains, "You don't care about marriage, I know this, it means nothing to you. Just a piece of paper, you said. I know that you're doing this because you love me so much, but I'm saying no because I love you just as much, and I don't need for us to be married to be happy. You've given me this beautiful home, even though I know you'd be just as happy at the clubhouse. You don't have to give any more, Vinnie."

She stands up and wraps her arms around me. "The fact that you'd do this for me means more to me than anything, but I can't accept, Vinnie. I love you so damn much, and I know you love me. I don't need for you to propose to prove that. Although the fact that you did just makes me love you even more."

I lift her chin with my fingers and kiss her deeply.

Everyone at the table claps.

"That was the most romantic proposal rejection I've ever seen," I hear Faye say.

"I'm sorry I said no in front of everyone," Shay says, cringing. "I just couldn't say yes, Vinnie, when I know this isn't really what you want. You've already given me two of the three things you said you'd never give, so this time it's me who's going to give up something."

"Fuck, I love you," I say, kissing her again, and kind of wishing everyone would go home now so I can carry her up to our bed and have my way with her.

"I love you more," she says, smiling at me, the happiness in her eyes proof that I'm not as bad of a man as I thought I was.

In fact, I might even be one of the good ones.

EPILOGUE

Shayla

"OH my god, she was right; it's like knives!" I yell, closing my eyes and trying to manage the pain.

Holy fuck.

It hurt so badly.

I want to scream.

I open my eyes and glare at Vinnie, who is holding my hand and telling me to breathe. "I don't want to breathe!" I yell at him. "Why don't you try and breathe through getting stabbed?"

"Do all women get this mean?" he asks the nurse, whose expression doesn't change at his question.

"For the most part."

"I don't know why you're yelling at me," he says, staying completely calm. "You're the one who didn't want the epidural, trying to be some kind of warrior woman."

The nurse hands me some gas, I suck it like it's going to save my life, which I'm kind of hoping it will. Yes, I fucked up by saying that I didn't want an epidural, but he didn't need to keep reminding me of it. Now it was too late to have one, as the baby was almost crowning, or so the nurse keeps telling me.

"Fuck!" I yell as another contraction hits me. I want to cry, but it won't help, so there's no fucking point.

Finally, the midwife tells me it's time to push. I don't really want to, but I want this over with, so I push, through all the pain, I push.

"The head's out," Vinnie says, eyes wide as saucers. I don't know when he moved to the other end, right in front of my vagina, but I'm pretty sure I told him not to look down there.

"Don't look!" I all but beg, only to be ignored, again. Even I don't want to look, and I'd rather he remember what my vagina was like before—not when it's stretched out with a giant baby head coming through it.

"Vinnie, stand by my head!" I growl, then start whimpering. They keep on telling me to push, so I keep pushing.

"Almost there," the midwife tells me, acting all calm. How is she so calm? I feel like punching her based on that alone. I close my eyes, block out Vinnie, still standing where he isn't supposed to be, and the midwife telling me to keep pushing, and I just push. With everything I have, I push.

And then, something amazing happens—the pain stops. I hear a baby crying, and I feel nothing but relief.

"We have a daughter," Vinnie says in awe. The nurse asks if he wants to cut the umbilical cord, and he does. I start crying. They place our little girl on my chest and she stops crying. She has a thick head of silky, dark hair, which I know she got from me, but when she opens her eyes, all I see is Vinnie.

"She's perfect," I say, tears running down my face.

After a little while, the nurse takes her from me, cleans her up and wraps her. The nurse then hands her to Vinnie, who holds her awkwardly, but without complaint. He sits down, and just stares into her eyes.

When a tear drops from his own, I know that Faye's words were true.